To Zack—
Who lived it too
before it. Thanks for all
the laughs and
memories over the years.
Cheers!
Jay

SOUL
FOR
SALE

a novel

by

jay williams

Portland • Oregon
INKWATERPRESS.COM

For my wife...
who always believed I could

And, of course, for Brendan...
who left us much too soon

CHAPTER 1

The briefing was being held, as usual, in a room too small to raise a veal calf.

The object of all meetings at Concordia Telecom appeared to be to assemble as many people as possible, in as small a space as possible, remove all physical comforts, visual distractions, and air—and then yell at you.

This one promised to be particularly medieval. They had invited not just our band of thieves from Cracknell, Burroughs, but a group from each of their ad agencies.

"Who the hell are all these people?" my boss, Larry Feinstein, whispered to me as we entered the room.

"They're from the other agencies," I said. Pointing discreetly, I continued. "Those guys are from Burton, those guys are from TMB, and those guys might be from that agency in Houston."

"Explain to me again why they have more than one agency?" he said.

"Do we have to go over this again?" I sighed. In an age when most large clients were preaching the gospel of consolidation, pooled resources, and economies of scale, our client had steadfastly maintained a stable of at least 5 agencies. We each had our own turf—land lines, mobile services, high-speed Internet, cable service, business products, whatever. But as new projects or divisions arose, they would invite all of us to pitch for it.

"They maintain," I continued, "that this method assures that they're being fair to everyone and that they get the best work. I believe it's because cock fights are illegal in New York and so this is the best they can do."

Mike Haggerty, our eternally optimistic head of Account Service, walked up. It was unusual for Larry and Mike to be at a Concordia meeting—especially on Concordia's home turf. But because it was a multiple agency briefing, and therefore technically, a new business opportunity, protocol demanded that the two top dogs be there, despite the fact that about the only thing they knew about Concordia was that that was the name on their phone bills at home.

"Hey guys!" Mike said, in his high-pitched chirp.

"Hey Mike," I said, shaking hands.

"Where's the coffee?" Mike said.

"Outside at a Starbucks," I said.

"There's no coffee?" Larry asked in horror.

"No."

"How can that be?" Mike asked.

"Guys, I have been coming to meetings at Concordia for 3 years and I have never been given coffee. Ever. Not once. Never been offered a meal, never had a sandwich, never even seen a bagel on the premises. I think it's because they're actually evil replicants and don't need to eat."

"Why don't they just torture us?" Larry said.

"Oh, they are," I smiled.

The Chief Marketing Officer, Anne Wheeler, swept into the room, reeking of cigarettes, bitterness, and fear.

"Guys, could you please take your seats?" she announced in a voice that sounded as if it had been dragged on the pavement. "We need to get started."

One of the truths of life at Concordia was that a C-level executive like Anne never went anywhere, particularly to briefings, without several surly, incompetent acolytes. Seated next to Anne at the head table were Jessica Moore, Martha Knocklemeier (honest to God, that's her name), and Tad Willoughby.

One of the other truths about Concordia was that, in mid-level management anyway, the women were almost without exception big, loud, abrasive, and masculine—while the men were predominantly tall, slender, impeccably dressed gay men. As the saying went: *Concordia…where the women are men and the men are women.*

The acolytes' job was to sit somberly and say nothing until Anne turned over the day-to-day management of the project to them—at which point, they would turn an already murky assignment and into a marketing Rubik's Cube.

"All right," Anne rasped. "The first thing is this." She scanned the room, her eyes looking enormous and slightly crossed behind the huge, Coke-bottle lenses of her glasses. "Your agencies are not diverse enough."

We all sneaked a peak around the room and saw nothing but white, primarily male, faces peering back at us. She was, of course, right—although there didn't seem to be a lot of diversity up there at the head of the table, either.

Well, not ethnic, anyway.

"This is an issue that's not gonna go away. Fix it! You need more ethnicity."

Larry leaned over to me.

"I'm a Jew from Brooklyn. Doesn't that count anymore?"

"Nah," I whispered. "Two generations of assimilation. You're white bread now."

"We're here to talk about the branding project, which, as you know, will be in two parts, two separate assignments. We will brief you on the first part; you will come back in two weeks, on the 26th, and present your work and we'll pick a winner. Then, whether you're the winner or not, you will begin on the second phase. That will be due two weeks after that—sometime around the 10th."

I groaned quietly. This was the most screwed up way of doing this I could possibly imagine. Not least because it meant that my teams were going to be doing two gangbangs back to back, which would do wonders for morale.

Ah, but there was more.

"The first assignment, Phase I, will be a retail promotion. We need to drive a lot of volume in the third quarter."

She leveled a long, nicotine-stained finger at the room.

"*You* need to drive a lot of volume in the third quarter." She paused to look at us threateningly through the Coke bottles.

"The second phase of the assignment will be a branding campaign to introduce the Concordia name in our new markets across the country."

The assembled group stared blankly back at Anne. There was a little shuffling of paper; we all furrowed our brows as if deep in thought. Someone finally raised his hand to ask the question that was hanging over us all. It was Andy Hawley, the Account Director from Burton, a tremendous bootlicking toady I'd seen in these meetings endless times before. He always made a point of addressing Anne as if they were the only ones in the room, and he always made sure to lace his speech with as much hackneyed, clichéd marketing-speak as humanly possible. There were times, I was convinced, that what Andy was saying was unintelligible even to him.

"Excuse me, Anne. So the Q3 promo will be deployed tactically within the current footprint, and then the branding launch will be deployed across all markets sometime late-stage Q4?"

Anne didn't always respond to Andy's attempts at corporate intimacy, and this turned out to be one of those times.

"I'm sure you'd all like it to be that way—*'cause it'd be easy. But that's not how we're gonna do it!*" She screeched. "The promotion will run in all our markets, old and new. The branding will follow."

This made so little sense even Andy Hawley couldn't pretend to like it.

"But, Anne..." he began.

"Andy, could I please get through this without being interrupted?" she snapped. "We've got a lot to cover here."

I was barely able to conceal my smirk at Andy the Toady getting publicly spanked. However, the other portions of my brain were grappling with the flaw in the information Anne had just unveiled.

I felt a tap on my elbow.

It was Larry.

He looked at me blankly. "Am I hearing this right?"

"Yes, you are." I said.

"They're going to do the retail first—and branding second?"

"Yes, they are."

"Shouldn't it go the other way?" he asked.

"Well, of course it should go the other way," I smiled. "But that's not what they're going to do. What they're going to do, is actually run a price promotion to get people to sign up for service—in markets where people have never heard of the company and don't even know they offer this service. At any price."

"That'd be...that'd be like..." Larry struggled for a metaphor. "Like running an ad about how many miles per gallon you get when people don't even know you make cars."

"Exactly."

Larry blinked. "They're insane."

I smiled.

"Welcome to my world."

CHAPTER 2

The morning after the inspirational and motivational Concordia briefing, I sat in my office at Cracknell, Burroughs & Partners, sipping bad coffee from the kitchen because I was too distracted to go downstairs and get the good stuff.

I was scribbling names on a notepad. I figured I needed about 5 creative teams to get us through the Chinese fire drill that the next six to seven weeks promised to be.

Seated in one of the black leather chairs I had inherited from my predecessor was Ellen Kaplan—Director of Creative Services, Head of Broadcast Production, Creative Den Mother, Mother Confessor, Larry's Right-Hand-Woman and All-Around Hot Shit.

"So, what have you got?" she asked, as she looked at one of her many staffing charts.

Staffing in the Creative Department here at The Crack was fluid, to say the least. We ran very lean and as a result spent lots of time with Ellen, moving people around like chess pieces to cobble together the coverage we needed for any given project.

"Well, I figure Mary Anne and Nicole for sure."

"Right."

"Jimmy and Ivan."

"Yup."

I paused.

"What?"

"What I'd really like" I said "is a team like a Gail and Mark—but I'm not sure I can do this to them."

"Do what to them?"

"Inflict this mess on them."

"Oh, please."

I laughed. "I know, I know—you think I treat creative people like such fragile flowers."

"Please! It's their job!" She sighed. "I'll ask them."

"Fine. Think we can hire freelancers?

"Why?"

"You know who'd be great to get?"

"Who?"

"Sarah Higgins and John Rogers."

"From LA?"

"Yeah—they have telecommunications experience. And they don't have the baggage that we all have. They could do something different."

"Maybe—but they need so much lead time. By the time they were clear to get involved, it'd be time to present."

It was my turn to sigh. Ellen was right. Sarah and John were a terrific team. I'd admired their work for a long time and had met Sarah while we were both judging the One Show in Barbados. We'd been trying to do a project together ever since. But this was the conversation we always ended up having: we only needed them when we were crunched for time and being crunched for time meant we couldn't have them.

Another in a long, painful line of advertising conundrums.

"You know who has time?" Ellen asked, still studying her staffing charts.

"Who?"

"Bob Berk."

I winced.

"Oh come on," Ellen said. "He could come up with something tasty."

"Oh, I don't know, El," I said.

"He used to work on Concordia."

"That's exactly my point—I think he'll come up with some tried and true solution."

"And that would be wrong be-c-a-u-s-e..."

"Look, if it was any other assignment—if it was the usual first-quarter promotion or something, he'd be exactly what we need. But this could turn out to be our chance to grab the brand assignment. We need something different, something fresh."

"I thought you said the first part was a promotional assignment?"

"Well, it is, in their warped way of working. But to really do this the right way, you'd have to know the branding piece before you could even attempt to do the promotion."

"So what are you suggesting?"

"That we treat this the way we treat new business. We do the whole thing, soup to nuts, show them a complete campaign—within which is their precious promotion."

"We serve the whole thing up at once instead of in two parts?"

"Yeah. We do it our way."

"Ignore the rules."

"It's the only way to it right, El."

"Does Larry know about this?"

"No. I'm meeting with him at 10—wanna come?"

"Yes."

CHAPTER 3

Cracknell, Burroughs & Partners was a typical agency story.

Two guys, Justin Cracknell and Ross Burroughs, had worked together for years at Durham & Elliott. Eventually they had decided that they could do better on their own.

Cracknell was a transplanted Brit whose specialty was that he was arguably the world's greatest account guy: smooth, street smart, born salesman, great political instincts, relentlessly ambitious.

Burroughs's specialty was that he had money.

Well, in fairness, he was a creative guy who was a pretty good writer, but his principal attraction to Cracknell was that Burroughs's family had made a fortune in real estate and so covering the initial nut of opening an agency without any clients wouldn't be a problem.

So they opened as Cracknell, Burroughs, Inc. in February of 1980 in a small space over a dentist's office. According to advertising legend, the phones went out that first week and Cracknell spent every day using a phone in the dentist's waiting room to call prospective clients.

He often recalled it during client dinners and in new business meetings.

"Nothing they were doing to people in the dentist's chair," he always said, "could have been any more painful than what I was going through out in the lobby!"

The hard work paid off, though, and the agency began to

grow almost immediately. Soon they moved from their boutique space to a floor in the newest, coolest, most desirable building in the city. They did the interior walls all in glass so that there were views from virtually everywhere in the office and you could see into everyone's office—except of course, Cracknell's, which was designed as a mahogany bunker with huge, paneled double doors guarding the entrance. Even in the beginning, he knew that for all the openness and spirit of sharing he was trying to foster everywhere else, there was going to be some ugly shit going on from time to time and it had best be contained.

He had the entire floor covered in green carpet—British Racing green.

"To remind us," he always said, "that we have to go faster than everybody else."

And they did.

Within a few years, Cracknell, Burroughs had a reputation as the hottest, coolest agency around.

It seemed for a time that every client wanted to move their business there, and talented creative people flocked there like lemmings, clutching their portfolios tight on the elevators—this being back when portfolios were actual physical portfolios and not accessed off web sites.

Cracknell also quickly developed the reputation, among people in the ad business, as being a lot like the galley scenes in Ben-Hur. The 40-hour workweek was something you were expected to accomplish by lunchtime Wednesday. If you were seen boarding the elevator at 6 o'clock at night, someone was sure to sneer "Half-day?" as they walked past. And on weekends, the saying went at Cracknell, "If you don't come in on Saturday, don't bother coming in on Sunday." People came in early and went home late—if at all. The place was fully functional by about 7:30 every morning. One year at the company outing (people were always in shock that they even had one), they handed out t-shirts that said "Up At The Crack" on the front with the Cracknell, Burroughs logo on the back—in British racing green, of course.

This was all in the go-go '80s. By the time I joined Cracknell from their cross-town rival Rothman, Simon and Clark in the late '90s, things had calmed down a little. Oh, the work ethic was still in place, as was the importance that was placed on creative. But the agency had grown to $850 million dollars in gross billings, they had big corporate clients like Concordia, and it was getting harder and harder to play the role of rebellious upstart. There was still a desire, even an addictive need, to be different, to make waves, to create the all-important and ever-elusive 'buzz'. That would always be part of the agency DNA. But more and more, it was about making good, old-fashioned, boring profits—and lots of them. Which is why accounts like Concordia and a handful of others were allowed to remain—they may have been contributing very little to the agency's creative soul, but they fed the bottom line. Actually, fed it is an understatement—the bottom line was positively feasting on accounts like Concordia—gorging itself like Mr. Creosote in the old Python bit.

So basically, everyone pocketed their paychecks and their fat bonuses and worked hard at turning a blind eye to the ugly, money-generating business—all the while dragging the more prestigious, award-winning creative accounts out into the hot, bright light of the PR stage.

It was a sort of silent agreement, a culture of ongoing denial.

It was the Cracknell way.

CHAPTER 4

I walked out of my office and headed toward Larry's office down the hall to discuss the Concordia situation. As I looked up from my staffing charts, I was suddenly aware of someone walking toward me.

"Yo, dude, what's goin' on?"

The sun coming through the windows obliterated all detail in the long hallway, but that greeting, the corona of curls, and the round, bouncing silhouette approaching me could only be one person.

"Yo, have you seen the sick shit we're doin' for The Vision?"

Keith Farner was, along with me, one of the Creative Directors. He was 34, with a couple of kids, and more than anything else on Earth he wanted to be fourteen.

OK, eighteen.

"Man, I got Mickey and Spike crankin' on this sick campaign—it'll be like totally underground, totally guerilla, like this subversive kinda thing. Kicks ass!"

Keith had an ability to talk about the work his group was doing in a way that got under my skin in about a nanosecond. And talking about how great The Vision was doing was a particular hot button with me.

Keith always operated on the assumption that anything he was doing was cooler, better and more creative than anything you could possibly be doing. He was cocky, arrogant, and opinionated, and fancied himself a revolutionary iconoclast. He was also very, very good. He was particularly gifted in television and had a great editorial eye. However, he worked a little too hard on his persona to suit me, and was such a relentless self-promoter that there were times when I couldn't stand to be in the same ZIP code with him.

Unfortunately, there were times when I didn't have much choice, because we occasionally partnered on things, new business especially. Larry and Mike felt like we were a great new-business team and we had had a fair amount of success together. Conceptually, I actually liked working with Keith. The work we did together was pretty good, if I may say so myself. We were both good presenters—me a little more measured, Keith bouncing around the room like a lunatic.

"Keith has the energy level of a 7-year-old girl," Larry had once said about him.

Unfortunately, Keith also had the maturity level of a 7-year-old girl.

This meant that if you were working on something with him, eventually he was going to do something completely irresponsible.

Now, being somewhat irresponsible is not an altogether bad thing—especially in the part of the business we're in. I mean, every good creative person has a little of the irresponsibility gene, or at least they should. Otherwise you don't have the healthy disregard for rules that are a prerequisite for doing fresh work.

But that wasn't the problem with Keith. No, what happened with Keith again and again was that in his quest to look like the world's biggest iconoclast, he would eventually do something that he felt made him look cool and that other people thought made him look like he was either crazy or didn't give a shit or both.

Actually, even this wasn't the biggest problem.

The biggest problem was that when the time came to take the rap, Keith always managed to make sure other people took the fall instead of him. It was a neat trick I'd seen up close more often than I wanted to.

For example, he and I were at one point working on a small airline account. One of the teams working for us showed me a newspaper ad they were going to present. The headline said, *"There are few things that worry our competition more than our new prices."*

The visual was a photograph of the smoldering remains of a plane crash.

"Guys," I said, kind of half laughing. "I admire your boldness, but a plane crash? In an ad for an airline?"

"That's why it's so cool, man," said Dale, the art director. "That they would have the balls to run this."

"But they won't have the balls to run this—and they probably shouldn't. We need another idea, guys."

Well, with that I headed out to a couple of meetings. In the meantime, my two creative geniuses went down the hall to play a little game I call "Ask Your Mother/Ask Your Father".

They went in to Keith to plead their case.

Of course, Keith was particularly fertile ground on which to sow this seed. He immediately overruled me (telling the team that I shouldn't "wimp out like that") and told them to put the ad into production. It turned out to be one of those tight deadlines when the ad was going back to the client but was simultaneously going straight to the publication digitally—and since it was over the weekend there really was no further checkpoint.

The ad ran in the Monday paper in Atlanta where our client was based.

The calls from the client began about 7:15.

The Chairman wanted us fired by the end of the day, the President wanted us fired by the end of the week, and our client, who had only recently hired us, was trying to figure out how not to fire us at all without getting fired himself.

It was a catastrophe.

Our client called and said he was flying in that night to discuss the whole mess. He wanted me, Keith, and Paula Hansen the Account Director to have dinner with him.

That evening, I showed up at the restaurant and ordered a drink at the bar—figuring I was going to need one. Paula arrived next and had the same idea. As we stood there alternating sips of liquor and gulps of dread, my cell phone rang.

"Hello?"

"Terry?"

"Yeah?"

"Terry, it's Jennifer." Jennifer was Keith's assistant.

"Ye-e-e-s-s." I said, my voice loaded with apprehension.

"Keith asked me to give you a call—he's stuck in an edit and won't be able to join you."

"You're kidding."

"Um, sorry."

"Yeah. Hey, be sure to tell Keith I said thanks."

"Um, bye."

I snapped the phone shut. Paula was looking at me over her wineglass.

"What?" she asked.

"Keith's not coming."

"What? This is basically his fault!"

"Oh, he's stuck in an edit," I said, heavy with sarcasm.

Paula was looking past me. "Here's Mike..."

So the two of us sat through dinner getting verbally reamed, taking our lumps for the agency, making passionate assurances throughout the meal that this kind of thing would never happen again. Somehow, we dodged the bullet and didn't get fired— although we both knew that we'd be digging ourselves out of this hole for months.

In the days that followed, Keith never said a word about it.

Well, actually, he did say, "C'mon, they shouldn't be so sensitive." But that was not exactly the word I wanted to hear.

"It's unbelievable," I said when discussing it with Ellen later. "It's like he wants the thrill of throwing the rock through the plate glass window but when the cops show up he wants to make sure I'm the one standing there."

Ellen kind of laughed. "Good analogy—this seems to happen a lot."

"Hell yeah! It's his standard MO. Why do you think his last partner moved to London? Probably couldn't take it anymore—and there were no jobs in Phuket!"

"All right, I'll talk to Larry about it."

CHAPTER 5

In my meeting with Larry, he completely agreed that doing the Concordia assignment as assigned was a recipe for failure.

"It can't be done the way they want to do it," he said, spreading his arms in frustration.

"That's what Terry said," Ellen nodded.

"Well, he's right," Larry, said. "There isn't another one of our clients who would ask to do it this way."

"It just means more work for us," I said.

"Have you got enough teams?" Larry asked.

"Yeah, we've got Mary Anne and Nicole, Jimmy and Ivan, Gail and Mark."

"Gail and Mark?" Larry asked.

"That's what I said," I laughed.

"I talked to them—they'll do it," Ellen said putting her verbal foot down on that one. "We've got two or three others, I'm just waiting to hear."

"You're fine."

The next morning, we held the briefing for the Concordia assignment in the Creative conference room. There were five teams, plus myself and Ellen, and a contingent from the Account group.

The briefing itself was going to be led by Rob D'Angelo, the Account Director. He sat to my left with two piles of presentation decks in front of him. Rob was fairly new to Cracknell, having taken over Concordia when Ethan Holland, the long-time

Account Director, had left to make a fortune in a new media venture. (Although, it tanked and he didn't.)

Rob was a good enough guy and gave the impression that he was a champion of creative. But lately he seemed to have been drinking a little too deeply of the Concordia Kool-Aid.

I was getting worried.

"Good morning," I said. "And welcome to our show. As you probably know from talking to Ellen, we're here to brief you on the Concordia brand assignment."

"Well, wait a minute," interrupted Rob.

"Rob, do you have something to add—*already*?" Ellen said laughing.

"Yeah, Rob," I smiled. "I mean, I'm sure I'll get it wrong eventually, but I've only said about 20 words."

The whole room cracked up.

Rob instantly became flushed and fidgety.

"Well, the client has been very specific about this whole thing. They've set down some very distinct ground rules."

"Yes, which I plan to ignore."

Rob blinked several times. "How?"

"We're going to do the whole assignment at once—we'll do a complete brand campaign, within which is the promotion. It's the only way to make them be consistent with each other."

"But they don't care if they're consistent with each other."

I smelled Kool-Aid.

"Rob—they have to be consistent with each other. Why would you possibly not want them to be consistent?"

Rob was crimson and his head was beginning to break into this sort of pre-Parkinson's shake it did when he was frustrated with us.

"It won't matter if they're consistent *if we go in there and arrogantly ignore the rules of the assignment. Because they'll throw us out!*"

"*Well, I'd rather get thrown out for doing it the right way than continue to produce crap the way they tell us to do it!*

"Guys, guys!" It was Mike Haggerty who had entered the room while Rob and I were going for each other's throats. "What's the problem?"

"Well, we have a disagreement over how to approach this Concordia assignment," Ellen said. "And for the record, I agree with Terry."

"Look," I began. "I'm sorry, Rob, I don't mean to get so upset, but I've been working on this business for a long time, since way before you were here. And this is the first opportunity we've had— and it may be the last one we get—to put something on the table the way we'd want it to be. Who knows what'll happen when we do it? I mean, the chances of them buying the right thing are about zero, but at least we should give it a shot. What you're describing feels like we're coughing it up from the word go."

"So what are you suggesting, Terry," asked Mike.

"I just think that rather than treating this like just another Concordia assignment, we should treat it like we treat new business. Who'd understand that better than you, Mike?"

This was, in fairness, pretty damn good bootlicking on my part—Mike, of course, ran New Business.

"Treat it as if this just landed in our laps," I continued. "And we had to figure it out. No baggage, no preconceived notions, no trying to appeal to Anne and Jessica's weird taste—just putting the best idea on the table that we can come up with."

Mike kind of wheeled and looked at Rob.

"And all I'm saying," said Rob, "is that if we're arrogant and ignore the rules–"

"*Where is this arrogance thing coming from?*" I exploded. "*Since when is my desire to do the right thing arrogant?*"

"Guys," Mike broke in. "Could we just–"

"Look," I said. "We've got all these teams here—they need the information. Rob, why don't you just give them all the background on both assignments? They need to have it regardless of which way we go. We can figure the order out later today. This is wasting their time."

I stood up.

"And mine."

CHAPTER 6

Bistro Jo-Jo was just across the street from the office. Every problem in the history of the agency had been solved many times over at the worn marble bar, while a framed honey from the Moulin Rouge lifted her skirt behind the vodka bottles and smiled down on us pathetic ad hacks.

I was sitting on a stool, nursing a Scotch and talking to Gail Meadows, the writer I had told Ellen I was embarrassed to inflict the Concordia mess on. Gail was, in my opinion, maybe the best writer I had. Hell, she may have been better than me. She was smart, funny, dedicated, and could write with range. When we were up against it, Larry usually came looking for me and I usually went looking for Gail. We had a lot of mutual respect, and early on Gail had taken it upon herself to watch my back.

"So what happened after I left?" I said to Gail.

"Well, Rob hemmed and hawed a little, figuring that he had driven you out of the room and that we'd all be pissed at him," Gail said. "Which we were."

"Oh, Rob's all right—maybe I was kind of an asshole in there."

"No," Gail said firmly. "You weren't. You were right."

"Although Rob probably tried to persuade you all that I wasn't."

"No, actually he made an embarrassing speech about how he wasn't the enemy of creative. How he always gets painted as the bad guy and it doesn't make him feel good about himself and he's got a wife and family he has to go home to and on and on. I actually think it was pretty heartfelt but it made my skin crawl. Way oversharing."

"And then Mike made it all better," I smiled into my drink.

"Oh, yeah—'*this is gonna be great, guys!*'" Gail said, mimicking Mike's odd falsetto.

We both laughed.

"God love him."

"Yeah, but everyone was cool. You know, they got the info, we all know what we're up against, but we'll try to do something cool. See what happens."

I clinked her glass with mine. "Thanks for bein' you."

"How're you doin' these days?"

"You mean other than this hemorrhoid of an assignment?"

"Yeah" she laughed. "I mean in general. You seem a little down."

"Me? Nah."

"T-e-e-r-r-y..."

I took a huge swallow of Dewar's.

"Ah, I don't know..."

"What?"

"Well, look at this Concordia thing."

"Yeah?"

"I mean, everything on my plate looks like this."

"Like what?"

"Like—I don't know...like...remember that scene in 'Good Will Hunting'? When the professor puts that big equation on the board in the hall? Numbers everywhere, connecting to each other, over each other, a wall full of numbers?"

"Yeah—I think it's called an advanced Fourier system."

"Right. Well, every assignment I have looks like an advanced Fourier system. Every other group's assignments are like "Here—sell this." Or "Here—get people to stop using handguns." But my assignments all are like "Here—sell these two completely unrelated products to three different markets, none of which want them, using four different distribution systems." I'm telling you—every strategy I read? Will Hunting himself couldn't figure them out!

"I know, I know." Gail was laughing.

"Well, have you noticed that?"

"Yeah, we all have. We've taken to calling ourselves The Mensa Group."

"Really?"

"Oh yeah, all of us. We kind of take pride in it."

"You do?"

"Yeah. Don't you?"

I paused for another sip.

"Yes, actually. Perverse pride, but pride nonetheless."

"Jason," a voice behind me said. "Give me a Cape Codder the color of the blood of a Hapsburg prince."

It was, and could only be, Sean Healy.

In addition to being the only person I ever knew who could order a drink by referring to the legendary hemophilia of the excessively inbred House of Hapsburg, Sean was an old friend and fellow toiler at Cracknell. We had actually known each other in college, although we moved in different circles. But several years later, we found ourselves in the same Creative Department at the now defunct Lewis, Childs & Gilman—both over-worked junior writers, both making no money, both in search of girlfriends and so both willing to spend hours at various bars lamenting all those facts. Sean now worked in Carolyn Kelly's group. My counterpart Carolyn was an average creative talent, an iron-fisted adminis-trator, and a legendary bitch.

"Miss Meadows," Sean said to Gail, taking the barstool on my other side.

"How are you, Sean?"

"Lovely, thank you," he answered. Turning to me, he said, "Your Excellency."

"Your Grace," I replied. It had been our standard greeting for years, born of Sean's hopeless and virulent case of Anglophilia. (How an Irishman ended up with such an affliction I had never figured out.) "How goes the battle?"

"Heavy casualties, I'm afraid. Ilsa, She-Wolf of the SS, was striding up and down the halls this afternoon."

"Ah, the lovely and talented Carolyn. Looking for young Aryans to fall in step?"

"Precisely."

"Richard Markson in tow?"

"No, actually, the bootlicker was MIA. But she did stop long enough to sing the praises of..."

"Let me guess—Maggie Loughlin."

"Exaaaaactly! And loud enough so that Andrew, Eric, and I were sure to hear. And find ourselves lacking."

"Which of course, you are. Particularly in testosterone."

"Compared to her? You bet your ass."

Jason arrived with the Cape Codder, thinly pink and perfectly Hapsburgian.

"What the hell is it that endears Maggie Loughlin to her?"

"It's simple" Gail chimed in. "Maggie's about the same talent level so she's not a threat. She's willing to be the good lieutenant, the loyal number two. And because of her weight she doesn't have a lot of self-confidence, so she's easily manipulated."

Sean and I stared silently at Gail for what must have been a full 15 seconds.

"Not that I've given any thought to it or anything," Gail said with a smile.

"You know," I said. "If the writing thing doesn't pan out, I think you've got a career as a therapist."

"I would gladly unburden myself and have you sort out my myriad issues," Sean said, raising his glass.

"I don't think we have that kind of time, Sean," Gail said, reaching over to clink his glass.

"So, anybody working on anything good?" Sean asked.

"Well, Gail and I have got this *fantastic* opportunity on Concordia."

"I can only imagine."

"And you?"

"Did you know that prune juice is an excellent source of fiber?"

"You don't say?"

"Oh, I do say. In fact, I say it again and again and again. I say it endlessly. In everything we write for Sun Grove Juices. And speaking of juices...Innkeeper!" He wagged his glass at Jason. "Excellency? Gail? Another wee snifter?"

"Not for me thanks," said Gail. "I've gotta have it together tomorrow." She stood up. "See you guys."

"Oh, I'll have one more with you, Your Grace."

"A gentleman, you are, sir. Let us settle in and regale each other with who we hate and why."

It was going to be a long night.

CHAPTER 7

"The Vision" was a 3-year-old account, essentially a public service effort, whose purpose was to promote information and legislation to reduce handgun violence in the United States.

Now, public service groups like this exist everywhere, looking to do everything from stopping violence to stopping drinking and driving to saving the rain forest to protecting the snail darter to having Elvis declared alive.

These kinds of groups generally share two characteristics—they have high ideals and they have no money. It's easy getting people to work on projects like this because there's usually a lot of good emotional stuff to mine and so everyone starts dreaming of One Show Gold Pencils as soon as they see the work order. The hard part comes later when it's time to produce the work and the agency is forced to a) beg for favors, b) tack the production onto a real, paying job or c) actually pay for it themselves.

c) is almost never considered to be an actual option.

The Vision was every bit a creative opportunity, that was for sure. I mean, c'mon, a kid dying from handgun wounds is a pretty powerful emotional place to be starting from.

But what made The Vision truly unique was that they actually had $100 million to spend.

The Vision's actual legal name was The Jenny McManus Anti-Violence Fund. It seems that several years earlier a young girl in Minnesota had been killed with an illegal handgun. Her father, a multi-millionaire technology CEO, had filed all sorts of lawsuits against the shooter, the gun shop, the manufacturer of the gun, the manufacturer of the bullets, and the state of Minnesota. He had won them all, the settlement totaling hundreds of millions of dollars. In an inspired bit of thinking, he asked that a portion of the settlement be earmarked to fund an anti-handgun marketing campaign. His desire to make sure that no one else suffered the loss that he and his wife had suffered was pure and admirable. The fact that he had also worked it so that the handgun manufacturers had to fund advertising to stop people from buying their products was an exquisite bit of irony.

The name 'The Vision' was what the agency had come up with when we pitched the business. It had come right out of the McManus Fund's mission statement– *That we share a vision of a safer country in which to live and raise our families. And that we shall make the vision real.*

Actually, Keith and I had come up with it. We had been reading through the mission statement along with the other reams of information you get at the start of a pitch, when Keith drew my attention to that line.

"That's it," I said.

"What?"

"That's what we should call the effort." We had both already agreed that, with all due respect and sympathy to the McManus family, The Jenny McManus Anti-Violence Fund didn't sound big enough. It lacked scale. It sounded like it could have been a tiny, local effort instead of the sweeping national campaign the founders imagined.

"What?" Keith asked again.

"The Vision."

"Dude, that's awesome," he said.

"Instead of making it just an organization, it becomes a way of life."

He had started sketching on a pad. "We can give it a cool type treatment."

"I mean, it's a logo but could we make it more than a logo?"

"Make it into patches, stencil it on stuff, kids can even spray paint it on buildings in tough neighborhoods..."

"Graffiti as part of the media mix?" I laughed.

"Yeah, man, it'll become part of the culture." Becoming part of the culture was always Keith's goal. I assumed that even if he was selling remedies for painful, rectal itch he'd somehow want to make it a part of the pop-culture milieu. In this case, though, I shared his optimism.

So 'The Vision' it became.

We built the campaign around it, pitched with it (I wrote a strategy video that had the clients weeping openly in the meeting—always a good sign), showed the work, won the assignment and went on. Sure enough, by the end of the first year, 'The Vision' had started to become a well-known cultural thing, like MADD or Partnership for a Drug-Free America.

But a funny thing happened on the way to this success.

'The Vision' stopped being my vision.

I don't mean I stopped believing in it. But a strange metamorphosis took place, part of which was business driven and I understood. But part of it I still don't quite understand—it was like waking up in another city and not being quite sure how you got there.

It started gradually: being pulled away, missing a meeting here, a meeting there, usually because the shit was hitting the fan on Concordia or we were pitching something else that Larry needed my help on. But Keith was always available, so he went to the meetings, got the face time and began to exert more and more authority over the business.

It was like getting posted-up in basketball—you're both maneuvering and then all of a sudden the guy makes one last move, sets his feet, leans into you and you realize you can't get to the ball. I became more and more a peripheral presence until finally, one day in a Creative Directors meeting when we were re-organizing the Creative Department for the umpteenth time, I looked at the staffing charts and noticed that I was no longer anywhere to be seen on The Vision's staffing chart.

I had been eliminated.

Rubbed out.

Oh well.

At least he didn't use a handgun.

CHAPTER 8

The Concordia work had started to percolate. Even under the time constraints, I knew it'd be a while before we saw anything.

Which was just as well.

The thing was that while Concordia was giving us this giant hairball of a corporate assignment and attaching all sorts of importance to it and demanding all the resources they could get their hands on, it was still just one other item on their list of assignments. While Ann, Martha, and Tad had dispatched us to sort through their promotional and branding issues, there were whole legions of incompetent middle managers whose jobs had nothing to do with this assignment. They had their own hairball assignments and didn't want to hear about how we couldn't service their needs because we were handling some big assignment for corporate. As far as they were concerned, it may as well have been an assignment from another company altogether. In fact, they were probably going to become more demanding instead of less—hoping that we'd stub our toe somehow and then they could scream bloody murder and claim that they weren't getting the attention and resources they needed.

All of which explains why, despite the work swirling around in the office, I now found myself on a plane to New York to attend a shoot for the Out Of Home Division—known as OOH.

OOH was introducing a new pre-paid cell service and aiming it at teens and college kids. The spots were going to be like music videos—stories of life and relationships set to original music we had commissioned from a kick-ass music house in London. The service was not going to be shilled so much as simply placed, woven into the story organically. The director was the reigning king of the thoughtful, sophisticated music video. He had recently worked with Radiohead, Coldplay, and Badly Drawn Boy.

I was uncharacteristically optimistic about this campaign. It had, somehow, navigated the gauntlet of the Concordia approval process and actually made it to production. This was almost completely due to the fact that it was aimed at teenagers and everyone at Concordia acted as if we were speaking to aliens. I had kept using that as leverage—so every time there was an objection to the script, the music, the casting, the wardrobe, all I had to say was "Teens dress like this" or whatever and they would all nod and say "Oh" and back off.

In any event, the campaign was actually happening and I was, as I say, cautiously optimistic. The creative team, Jimmy and Ivan, had already been shooting for two days and by all accounts it had been going great. I was arriving for the morning of the 3rd shoot day. Jimmy and Ivan were terrific and certainly not in need of my help supervising a shoot.

I was just there to "troop the color", as Sean said before I left the office.

Today's shoot was taking place in a second floor loft on Broome St. in SoHo. It was actually two separate lofts—front and back—that had been rented from their owners and opened up for us. Shooting was going on in the front portion, where an absolutely gorgeous actress was rehearsing throwing all of her suddenly-ex-boyfriend's possessions out the front window onto a rainy sidewalk—where a crew of production assistants stood out of camera range, waiting to catch them. The make-up people had made her up to have mascara running down her cheeks with her tears. To go with the tears, she was wearing a spaghetti strap, champagne-colored satin nightgown, and nothing else.

The effect was absolutely knee-buckling. Only in a commercial would a man ever leave this woman.

In the back portion of the loft, the grips and prop departments had claimed their corners and were all busy rigging, prepping and keeping up a steady crackle of walkie-talkie conversation. In the middle of the room, sat video village—the encampment of playback monitors and director's chairs reserved for the agency and its clients. Because Concordia was based in New York, and there were therefore no travel costs involved, they had sent what seemed like every man, woman and child in the company to observe the shoot. There were about twelve chairs lined up in a semi-circle facing the monitors—six short ones, six tall ones. Of course, for our Account guys, the first commandment of shooting is that no client shall be unattended. Sort of like man-to-man defense. So there they all sat—six Concordia clients in the front, six Cracknell account people in the back. All reading the newspaper, talking on cell phones, and drinking coffee from the craft service table.

When I walked in, Jimmy and Ivan were actually standing several feet away with our producer Mike Banaszac. "Zack", as he was known, was a great producer, talented client handler, and about the funniest man on the planet. He and I had worked together on a ton of jobs.

"Oh my God," I said, eyeing the entourage. "How many of them are there?"

"Oh, the magpies?" Zack said, shaking hands. "About 50—I think they're doing it in shifts."

"Have they been here both days?"

"Not the same ones," answered Ivan. "We had a few different ones yesterday. But Winnie and Anna have been here throughout."

"How's Winnie been?" I asked. Winnie O'Brien was the lead client for OOH—she knew absolutely nothing about her job and seemed convinced that she knew everything about ours. She was constantly tossing out what she thought were insider production terms so that she'd seem hip. We could never figure out where she got this stuff.

"She's beautiful, man," laughed Zack. "Last night, we're prepping this sidewalk shot for the second spot?"

"The one where the two guys go into the bar?"

"Yeah. Shot it in front of the Old Town Tavern. So we're rigging the shot and she comes up to me and says 'Mike, are we shooting this night for day?' "

Jimmy started laughing.

"Zack looks at her like she's insane and says, 'No, Winnie, we're going to shoot this night for night. You know, regular night. Like God made. Night.'

"What did she say?" I asked, laughing.

"Nothing!" Zack says. "Just walks away until she can look up some other term in her production handbook or wherever it is she gets this stuff."

"I better go say hello," I said, turning toward the amphitheater of chairs.

Rob D'Angelo saw me approach and stood up.

"Hey, Terry," he said, shaking hands warmly. Our heated exchange of last week seemed to be forgotten. "Thanks for coming. How was the trip?"

"Hey, Rob. Hi Winnie."

"Hi Terry!" Winnie struggled up out of her chair. She was a big gal. "How you doin'?"

"Good. Things going well, I hear?"

"Great, just great. Little concerned over the filters on the CU's last night, but we could fix that in post, right?"

Oh, man. "Yeah, Winnie, we can fix it."

"'Cause you promised me, it wouldn't be too dark."

"I know Winnie. It won't be too dark."

"'Cause we don't like dark."

"Oh, I know it, Winnie."

"Long as we're clear. Get some coffee."

"Gee, thanks." Like she was hosting a dinner party or something.

"Terry, you know Anna."

"Hey, Anna."

"Hey, Terry. Nice to see you."

Anna Rosso was a junior client who we all thought had potential. She had worked on the agency side and, occasionally, recognized and fought for good work. The problem was she had fallen in with bad companions and I worried that her potential would be beaten out of her before long. Rob went on to introduce me to the rest of the Concordia brain trust. I went for the coffee and returned to Zack and the boys.

"How long before we roll?" I asked.

"I don't know—ask Winnie," Zack said.

I barely managed not to spew my coffee all over him.

"About half an hour," he said laughing and patting me on the back.

"You guys go out last night?" I asked.

"Cafecito," said Jimmy, pumping his fist.

"Mojitos?"

"Multiple Mojitos."

"Ve-e-r-y nice" I said.

"You hangin' tonight?" Ivan asked.

"Yeah."

"Cool. We're thinking of going over to Markt."

"For some large Belgian beers?"

"Among other things."

"And then maybe up to the roof bar at The Gansevoort," Jimmy added.

"Oh, what the hell is she doing now?" Zack was looking over my shoulder.

"Who?"

"Who else? Cecilia B. DeMille."

I turned and looked. Winnie was up from her seat at video

village and seemed to be canvassing the loft. As we watched, she disappeared down one short corridor and then returned. She opened a closet door, examined the contents, and then closed it.

"What the–" Zack's mouth was hanging open.

Winnie continued around the back of the room past the grips and everybody, opening closets, looking in drawers, generally casing the joint. Zack and I walked over to her.

"Hey, Winnie," Zack said. "You know, somebody lives here."

"I know," she answered.

"Well, it's kinda not cool to be goin' through all their stuff."

"I'm not, I'm not, just looking around."

"Well, could you not?"

"Oh, Zack. Stop worrying." She walked away and continued on her exploration.

Zack was the color of an eggplant. I gently took his arm.

"C'mon, you said your piece. If anything happens, it's on her."

We walked back to video village.

"What's going on?" Rob asked nervously.

"Nothing—we just told Winnie maybe she shouldn't be casing the joint since someone actually lives here."

We turned to check Winnie's progress. She had reached a door just beyond the monitors. She turned the knob and pulled it open.

It was the bedroom.

And there, on the bed, was the owner of the loft and his girl-friend. They were on top of the sheets, buck naked and going at it like farm animals. In mid-stride they turned and looked out at us—12–14 people sitting in director's chairs as if in a theater.

Winnie screamed.

The happy couple screamed.

Winnie slammed the door, walked quickly back to her seat, and sat with her face in her hands as if she had just witnessed an atomic blast.

Zack and I, in the same instant, turned and headed for the back stairs out to the street, where we leaned against the building and each other, laughing so hard that no sound came out.

The best part was that there was no other way out of the building for our libidinous pair. A couple hours later, the door opened and they walked out, fully dressed, heads down, and headed out the back stairs. I was surprised that they didn't have raincoats over their heads like Mob figures leaving the courthouse. They didn't look at us and we didn't look at them.

Well...we looked at her.

A little.

After that spectacular beginning, the rest of the shoot day was uneventful. Winnie never fully recovered enough to offer any production tips and things went smoothly until we wrapped at about 6.

"Are you guys going straight to Markt?" I asked the boys.

"Nah, not till about 9:30. Have you checked in yet?" asked Zack.

"No. Why don't I go check in and meet you there?"

"Cool."

CHAPTER 9

I was staying at a new hotel in town. Well, it was newly renovated anyway. It had been a residence hotel for young, working women for about 40 years and had recently been re-opened. Because the hotel was trying to drum up business, our travel people had gotten a discount on suites.

The red message light on the phone was glowing as I entered the room. Not blinking like it did in some hotels, man, I hated that. The phone sitting there on the bedside table basically saying *"Look at me! Look at me! Answer me! Don't turn on ESPN! Don't look out the window! Don't take a leak! Don't do anything except deal with me—right now!"* Arrogant piece of goddam plastic.

This one was a little more demure—it just sat there and glowed.

I put my briefcase on the desk and the rest of my stuff on the bed. Walking past the foot of the bed, I opened a set of French doors and walked out onto a stone patio that looked out over the city. It wasn't the most picture-postcard view of Manhattan. Not one of the icons of New York architecture was visible from here— no Chrysler building, no Empire State, just some standard-issue skyscrapers.

But, hey, I thought, evening is falling, the lights are coming on and it looks great. Besides, it was a patio, outside, 19 floors up, on the Upper East Side of Manhattan. Excuse me? When was the last time I had had a hotel room like that? Exactly never was the answer. It made me feel like Henry Kravis, Steve Schwartzman, and Bruce Wasserstein rolled into one.

I looked west where the sun was setting over Central Park. OK, technically the sun was setting over New Jersey, but if I was going to fantasize that I was in a Fred Astaire movie, Jersey was going on the cutting room floor.

I took in the view for a few more minutes. It was a beautiful, mild night. A light breeze ruffled the flags over the hotel entrance below, people were strolling down Lexington Avenue. Even the planes leaving LaGuardia seemed to bank a little more leisurely overhead.

I looked at my watch. "Better go for that run if I'm gonna go," I thought.

I walked back into the room. It wasn't that big—they made up for the kick-ass, Master-of-the-Universe patio with a very ordinary-sized room.

Grabbing my running stuff out of the bag, I flipped on ESPN, hit the mute button and then leaned over and pressed the speakerphone button. The raw, discordant speakerized dial tone burst into the room. As I stripped out of my clothes, I pressed the Voice Mail button.

"Hello, Mailbox 1940" said the disembodied voice.

I laughed out loud.

"Thanks. It's important that you say 'Hello'. It's so personal—right before you address me as Mail Box 1940." I pressed the "1". The Voice said:

"You have (PAUSE) one (PAUSE) new message. (PAUSE) 5:51 PM"

It was one of my Account Service counterparts, Linda Usher. We didn't work together on any existing business, but we had just pitched something together and were waiting to hear. It was a project from a TV network; not a lot of money but the work we had presented was killer. Linda was great to work with because her enthusiasm was more infectious than herpes. Only she didn't sound anywhere near as amped-up as she usually did.

"Terry, hi, it's Linda—sorry to be bugging you at the hotel, but I just got a call from Robert and...we...well, we didn't win. We didn't get it. I...I don't even know what to say...I'm...they've made a gigantic mistake. They've really...I mean we all worked so hard, you worked so hard...it's, I'm sorry...call me."

I stood stark naked with my hands at my sides.

What? How could this be? How could nine weeks of work come to this? Nine weeks of commitment, nine weeks of investigating, nine weeks of getting inside their heads come down to this? What about the work? The work? My God, the work was awesome! They said so themselves! Hell, the goddamn president of the network had stood up and said the work was smart and funny. The rest of them had applauded! What the hell was that all about? All that glad-handing and backslapping at the end of the presentation—so they could do this?

I could feel the anger starting to rise. The feeling of betrayal that I always felt when I put my heart into a project and it didn't pan out. The truth was, I didn't always put my heart into it—not into every assignment, every presentation. But there were some that struck a chord, that seemed to tap into something inside me and I was willing to lie on the tracks for one of those.

This had been one of those.

Alongside the anger there was another feeling bubbling up, a dread that I always fought when I came this close to something big. It was the feeling that if we'd gotten it, if we'd been able to produce the work we'd done, it would have been noticed. It would have been big and noteworthy and visible, and the greatest fear I had, the gnawing that I battled all the time, was that what I was doing was invisible. So now, after all the work, after investing myself again, after weeks of tiptoeing quietly and relentlessly up on something great, it was over.

I felt like I was being slowly erased.

I thought of dinner with everybody that night.

Yeah, that's just what I wanted to do, sit there and clink glasses an smile and listen to their bullshit. I didn't have the energy.

I pressed "3" and banished Linda's depressing message into the ether. What the hell, I figured I'd go for a run anyway, maybe feel better, get my energy up. Then see about going to dinner.

I've gotta tell those guys, I thought. Jimmy and Ivan had worked on the pitch. *They should hear it from me.*

I started to pull on my shorts, but I couldn't shake the feeling of depression. Why is it called *depression?* I often wondered. Should be called *submission* instead. Submission to the weight of all the bullshit.

It wasn't like I'd never had any new business wins before; I'd had my share, I thought, as I laced my Asics. But lately they hadn't been the kind of career- and reputation-making wins that I wanted.

I took the computerized room key off the desk and slipped it into my shorts. I went out the door and into the small, marble lobby, pressed the button for the elevator and walked over and looked out the leaded, mullioned windows looking down Lexington Avenue. After a few minutes the elevator arrived and I stepped in and rode to the lobby alone.

The lobby opened onto East 63rd between 3rd and Lex. Turning left, Central Park was only three blocks away. I walked to the corner of Lex, stretching a little as I went. I waited for the light and then began running down 63rd. In the first block, there was a small knot of interesting looking people standing on the sidewalk. As I ran by I could see a plaque on the wall that indicated that it was The Society of Illustrators.

Well, that's pretty civilized, I thought.

Visions of Peter Arno, Charles Addams and William Steig danced through my head.

"See, that's it," I said aloud as I ran. "Those are people you can point to and say 'They did that'. Just once, just once I want to do the campaign where people say 'Oh, Terry Wilson? He did the so-and-so stuff.'"

I caught the light at Park and ran on toward Madison. On my left, more well-heeled types milled on the sidewalk. I knew without looking that the first group was waiting to enter The Post House and the second was heading into the Club Macanudo. A little early for cigars, but both places were tailor-made for celebrations. I gave both places a long look as I ran past. I jogged in place at the light on Madison, and then when the light changed, headed on toward the Park.

When I reached Fifth, I had a choice—I could turn left and enter the Park at 59th, running North to 90th. Instead, I chose the opposite route, heading up Fifth along the stone wall that guarded it in the 60's and 70's.

Maybe I just don't get it. There's some secret to getting that kind of work done—and I just don't know it. Maybe I never will. Maybe I'm not supposed to...

By now I was talking out loud and people were looking at me as I ran.

It was uphill this stretch of Fifth, and I had started to sweat already. The sidewalk was broad and it was easy to avoid the other pedestrians and dog-walkers. There were a lot of spots where the tree roots had begun to lift slabs of sidewalk and I kept half an eye out for those. With my concentration split between pedestrians and roots and the beginnings of the endorphin rush coming on, my rant began to lose a little steam.

A few blocks up ahead, I noticed a group of runners cross Fifth and head into the Park. Men and women, they seemed to be somewhat organized, as if participating in some Corporate Challenge or other. They disappeared down a stone stairway and were gone by the time I passed the entrance.

Up ahead stood the Met, and the sidewalk in front of it was thick with visitors, strollers, painters, vendors, and people waiting for their buses. Just past that, across the street, stood my favorite, the Guggenheim, Frank Lloyd Wright's monument to art.

Well, to art and his own ego, I thought. *Maybe that's the secret. Maybe you just have to be a world-class, Grade-A prick like him.*

I turned into the Park through the gates at 90th Street.

As I ran through the marble gates, I saw that the Park was mobbed with runners—thousands of them, clogging the running lane and all coming straight at me. I slowed for a second on the other side of the road wondering if this was a road race. Was this where those runners had been headed? But none of the runners seemed to be wearing numbers or race t-shirts or any other indication that this was an organized event. They were all just running in the same direction, North through the Park. There were skaters, too, and people on bikes, all headed North toward 90th and beyond.

A town car wound its way cautiously up the road headed out of the Park. As it passed, I stepped tentatively out into the road and began to cross over to the running lane. As I reached it, I saw that it was actually a two-lane kind of deal and that the right hand lane, the lane headed South, was wide open.

I dodged between two women in high-cut running shorts and jog bras, turned left and headed south. Within a few minutes, I had settled into my rhythm, breathing in for four steps, breathing out for three. The road swung around to the right, revealing a long stretch of straightaway before it curved left and disappeared over the hill. Coming toward me were hundreds of runners, their faces bobbing, their legs pounding, wearing looks of determination or contentment or, occasionally, pain. They wore everything from the most expensive Nike F.I.T running gear to old, faded law school t-shirts. They were old and young and men and women and they ran in pairs and alone. There was a steady stream of them coming over the hill.

All heading north as I headed south.

CHAPTER 10

"They were just in there doing it?"

I was having dinner with the lovely Alex Clarke, my girlfriend of two years.

"Yeah."

"How far away?"

"About as far away as the bar."

"You're kidding me!"

"No, it was unreal. I thought Winnie the client was gonna turn into a pillar of salt."

"Can you imagine? I mean, what could they have been thinking? How many people are around at a shoot?" Alex was a lawyer.

"Including us? Probably 25-30 standing right there, more out in the front loft."

"My God! And the door wasn't even locked?"

"No, Winnie just yanked that thing right open—like 'ta-dah!'"

"I can't even imagine."

"Maybe that's their thing, the element of danger."

"What did they look like?"

"In bed?"

"No, you pig, when they came out."

"Well, they looked pretty sheepish when they came out. Unless looking sheepish is just part of the whole role-playing thing."

"Oh, that's creepy."

Alex shook her head hard to clear it of that vision. She was quiet for a minute as she twirled some linguine.

"I'm sorry about that new business thing."

"Yeah, me too."

"Have you talked to Larry about it?"

"Yeah, I talked to him today for a few minutes."

"What'd he have to say?"

"He said what he always says in situations like this."

"What's that?"

"'Screw them—they don't deserve it'."

Alex looked at me. She had her serious face on which was every bit as beautiful as her silly face—maybe even more so.

"Well, that's childish."

"I guess it is," I laughed.

"Does he think that actually helps?"

"You know, the funny thing is—it actually does kinda help."

CHAPTER 11

The time had come to take a first look at how we were doing on the Concordia stuff.

I asked my assistant, the young, wise-beyond her years, practically telepathic Meghan Addison, to schedule a meeting with the teams.

"Do you want them all together or one at a time?" she asked.

"We can do them one at a time."

"Good."

"Why?"

"Because that's the first thing they're all gonna ask me—and if you're seeing everyone together, they're all gonna freak out on me."

"I know—no one wants to be the first one to show their stuff."

"Can you blame them?"

"No."

"Do you want to do it in your office?"

"Can we get The Hole?"

"Yeah, no one's using it today."

The Hole was a small, windowless conference room down the hall with cork-covered walls and a large central table. I used it a lot for creative sessions like this one partly because the cork allowed us to pin all the work up and partly because it was neutral turf—if things were going badly, I could always escape.

"Do you want them in any particular order?" Meghan asked.

I thought for a minute.

"Yeah, give me Gail and Mark first."

"I knew you were going to say that."

"Why?"

"Because Gail will have something good and you'll feel better immediately."

"Meghan?"

"Yeah?"

"Could you stop peering so directly into my brain?"

She laughed. "Hey, I know you."

"Apparently. I'm going to get a coffee. But of course, you already knew that."

She stuck out her tongue.

"Lovely. When I come back we'll get started."

I went for the good stuff today, a large at Jonathan's downstairs, figuring it would take me through most of the review session. I came back up the elevator and headed down the hall toward The Hole. Rounding the corner, I almost bumped into Sean.

"Excellency!" he smiled.

"Your Grace!"

"And where are you headed so purposefully? High matters of State?"

"Hardly. Heading to The Hole for a tissue session."

"Ah, a dreaded skirt-raising" he nodded.

"Skirt-raising?"

"You know—I'll show you mine if you show me yours."

"Haven't heard that one, Your Grace," I laughed. "And I'll be stealing it immediately."

"With my compliments, sir," Sean said, bowing before he continued down the hall.

Inside The Hole, Gail and her art director partner Mark Rockford were waiting, talking quietly at the table, piles of paper in front of them. Mark was a quiet, thoughtful guy with a Southerner's tempo—which you wouldn't think would mesh with the crazy pace at The Crack, but it did. Mark was one of those guys who didn't always need to come up with a million ideas, because somewhere in his first five was something brilliant.

"Hey guys."

"Hey Terry."

"Terry, how you doin', man?"

"So," I said plopping myself down. "How we doin'?"

A session like this takes anywhere from an hour to two hours plus—depending on the number of teams. In my experience, the better it's going, the longer it takes. That's because you see something you like and start refining it, thinking of other executions, seeing how it can extend to magazines, outdoor, digital, you name it.

When you're out in under an hour, you know you're screwed.

This one lasted an hour and 45 minutes. Not bad. There were a handful of good ideas—and Meghan had been right, two of the best had come right off the bat from Gail and Mark.

"Work on those two, guys—I would flesh those out and forget everything else."

"Great."

"When do you want to get back together?"

"When you think it'll knock me on my ass."

They both smiled.

"Sounds good, man," Mark said in his soft drawl.

The problem with these sessions is there is always a team involved who just misses the boat completely. Misses the tone, does work that's generic, whatever. Unfortunately, this team tends to be not only wrong but also prolific. They'll have 147 TV spots for an idea that was no good halfway through spot #1.

Now, I don't say this to be mean. I have, on occasion, been this team myself.

This time, that team was Mary Ann and Nicole—unfortunately, the lead team on Concordia.

"So what should we do?" Mary Ann asked.

"Well...let me see the, what did you call it—the Suburban Blender campaign?"

"Yeah." Nicole was pulling sheets of paper out of the pile.

The fact was, I didn't like Suburban Blender even a little. It had no shot at being the answer. But half of me was stalling and the other half was trying to find some nugget they could build off. This was compounded by the fact that they knew they had nothing and furthermore, they knew that to be the lead team on the business and have nothing didn't look good. They should be the ones making me feel better and more confident about our chances—not Gail and Mark.

"I think this thought of people being busy is OK" I began cautiously. "I mean it's not a revelation, but it is true."

They both nodded.

"But," I continued, "to make it work, I think ya gotta go one way or the other—you've either gotta drop down and get really specific, ultra-real with it, almost like a documentary...or, you've gotta go the other way. Make it so over the top, so exaggerated, so high concept, so stylized, that it's entertaining. Right now, it's in No-Man's Land."

"Yup," Nicole answered for both of them. They gathered up their stuff.

"And then I'd put it aside and see what else is out there," I said as kindly as I could.

They nodded unenthusiastically.

They knew that what I'd just said was code for start over.

CHAPTER 12

That night, I sat in my apartment drinking a beer and watching *Run, Lola, Run* on DVD. I'd seen it before, 3-4 times in fact, but I was looking for something.

It had struck me while I was talking to Mary Ann and Nicole about the whole busy-ness of life thing. As I'd been heading home, it had been percolating and so I stopped at Hollywood and grabbed a copy of *Lola*. As I watched Franka Potente running through the German streets with that red fright wig of a hairdo, playing out all the possible scenarios of how she was going to save her drug mule boyfriend, I kept wondering.

What if Lola was a suburban housewife? In a series of spots, she'd be running around getting kids to soccer practice, piano lessons, etc. It'd have to be a series of spots, since it took a whole movie to do it justice. Maybe 3 spots in a half-hour segment. But maybe that was the shtick—(big swig here)—maybe you could buy the media so that when you were talking to housewives it was one series of scenarios, when you were talking to guys on ESPN or something, it would reflect their testosterone-fueled needs, teenagers, college kids, etc.

I started to pace.

It would work. I mean, I didn't know if it could be great. I didn't even know if it was good. But it would work. I knew that much.

But it would also cost a fortune—you'd be talking about as many as 15 different spots, three spots each for five different segments. They'd have to run sequentially, too, placed just so in the pods so that would make the media more expensive to buy.

I shook my head hard. Who cared about the media at this point in the game? We didn't have a decent idea on paper to show them. And this could be that.

My pacing was interrupted by the phone. Which was perfect—concepting for the phone company interrupted by the phone.

I checked the caller ID. It was Sean. I hesitated for a minute—and then let the voicemail pick up.

The stories would have to be interesting, too, obviously. The ordinariness of life wouldn't cut it; we'd need some tension in the story, something to suck you in. They'd have to be mini-movies, hell, maybe even get the guy who directed 'Lola'...

I opened another beer and began scribbling all this madness down. It may not have been much, but it would work.

CHAPTER 13

"Excellency!" I said as I caught sight of Sean walking toward me in the elevator bank.

"Ah, Your Grace," he said. Although without much enthusiasm. He looked tired.

"Sorry I missed you last night," I said, clapping him on the shoulder. "Was up to my ass with this Concordia thing."

"Not a problem, Your Grace," he said with a wave of his hand. "Totally understandable."

"You said you were interested in some 'mid-week merriment'" I smiled. "Did you find any?"

"Sadly, no," he said with a crooked smile. "Merriment seems to be in short supply these days.

The elevator arrived.

"Well, we mustn't stop searching, eh?" I said, holding an arm out and inviting Sean into the elevator.

"No," he said as he headed into the car. "No, indeed."

As he passed by me, I got a whiff that told me that Sean must have been very diligent in his search for merriment last night.

Turning over every stone.

And, apparently, more than one bottle.

CHAPTER 14

"Terry Wilson, dial 5600. Terry Wilson to 5600."

Perhaps more than anything else, the paging system at The Crack contributed to the atmosphere of urgency, pressure, and sense of mission that everyone had. It was like working in an emergency room.

That being the case, being paged to Ext. 5600 was like being paged to the neurosurgical amphitheater where it's all gone horribly wrong—where not even Dr. Meredith Grey, McDreamy, and House put together could possibly set things right.

Ext. 5600 was the home of Justin Cracknell himself. If Justin wanted to tell you what a swell job you were doing (which happened slightly less often than the appearance of Haley's Comet), he called you himself and either gave you the attaboy over the phone or asked you if you could "pop down for a minute". If you were paged, it meant that someone had screwed up in an epic way—and either it was you that screwed up or you that was being called in to fix the screw-up.

"What are my chances?" I said to Glynis, Justin's gatekeeper and the one who had delivered the page.

"Relax, it's not you. Well, it's not you who messed up."

"Imagine my relief."

"But I do believe they want you to fix it."

"How unusual."

"Isn't it?" Glynis laughed. "Come on down."

As I approached Justin's office, the narrow, green carpet of the hallway opened out into a wide green foyer in front of the mahogany doors. The doors were open, which was a good sign—closed doors meant it was really ugly.

I slowed my nervous stride as I reached the doors.

"Hey Glyn," I said to Glynis. "Go right in?"

"Hey, Ter. Yeah, he's waiting for you."

I walked slowly into the inner sanctum.

Justin's office was the office of a captain of industry if ever there was one. It was the obligatory corner office; floor-to-ceiling windows wrapped the room on two sides. The green carpet extended from the hall but once inside changed to a slightly richer green and slightly plusher thickness. The walls were the same burnished mahogany as the doors, complete with wainscoting and hand-carved accents. (I'd heard that when we moved into the space, Justin had flown a woodworker over from England just to craft the grooved wainscoting, the burled chair rail and the rest.) The chairs were burgundy leather, the couches, of which there were three, were tastefully done in Ralph Lauren prints, and there were original oils on the walls of scenes in England and Scotland. If it sounds like a lawyer's office, that's because that's what it looked like. It was beautiful, but weird—outside the doors, it was all chrome and glass and contemporary buzz; inside it was like a London men's club. But that was Justin—he preached new school, lived old school.

"Terry," Justin said. "How are you, my boy?"

"Good, Justin...thanks. How's things?"

"Well," he smiled, a smile that had launched a thousand deals. "That's what we're going to talk about."

He waved his arm to include the rest of the group that was gathered there. They'd been sitting in silence since I came in—I hadn't really noticed exactly who was there until just now. That was the way it was when you were summoned into Justin's lair—no matter who else was there, you were there to see him, so for the first few minutes he was all you noticed.

Seated with him was Mike Haggerty, which led me to understand that the problem was of the new business variety.

"Hey, Mike," I said, taking the spot on the couch next to him.

"Hey, Terry, how's it going?" he chirped. Mike always greeted you as if he'd just run into you on the street after a five-year absence. I'd just seen him in the elevator 20 minutes earlier.

In the chairs sat John McGinley, whom I liked, and Jane Fontana, whom I didn't. John was a young account guy, viewed as a comer in the agency and his presence meant he had earned the right to help direct this pitch—and to run the business if we won.

Jane was our Chief Strategy Officer. This meant that she and Mike were engaged in an on-going taffy pull over who actually ran New Business. The fact that she was in charge of Strategy was the laughingstock of most of the agency. As far as anyone could tell, the only successful strategy she had ever mapped out was that she, reputedly, had slept with Justin.

Seated in the chair next to Justin, which was about the most improbable place on earth to find him, was Ross Burroughs.

"Hey, John...Jane. Hi, Ross."

"Hey, Terry," said John.

Jane stared at some papers in her lap. Maybe she was trying to teach herself to read.

"Hi, Terry." Ross said this with actual affection. He seemed uneasy being here and seemed to welcome a face from Creative, technically his home turf.

Cracknell and Burroughs marriage was, as I've said, arranged. And like many such marriages, they had begun to grow apart almost immediately. At this point, Ross was a figurehead. In fact, Justin had made several attempts to remove him, fire him or otherwise banish him from sight. The problem was that when they'd started the agency, Justin and Ross had each agreed to own 50% of the agency. Not a share more for either of them. And since the place was privately held, there had never been any other shares issued. So while Justin was willing to ignore, double-cross, coerce, and otherwise run roughshod over Ross, the simple fact was Ross was not going away, until Ross felt good and ready to go away.

None of which explained what the hell Ross was doing in this meeting.

"How much do you know about the Global Petrol pitch?" Justin asked.

"A little," I said. "I mean, I know a little of the background, I...don't know...the work..."

"That's all right, Terry," said Justin, holding up a hand and putting an end to my nervous babbling. "Carolyn's got the work well in hand. We want you to help us with something else."

I looked around quizzically.

"Well, Ter," began Mike. "Here's the thing—the guys at Global are older guys. They've been in the business a long time; most of 'em are lifers at Global. They're conservative. They don't meet a lot of guys like us—younger, hipper, cooler."

"They hate younger, hipper, cooler," McGinley added. Which was fine for John, because he was one of those guys who were 35 going on 55. He'd fit right in at Global.

"And they hate women," snapped Jane.

"They don't hate women, Jane," said Justin quietly.

"Then why aren't I going?" she snapped back.

There was a lot of silence and some clearing of throats.

"Terry, we want the group we send to look as much like them as possible," Mike said quietly, probably fearing that if he made any sudden moves or noise, Jane would strike him like a cobra.

"Um, do I look that old? I mean, I know I haven't been getting enough sleep, but..."

It wasn't that funny, but the tension in the room magnified my feeble attempt at humor. Everyone laughed.

Except Jane.

Jane never laughed.

"No, dear boy, no," Justin said. "What we're trying to get round to is this—given the audience, we'd like Ross to present the creative."

Ross probably hadn't been to a pitch since Reagan's first term in the White House.

"OK." And, uh, my role would be?

"And we'd like you to help him prepare his presentation."

"I haven't done this in a while," Ross said sheepishly.

"Uh, sure. You mean like write up an outline, a rationale?"

"Yeah, partly that." said Mike. "And, you know, a little coaching—how to present the work and stuff."

"But shouldn't Carolyn..."

"She's got all she can handle getting the work together. We don't want to distract her." Justin explained diplomatically. "And you're an excellent presenter, Terry. One of the best."

I looked at Ross. For a man in his late 50's, he looked as much like a nine-year-old boy as you could imagine. He was looking straight at me, his eyes almost pleading. I suddenly understood— he needed help with this and he was embarrassed to death about it. But having to be lectured by a young woman on how to do his job would have been humiliating for him. (He was pretty old-school himself, in that regard.) To have to sit there, the Chairman of the agency, and be treated like the village idiot—my heart ached for him.

I looked right back at him.

"Hell, yeah, Ross—let's do it. You can knock those old birds on their asses."

Ross's face lit up.

Justin smiled.

Mike and John leapt in and started handing me decks, background briefs, you name it.

A thought struck me—an obvious thought that no one had mentioned.

"Uh, when is this meeting?"

"Day after tomorrow."

Great.

Late that afternoon, my phone rang.

"Terry, it's Sean." Meghan called in the door.

I picked up.

"Excellency."

"Your Grace. Care to join me for a tureen of the Loud Mouth Soup?"

I laughed.

"A martini might make this whole day make sense."

"Chez Jo-Jo, then. I will have the chef standing ready with ladle in hand at 6:30."

"I'll be there with bells on."

"Tassels will do."

CHAPTER 15

"You're *shitting* me!" Sean said when I told him about the presentation clinic I was expected to put on for Ross.

"No, I'm not."

"And will you be receiving a healthy slice of the Old Boy's monumental paycheck for your yeoman efforts?"

"Ah, Excellency, I'm quite sure my efforts come under the heading of 'my job'. At least in Justin's eyes."

"In Justin's eyes, Your Grace, anything up to and including a covert night jump into a foreign dictatorship would come under the heading of 'your job'," Sean said sarcastically.

"True," I laughed. "Anything for the cause."

"Yeah," he snorted.

Sean looked ruefully into the remains of his martini.

"You know," he said. "There was a time..."

"A time that what?"

"A time I believed it was a cause."

"What?"

"The Crack."

"Me too."

"You don't anymore?"

"I don't know. You don't?"

Sean laughed without a trace of happiness.

"Nah," he said with disgust. "The stuff I'm working on is invisible, Carolyn makes it a point to flog my ass every day whether it needs it or not, and I haven't won an award since Edward VII gave up his throne to boff Wallis Simpson."

"Ah, none of us are knockin' it out of the park these days."

"Maybe not...Jason! Another crock of your excellent soup!" he called up the bar. "And a bowl for Viscount Wilson here!"

He continued.

"Maybe we aren't all doing the Queen's wave on our way up to the dais. But, at least you seem to be advancing."

"How? I haven't won an award in two years! And Concordia isn't likely to provide that opportunity anytime soon."

"No, that's true. But you seem to be in the right part of the solar system. I mean, look at this thing with Ross."

"I'd prefer not to."

"I know it's a carbuncle of a thing to get handed, but it's important to the place. I mean, Justin himself is involved—it's high profile, big stuff. And when it hit the fan, they called you. Not even Larry."

"Well, you know how tenuous things are between Larry and Ross."

"Just the same, it was you they wanted to be the cavalry. In our particular solar system, that's like a visit to the sun. In fact, you seem to be moving constantly inward in our solar system— moving toward the sun. My star seems to be being sucked toward the darkness. Moving away from the sun as fast as you're moving toward it."

"Well, when we pass each other, let's grab each other and escape the orbit altogether," I said, raising my refilled martini toward him.

He raised his, but his face was blank.

"We already passed each other, Terry. Didn't you notice?

CHAPTER 16

The next morning, my hangover and I stood in front of my closet. I was not only figuring out what to wear, I was suddenly realizing I might be asked to travel to the pitch. If I'd learned one thing at The Crack, it was that most of the presentation preparation happened the night before. But since the meeting was in Chicago, those discussions would take place either on the plane or at the hotel where the pitch team was staying tonight. I figured I'd better pack a bag.

When I arrived at the office, Meghan told me my day was already in high gear.

"Ross's office is looking for you, Larry wants you to pop your head in for a minute, Mike's called twice, Jane Fontana called, of all people, and Carolyn sauntered by and asked if 'that cute Terry Wilson' was in."

"What does she want?"

"Your ass, if I'm not mistaken."

"That's nauseating."

"In the extreme. I'll tell Ross's office you're on your way. And then when you get a minute, you can explain to me what this shitstorm is all about, thank you very much."

"Aye aye. I'm just gonna stop and see Larry on my way."

I headed down the hall to Larry's. He was reading Stuart Elliott's advertising column in The New York Times. He had his new reading glasses on. Buying reading glasses was the kind of concession to age that made Larry break out in hives. The clean, white interior design—both here at the office and at his two homes—the Armani casual clothing, the Porsche...it was all a certain aesthetic. The glasses were Armani, too—clean, thin black frames that looked very European. They were actually quite handsome on him. But to Larry, the beauty of the design didn't make up for their purpose. To him, they may as well have been a pair of those glasses with the big nose and the Groucho moustache and eyebrows. When he saw me coming toward the door he whipped them off as if they were burning his face.

"What the hell is this thing with Ross?" he said.

"Ask Justin and Mike," I shrugged.

"Are you really gonna teach him how to present?"

"I guess I'm gonna try."

"Why didn't they ask me?" I knew it was only a matter of time before we got to this. Larry didn't like being excluded.

"I don't know. I had the same question," I lied.

"Course, I'm only the Creative Director. Why would they want to ask me about how to present creative?"

"I think they think I'm less of a threat." This was true. I was also a better presenter than Larry but I wasn't going to say that. I may have been hung over, but I wasn't drunk.

He looked at me. He had long wanted Ross's title of Chief Creative Officer and while he was pretty benign as corporate sharks go, it wasn't exactly a secret.

"Maybe you're right."

"I mean, it's bad enough he has to go through this exercise. Getting tutored by you would be political suicide."

"Well, why not Carolyn? She's running the pitch?"

"The next worst thing to you would be a woman."

"Oh...yeah."

"So I drew the short straw."

"I guess you did. Well, good luck."

"See ya, Larry."

I walked toward the door.

"Hey, Terry?"

"Yeah?"

"Don't make him too good."

"Don't worry," I laughed.

Ross's office was a floor below, just like Justin's, but at the opposite end of the floor. No English clubbiness for him; his design aesthetic was much more modern. Well, let's say the aesthetic of the people his wife had hired to do it for him was much more modern. Glass tables, Le Corbusier chairs, angular glass vases with sleek Calla lilies in them. It was the polar opposite of Justin's office. Even the green rug stopped at the doorway. Ross had his own beige carpet to highlight the office.

Ross jumped to his feet when I came in. "Terry, how are you? Jesus, it's good of you to come do this."

"Not at all, Ross. Us creative types have gotta stick together."

"Jesus, isn't that the truth? Here let's sit down."

We sat at the low coffee table in the corner of the office. I had been through all the decks and everything the day before and, despite my several martinis with Sean, had managed to make a few notes last night.

I hoped they made sense this morning.

"OK, near as I can figure, the part we have to go over is your set-up. I mean the work will present itself, you know? You read the scripts, read the headlines; I mean, in my experience at that point they decide for themselves, no matter what you say. And that part's already done."

"OK." He was hanging on my every word, which was completely unnerving.

"So, you're going to be coming out of the research portion—which Mike is going to present. He'll hand it over to you. You need to first continue the flow of logic. Our basic premise–" I flipped through the deck looking for the slide that held the golden strategic nugget. "Is that Global isn't a gas station. It's enabling people's lives."

Ross looked at me as though I were speaking in tongues.

"How do you mean?" he said. This was the point when you were describing things to Larry where he already got it, had decided whether he liked it and was already off thinking about how you would execute that. I was spoiled by it. I was going to have to lead Ross by the hand.

"Well, the things they sell—gas, oil, washer fluid, even coffee, soda, sandwiches at their convenience marts—are like pit stops in the race of life."

I watched as he wrote down "pit stop".

We were going to be here a while.

When Ross and I were finally finished or at least couldn't take any more, I headed back upstairs with the promise that we'd hook up again later in the day to go over everything.

"There's a rehearsal, I guess it is, at–" He walked over and, putting on his half glasses, examined his schedule. "4:00. Will you be there?"

"If you want me to," I smiled.

"Great!" he said with much more enthusiasm than he had reason to feel.

Back upstairs, there were four people waiting to see me, arranged in a loose line like you see at the deli counter—a junior team I didn't even know who wanted to show me a house ad; a woman from traffic who wanted to know when I thought boards for Concordia would be ready; and, last but not least, certainly not if you asked her, was Carolyn Kelly, dressed in one of her Sex and the City power suits.

"Hey cutie," she began as I approached. I didn't dare look at Meghan, who was probably vomiting quietly into her wastebasket.

"Hi Carolyn...Susan...Guys. Now serving #36..."

Carolyn laughed. "You're so funny."

Now I did look at Meghan.

"Who's first?" I asked her.

"I won't take a minute, hon," Carolyn said, grabbing my arm and leading me into my own office. The look on Meghan's face told me that Carolyn was nowhere near first.

"So," Carolyn began, arranging herself on one of the chairs so that she was showing *w-a-a-a-y* more leg than necessary. "How's Ross?"

"Nervous...like me."

"Well he should be," she snapped, her face suddenly angry.

The speed with which Carolyn could go from being Rebecca of Sunnybrook Farm to becoming Cruella de Vil always took my breath away.

"He doesn't know anything about this pitch. He doesn't know the clients; he doesn't know the work. This is my pitch!"

"I don't think anyone doubts that, Carolyn."

"Well, then why am I not going?"

"Whoa, whoa, whoa...this isn't my decision. I got drafted into this army. Believe me, I've got more to do than sit around giving poor Ross a primer on how to present."

"Well, why didn't they ask me?"

"Justin said he thought you were busy with the work. Didn't want to distract you."

"Bullshit."

"Well, that may well be. But that's what he said to me. Look Carolyn, I know this sucks. It's not right. But you're too old to think this game is fair."

"Fair is one thing—sexist is another."

"I know, I agree. You think I like the sound of these guys? Bunch of old, stodgy, sexist, racist SOB's? You think they hate women? Wait'll you see what they think of creative people."

Carolyn stifled a smile.

"Ah, c'mon, kid, we'll just slog through it and go on with life. We're probably not gonna win anyway, so let's get through it and go back to our accounts."

"You're right, you're right." She tossed her hair and let the smile out.

"How's the work? Do you like it?"

"Yes I do!" she barked. Ah, Cruella, nice to see you again. "It's great and I want you to make sure Ross doesn't fuck it up."

"Well, I can only promise so much, kid. I mean I'm concentrating on his set-up. Why don't you go through the work with him?"

"No one's asked me to."

"Believe me––he'll want you to."

"I'll call him."

"Why don't you just come to that 4:00 rehearsal?"

"Cause I'm not going to the presentation. I don't have anything to rehearse!"

"No. But Ross does. Bring the work and show him how to go through it. You can be Edgar Bergen and he can be Charlie McCarthy. Maybe he'll even sit on your lap."

"Ugh, no thank you." She shifted her weight a little. "You, on the other hand...."

"Good bye, Carolyn. See you at 4:00."

She uncoiled from the chair.

"See ya, cutie." She rubbed my back as she walked out.

"Meghan?" I called from the chair without getting up. She appeared at the door looking as though her stomach was still unsettled.

"Yes?"

"What's next?"

"Oh! Are you finished with that refugee from a Danielle Steele novel?"

"Yes, Meghan."

"Well, then you've got Mike and Scott with an ad for CEO night at the Symphony, whom I can probably make go away, Susan with a Concordia question, whom I can probably make go away and me with a question—whom you can't make go away."

..ng up my hands is if to shield

ʟet me look at this foolish ad and then

you what's happening."

you, Mis-ta Wil-sun," Meghan sing-songed as she went out the door. "Go ahead in guys," I heard her say in her normal voice.

The rehearsal at 4 was in the Empire Room—the main conference room that Justin had named for the fading glory of England.

There was no end to the whole Brit thing.

The table was horseshoe-shaped and deep mahogany like everything else. There were about 14 people milling around—Haggerty, McGinley, and Jane Fontana were huddled up at one end of the horseshoe with three people from Media on the other corner. In the center was the obligatory MacBook Pro, beaming the pages of the presentation deck onto the blank wall. Hovering over the computer were Maria Martinez, Haggerty's right-hand woman in new biz and a guy named Chris from MIS. There were two people from Research, assorted account executives and, as I looked up, Carolyn coming through the side door.

What there wasn't, was Ross.

"Where is he?" Carolyn whispered to me fiercely.

"He'll be here. He's the Chairman of the agency, for Christ's sake. He doesn't have to be the first one here."

"Guys, should we get started?" Mike chirped.

Everyone settled in around the table and pulled out their rough drafts of the presentation deck.

The purpose of these little get-togethers was primarily to make sure the presentation flowed. This was often harder than it sounds, because every department or discipline had its own section, which had all been prepared separately.

Good presentations flowed like water over granite. The bad ones were stitched together like Frankenstein.

And looked it.

The Creative section of every presentation deck was the same—one page on which it said 'Creative' and that was it. And the rehearsal wasn't going to get into the presentation of actual boards; the only part that needed rehearsing was the set-up, the lead-in, which was going to be Ross's moment in the sun.

We were about halfway through the research portion when Ross came in and took a seat next to me.

"Hey Ross," I said quietly.

"Hi Ross!" Carolyn said much less quietly and much more enthusiastically. Cruella had taken a coffee break and we were being treated to the full-on Rebecca of Sunnybrook Farm.

"How's it going?" I asked Ross, pointing to the fistful of notes and drafts he clutched.

"Good, good," he said unconvincingly. "Just trying to work up that whole, whole...what was it?" He shuffled through the papers. "That whole...ya know...pit stop thing...that's good...good stuff."

I was starting to smell fear and it didn't smell pretty.

The rehearsal was continuing, each presenter going through their particular 10 minutes or so, covering the agency's history, what we'd done for our other flagship clients, getting into Global's business—a look at the marketplace, the research we'd done, the obligatory interview tape of their customers talking, all of it leading up to our key insights and the strategy we had settled on.

As each presenter ran through their little speeches, Haggerty would interrupt every few sentences.

"Hey, you know, Richard," he said to a guy from Research—one of the only guys in Research in fact, but apparently we were ratcheting up the testosterone level across the board. "That stuff is really good but maybe you could serve it up this way." He went on to basically script Richard's entire speech for him.

The truth was, Haggerty would have loved to give every portion of the presentation himself—but it'd look bad. So he'd have to settle for completely micro-managing the thing and scripting everybody out. Anyone who'd been through this before, though, also knew that in the actual presentation, even if you followed the script to the letter, Haggerty was going to jump in at least once in your speech and try to make the point himself.

"So that's how that'll go..." Haggerty said at the end of the strategy piece.

Now it was our turn—in the meeting, this is where the baton would be passed to Ross.

"So guys, what've we got?" Haggerty said turning to look at us.

Haggerty was a big vocal proponent of creative, always beating the drum for it in new business presentations, agency meetings, when he was quoted in the press.

But the truth was he didn't like creative people.

In his heart of hearts, he thought they were erratic and unpredictable—and for a guy who wanted to be able to script out every turn of the planet Earth, this was catastrophic. He thought creatives were messy, something to be managed, pushed around like chess pieces to fit his master plan. So when he turned to you in a meeting like this, his voice, his body language, the tilt of his salt-and-peppered head all indicated that he was really excited to see what you had.

But when you looked in his eyes, you could tell he was thinking "OK, how did you guys fuck it up this time?"

Well, Ross didn't disappoint him.

He stood up and babbled through a segue into the creative section that sounded as if he was speaking Farsi.

Maybe an ancient, no-longer-used dialect of Farsi.

I recognized a few of the catch phrases and thoughts that we had talked about, but since I'd left Ross's office, he hadn't woven it into any kind of coherent piece. After all the outlining I'd done for him, he was freezing up, even here in the rehearsal. I didn't know whether to kill him or hug him.

Carolyn was not, shall we say, as emotionally conflicted as I was. She was slowly turning crimson and if there had been an axe in the room I'm pretty sure she would have buried it in the back of Ross's head. I could see her point. She thought she had some pretty good work to show. But with a set-up like this, you could show them the Sistine Chapel and they wouldn't buy it.

"...and so...then" Ross concluded, "I'll turn it over to...who?"

There was silence and a lot of looking at papers.

"Uh, you don't turn it over to anyone, Ross" Haggerty said as encouragingly as he could. "You'll be presenting the work."

"You can just go right into it, Ross," I said quietly. Then, to the room I said, "I thought maybe Carolyn could..."

She didn't need anymore introduction than that.

"Let me show you the campaign" she said, circling to the front of the table. "So that everyone can see what we've got here." She was looking daggers at Ross.

Ross didn't even notice.

CHAPTER 17

"Hey, Al, it's me," I said when I called Alex after the rehearsal debacle.

"Hey Babe! How are things?"

"Oy."

"That good, huh?"

"Well, for starters, I have to go to Chicago tonight."

"Tonight?"

"Yeah, I'm on my way to the airport right now."

"Why do you have to go?"

"Well, I told you about this whole thing with Ross..."

"Yeah, you were going to prep him on the presentation."

"Yeah, well, let's just say he's not an apt pupil."

"Are you gonna have to do it for him?"

"No way."

"But aren't they looking for a good presenter?"

"No, actually what they're looking for is an older man who won't step on his tongue while he's presenting. As long as he's got some gray around the temples and speaks English, he'll do."

"How bad is he?"

"Bad, kid. Really bad."

"I'm sorry, hon. Are they going to be pissed at you?"

"Why, because he sucks?"

"Yeah."

"Nah. They already know he sucks. In fact, part of me thinks Justin wants him to suck—further evidence in the case against him. But if I can make him 1/10th less sucky, it'll be a triumph. For me anyway."

"When will you be back?"

"Tomorrow night. Will you buy me a drink to ease my pain?"

"You sure a drink is all it's gonna take to ease your pain?"

"No."

"Good. Come by when you get in."

"I'll call ya."

"Good luck. Love ya."

"Thanks. You too."

CHAPTER 18

American Flight 180 banked into the evening sky and headed toward Chicago. I was seated in First Class next to Ross—a rare perk for me but since Ross always flew First Class he had me upgraded. In fact, we were the only ones from Cracknell in First Class—the rest of our traveling road show was back in Coach.

You could almost hear the steam coming out of Jane's ears from here. Although she wasn't presenting, she had wangled her way onto the travel team "to help make sure the presentation was strategically sound." This was, of course, complete crap—the presentation was what it was. All that was left was to present it. But by coming, Jane avoided the taint of being left behind, of being outside the innermost loop of the agency. Once again, her most astute strategic moves were in positioning herself.

Ross and I each took a cocktail when the attendant offered and then hauled out the notes and charts of the presentation.

"So whaddaya think?" I asked.

"Well, I think I get the idea that the gas station isn't just a gas station," Ross answered thoughtfully.

"Good," I said. We were making some progress. If the pitch were going to be next year, we'd be in good shape.

"But how do you connect the...what did Carolyn call it... paradigm shift," he mumbled as he shuffled through the papers. "There was a good nugget about that in the...dynamic..."

Jesus, he sounded like the Nutty Professor. It seemed like the more we went over it the less he got it. Listening to him, I wasn't even sure that I got it anymore.

The flight attendant came by and we each had another drink and then dinner. Conversation had stopped—Ross was reading through the deck again like a monk looking for illumination. I was concentrating very hard on coming up with Plan B.

"Look, Ross" I said after the dinner trays had been cleared away. "Forget all this stuff."

"What do you mean?" he said looking at me over his half-glasses.

"I mean, this is just confusing you," I said, pointing to the bouquet of papers he had in his hand.

"Oh" he smiled slightly. "Does it show?"

"A little" I smiled back. "But look—give me this shit."

I gathered up all the papers from his tray and grabbed the pile out of his hand. I stuffed them all in the seat-back pocket behind American Way magazine.

"Now, look at me" I said. "You've read through this stuff, you've listened to everyone talk about it, heard the presentation, listened to Mike, listened to Carolyn. Forget memorizing this. Stop trying to learn this like you were learning your lines as an actor. Think about it. What do you think? How would you explain it?"

Ross stopped looking at me and looked straight ahead, pursing his lips and looking thoughtful.

"OK, think about it this way," I said. "What's your favorite restaurant in St. Kitts?" He and his wife, Tish, had a home there that had been written up in Architectural Digest. Twice.

He looked at me. The introduction of something pleasant into this on-going unpleasantness was like finding a piece of flotsam just before you go under for the final time.

"Why, the Royal Palm!" he beamed. "At Ottley's Plantation! Have you been?"

"Uh, no—but I'm sure it's amazing. And whom do you go there with? Besides Tish?"

"Well, Joss and Glenda Maxwell." He smiled at the very thought of it.

"And whaddya order? What's your favorite dish?"

"The paella! Best I ever had!" He was going with it. Finally, a subject he knew something about.

"All right, then. You're sitting across the table from Josh and..."

"It's Joss."

Ross and Joss. Good God.

"Sorry—Joss and Glenda. You've got a big plate of paella in front of you, the sun is setting over the Caribbean and the waiter is pouring a bottle of vintage Rioja while you polish off the remains of your Mount Gay and tonic. Now...look Joss in the eye and explain it to him."

I stood up to head for the men's room. I turned back to Ross.

"And write it down."

We landed in Chicago, picked up all the luggage and presentation cases and climbed into two limos that were waiting out front. I purposely got into the one Ross wasn't in. I couldn't take much more.

"How's Ross doing?" asked Melanie, an eager young thing that was helping out in New Biz these days.

"God, he's great. Really—he's gonna be awesome"

We got to the hotel, got our keys, and started to scatter to our rooms. It was late and we needed to be up early.

"Hey guys," said Mike, perky even now at 11:30 at night. "Why don't we meet downstairs at around 9:00—we'll have some coffee and go over everything. Sound good?"

"Ross, how's your part?" asked Jane with all the warmth and feeling of an anaconda.

"It's good," I jumped in. "Two more things to go over."

Jane looked at me.

"All right, guys" Mike said. "See you in the morning."

"Mike, there's one thing I wanted to go over with you," said Jane. Ross and I seized the opportunity to head for the elevators.

"Want me to come by now or should we just hook up in the morning?" I offered to Ross.

"Morning's OK, don't you think?"

"Absolutely."

"What are the two things?" he asked.

"What two things?"

"You told Jane there were two things to go over. "

"Oh, that. Just a diversionary tactic."

"Oh. Are there two things?"

The elevator stopped at my floor. I stepped out into the corridor. I looked back at Ross.

"There are way more than two things."

Ross smiled as the doors slid closed behind me

The next morning, I got up, showered and looked in my hang-up bag. I figured I might as well put on the rig I had brought. Couldn't hurt.

When I was dressed, I headed to Ross's room. It was about 8:00, the meeting wasn't until 11:00 so I figured we'd have a chance to go through his piece a couple times.

Ross was staying in the Presidential Suite. It actually had a doorbell—which I rang.

Ross opened the door looking absolutely immaculate—blindingly white shirt with French cuffs, Hermès tie, silk braces, and chalk-stripe suit. He looked every inch the *eminence gris* he was supposed to be.

"Morning, Ross," I said.

"C'mon in, Terry" he said in a monotone.

I guessed the cheerleading had better begin immediately.

"This'll be great." I was following Ross across the enormous expanse of living room toward the dining room table at the other end. "I figure we'll run through this a couple times here and then once more in the room."

Ross had reached the dining room table where his notes were spread out all over one end. He slumped down in the chair at the head of the table.

"So we'll knock off the opening piece now," I said, still rattling the pom-poms. "And then–"

"I can't do it."

"What?"

"I can't do it," Ross said quietly.

I sat down in the chair to his right.

"Can't do what...exactly?" I said softly. I was grasping for something, anything.

"I mean, I can't remember...which campaign comes first, why, why are they in that order? Couldn't we just post them around the room and..."

A glimmer of hope.

"Hold on, Ross—it's the work that gets confusing?"

"Hell, yes, it's the work that gets confusing!"

"OK. OK. Well, what if you just concentrated on the set-up and someone else did the work?"

He looked up for the first time.

"Would that work for you, Ross?"

"Yeah—that would be fine."

"All right. Well maybe that's what we'll do. Maybe you'll do the set-up and I could do the work."

"Jeez, that would really help. What do you think of that?"

I smiled and lifted my suit jacket up by the lapels.

"I think it's a good thing I'm not in my bathrobe."

We spent the next hour in separate parts of the living room—Ross going over his set-up and me going through the work. The good news was Ross now had less to think about. The bad news

was I could no longer take him through how to do it because I had
to get my own shit together.

I had gone in the bedroom earlier and called downstairs to tell
Mike that we wouldn't be joining them for breakfast.

"Is it going OK?"

"Yeah. Well, pretty good."

"What?"

"I think I'm going to have to present the work."

"Oh shit!"

"Thanks for the vote of confidence."

"It's not that. It's...."

"I know, Mike. Just trying to keep my sense of humor."

"I know. It's fine, it's fine. We'll be better off, actually."

"Don't leap to that conclusion. I'm not much more prepared
than he is."

"Can I do anything?"

"Nah. We'll meet you in the lobby."

When the time came, Ross and I rode down to the elevator
in silence. We met the crew downstairs, everyone with their game
faces on. Particularly Jane, who was dressed to the nines and getting in one of the town cars even though she was still not part
of the meeting. I wondered if she was going to just walk into the
conference room and sit down, just claim squatter's rights.

Global's headquarters were up on Michigan Ave. overlooking
the Chicago River. We pulled up out front and were directed to the
37th Floor, where we were herded into a tiny conference room.

Mike almost fainted.

"This isn't the room, is it?" he asked the assistant who had
led us in.

"Oh, of course not!" she laughed. "Relax. This is just a place
to wait until the first agency is done. Then you'll have half an
hour to set-up in the boardroom and go. There's coffee in the
corner. I'm right down the hall if you need anything. My name's
Kathy."

"Thanks, Kathy," we all mumbled.

A little while later, Melanie, Maria and the rest of the AV team were summoned to the big room to set up. We all stayed behind rehearsing our parts quietly in our heads. Including Ross. I could no longer imagine what was going through his head—but I was sure it was really noisy in there.

Kathy the Friendly Assistant reappeared at the door.

"They're ready for you."

We stood up and trooped down the hall toward the boardroom.

We were about 20 feet from the doors when Ross, who was just ahead of me, stopped dead.

I stopped next to him.

"I can't do it," he said staring straight ahead.

"What?"

"Any of it."

Mike and I looked at each other.

Jane, who apparently was going to walk us right to the door before turning away, exploded.

"Oh, for Christ's sake!!"

"Shut up, Jane!" Mike hissed. "You want them to hear you?"

Ross still stood looking straight ahead.

"All right" Mike said. "Ross, you introduce the agency and Terry. Terry, you do as much as you can."

Jane turned and stomped back toward the waiting room.

I gently touched Ross's arm. "Let's go, Ross."

Alex had been right, I thought. It had never occurred to me that I would actually have to present. Now I just had to hope Alex wasn't right about the second part.

The part where everyone was pissed at me.

CHAPTER 19

"The trip home must have been awful," Alex said, her head on my shoulder. We were lying in her bed in the semi-dark.

"Yeah, it was pretty quiet," I answered, stroking her bare upper arm.

"What did Ross say on the way home?"

"Nothing to me. I was back in steerage with the rest of the gang."

"You didn't fly First Class home?" She raised her head a little to look at me.

"Ooooh no. On the way home, I was busted back to Private. Besides, I don't think Ross needed any company."

"God, the poor guy," she said, settling her head back on my shoulder. "He must be mortified."

"I think he feels pretty bad. But, hey, I don't know—the guy's a gazillionaire."

"You think money makes you immune to embarrassment?"

"No, no, no. I mean he could just chuck it all. Avoid being put in that position ever again."

"You think he'll ever be put in that position again?" she smiled.

"Ah, good point," I laughed. "I'm pretty sure his career as a presenter is over."

"What'll happen tomorrow?"

"You mean what will the fallout be?"

"Yeah."

"Probably nothing. I mean, the story will make the rounds—if it hasn't already—and everyone will go on with whatever they're doing. I mean, that's the thing with New Biz—it's really intense for the people involved, but for 99% of the agency it doesn't touch their lives at all."

"Litigation's like that."

"Yeah?"

"Oh, Sean called looking for you."

"Here?"

"Yeah."

"He left me a voice mail at the office, too. I'm sure he's dying to find out how it went."

"How's he doing these days?"

"Good."

"Yeah?"

"Well, he's a little down, not working on anything too good these days. Feels like he's out of the loop."

"How're he and Maggie doing?"

"He and Maggie are no longer doing—anything."

She lifted herself up, propping herself up on her elbows and stared at me.

"Guys are unbelievable."

"What?"

I mean he's one of your best friends."

"I know. What?"

"You tell me he's doing good? He feels lost at work, not involved, not working on any good accounts, he and his girlfriend just broke up and you tell me he's doing good?"

"He's fine."

"If that was one of my friends, I'd be at their apartment on suicide watch."

"Oh, stop it—Sean isn't going to kill himself."

"That's not the point. The point is you should be more aware of what's going on with the people you care about. You should really know how they're doing, not just 'Oh yeah, he's doing great'. He's not doing great! Maybe he needs your help."

"Oh, he's just like the rest of us—he needs a hit, something tasty to work on, something that'll be fun and cool and get noticed."

"What about a relationship?"

"Well," I chuckled. "In the short term, I'm sure Sean would gladly trade a nice, stable, fulfilling relationship for a handful of awards."

"Are you serious?"

"Absolutely."

"You people are nuts."

"Of course we're nuts. We're full of insecurity, anxiety and low self-esteem."

"Yeah, so?"

"So all of that drives us to seek approval, validation, and praise wherever we can get it. And, believe me, getting up on stage somewhere and accepting your silver bowl or your gold pencil is a heapin' helpin' of approval."

"I don't understand men."

"Oh, trust me, it isn't a guy thing—it's a creative thing. I could give you a list of women who feel the same way."

"Please don't."

CHAPTER 20

"Oh my God, Terry!" Meghan was saying, sitting in my office the next morning. "What did Mike say?"

"I think he was like the rest of us—too weirded out to even be pissed. I mean it was bizarre. Everyone mostly felt bad for the guy."

"Except the Viper Bitch."

"Jane?" I laughed. "Yeah, Jane didn't seem to be exactly welling up with compassion."

"What's gonna happen?"

"You know, everyone keeps asking me that. Nothing, I guess. I mean if it were you or I we'd already be shitcanned but hell, he's the Chairman of the Agency. Who's gonna fire him?"

"Justin."

"If Justin hasn't figured out how to get rid of Ross by now, it ain't gonna happen today. I think life'll just go on."

"Do you think we're gonna get it?"

"What, Global? Are you high? You can imagine how buttoned up we looked after that fiasco in the hall?"

"Carolyn called."

"Tell her I took a medical leave of absence."

"You've gotta talk to her," Meghan laughed.

"Fine, fine." I said getting up. "I've gotta go see Sean first."

Sean's office was at the opposite corner of the building from me. Not that he had the corner—that was reserved for Carolyn. Sean's "hutch", as he called it, was two doors down.

"Seano," I said cruising through the door. He was seated at his Mac, looking at what looked like some sort of animation on the screen.

"Ah, home from the crusades!" he smiled turning to face me. "And do tell of your travails."

"You heard about it?" I said slumping down in his company-issue chair.

"Did His Eminence really spit the bit at the last minute?"

"Oh, and then some."

"Poor bastard."

"Yeah it was kinda sad—but, you know, I don't know, this is another one of those things where Mike tries to orchestrate the whole world and it blows up on us. Where we try to be too smart for our own good. Sending Ross out to present because he'll wow these guys with his gray hair. Christ!"

"Well, I must present these new logo treatments to Sun Grove tomorrow," he said, pointing at his computer screen. "And if Ross wants to come wow them with his gray hair he's welcome. In fact, anything that'll distract the Visigoths from disemboweling me and Marty is welcome."

"That bad?"

"The treatments? No, they're actually lovely—but the gifted visionaries at Sun Crop will almost surely find them lacking. Not quite the stultifying, Eisenhower-era design of which they're so fond."

"Got time for a see-through tonight?"

"Sean!" screeched Carolyn's voice from down the hall. "What is this shit?"

"How about right now?" Sean said rolling his eyes. He got up. "Well, once more into the breach..."

"I'll go with you."

We walked out of Sean's office and turned right towards Carolyn's. We reached the door and Sean walked into a withering hail of insults.

"How am I supposed to present this crap to Sun Crop? Do I have to do everything myself? Are you guys so incompetent that you'd actually..."

I poked my head in the door.

"Morning, Sunshine," I smiled. Carolyn's office was a complete anomaly. In the sleek, black-and-chrome, all-Prada, all-the-time world of advertising, Carolyn's office was a paean to Pierre Deux—overstuffed French country florals everywhere, dried arrangements on the tables, lace-trimmed pillows on the love seat. The love seat was a particularly ironic touch—because there wasn't a lot of love available in Carolyn's office.

Sex, maybe, but not love.

"Don't even talk to me," she snapped.

"Oh, like it's my fault" I laughed.

"It's everyone's fault—I should have been there."

"Oh trust me Carolyn—you didn't want to be there," I said.

"All that work, wasted!" she said through clenched teeth.

"I know, I know."

"It was the right thing for them!"

"Yup, it was right on the money."

"Except we screwed it up!"

"Well, the Ross situation wasn't optimal."

"I did all that work and then it got packed up and wasted!"

"Well, you know, Carolyn," I said, starting to get my back up a little, "we did present it. I *personally* presented it. I mean, the whole thing with Ross was weird and surreal and unfortunate—but we did present the work. And they didn't react at all."

"What do you mean?" Carolyn blinked.

"I mean you're acting as if when Ross choked, we just packed up the bags and came home. I mean, we did the pitch, Carolyn, we showed the work, every piece—but it was like presenting to the stone heads on Easter Island. Not a smile, not a frown, not a glimmer of recognition or interest from any one of them."

"Bastards."

"Oh absolutely. Prototypical bastards. Look up bastard in the dictionary and it's a picture of these guys."

Carolyn looked out the window of her office at the roof of the department store across the street.

"See?" I said. "I told you it wasn't a chick thing. They hate everybody."

"Get out of here," she smiled, waving her hand at me as she turned back from the window.

I turned to go.

"Oh, by the way," I said stopping at the door. "Those logo treatments look good."

The smile disappeared, the eyes narrowed and the transformation into Cruella began.

"See ya, guys!" I said, making my escape.

Back in my office, the phone rang. I could hear Meghan pick up. A moment later, she appeared in the doorway.

"That was Fran," she said, referring to Haggerty's assistant. "Mike would like you to join them in his office."

"Must have got the glad tidings," I said heaving myself wearily out of my chair.

"What glad tidings?" she asked.

"The official word that we're not getting Global Petrol's business."

Upstairs, a small group was gathered in Mike's spacious office. Mike, Larry, McGinley the account guy who was now not going to be working on Global, a few of the key support people from new biz and, of course, the ever-present, ever-pleasant Jane Fontana.

"Hey, Ter," Mike said quietly as I walked in.

"Hey, Bud..." Larry smiled.

"Mike...Larry...guys," I said and took a seat. I looked around the office and noticed, as I always did, the appearance of Mike's office.

Every stack of decks or magazines or call reports stacked just so, perfectly squared to the corners of whatever surface they were sitting on, pictures on the windowsill arranged in even, precise rows like soldiers awaiting inspection. Framed awards on the wall in perfect alignment, not a stray scrap of paper or unruly pile of memos to be seen. Even his wastebasket was empty and pristine.

The place was a shrine to OCD.

"Well, guys," Mike said. "I got a call from the guys at Global this morning and we didn't win."

"No way!" I said.

There was a small ripple of laughter. Except from Jane who looked, as usual, as if she had been carved out of ice.

"Well, they said our presentation was actually good—they liked the people, liked some of our thinking. But they felt like we didn't demonstrate a firm enough grasp on their business, on the challenges of driving distribution and how to steal market share from the established brands."

Mike paused and sighed.

"So, they're going to go with Burnett ..."

There was a collective groan from the table. A guy named Tom Conner who had once been a protégé of Cracknell's now ran New Business at Leo Burnett . This was about the 3rd time in the past 18 months that we had been bested by him. Justin had been pissed the first time, so this time it was going to go up his ass a mile. A feeling of pain, discomfort, and distress that he would make sure to share with all of us.

"So—thanks for the hard work, everyone. Thanks for coming up."

We all filed out of the office and headed down the hall. As Larry and I turned out of Mike's office, we noticed that Jane Fontana remained behind and quietly shut the door behind us.

Larry looked at me.

"Probably just wants a minute to give him a consoling hug..." I said.

"Yeah," Larry snorted. "Probably."

CHAPTER 21

It had been, all in all, one hellacious week. So the chance for a weekend and a little time with Alex was more than welcome. We would, however, be sharing that time with her parents—visiting them at their home this weekend. This was not, let me hasten to explain, exactly a hardship—the Clarkes lived at the beach, about an hour-and-a-half drive from the city in a beautiful, rambling, weathered-shingle home I teasingly referred to as "The Manse".

I had thought we could stop for a quick one at Bistro Jo-Jo on our way out but Alex put the kibosh on that.

"No, the traffic is going to be bad enough. And Mom said they'd hold dinner until I called from the road to see if we'd make it in time."

"All righty, then." I always managed to forget that when visiting Chez Clarke, we were required to challenge all land-speed records in the process of getting there. I never really understood this, but it was a fact of life with Alex. After every lead-footed trip I was always waiting for the trophy presentation but it never came. Maybe it was a cumulative, season-long award, like amassing World Cup ski points.

"Made a little progress in the Hansen case today," Alex said as we hurtled out of the city in her bottle-green Jetta.

"Good...which one is that, again?"

"Terry! Only the most important thing I have going on!"

"I know, I know—I'm just...what portion of it did you make progress on?"

Huge sigh.

Pause.

Another huge sigh.

"I'm sorry, Al—it's not that I don't know that the Hansen case is important to you."

"I know, it's just..."

"Just what?"

"You're just always so distracted."

"No I'm not. I'm listening."

"Yeah, you're listening but you're not hearing. On the surface you're paying attention, but underneath you're somewhere else."

It was true.

"That's not true." I said.

"Yeah it is. You don't even realize you're doing it. What is it you're really thinking about?"

"I'm thinking about the Hansen case and wondering what progress you made."

I was, in fact, not even remotely thinking about the Hansen case and wondering what progress she'd made.

What I was thinking about was something that had happened at the very end of the day. I had been walking back to my office from a meeting, ready to pack up and meet Alex. As I passed Larry's office, I looked in and surprisingly found him sitting there in the low, and, of course, flattering, light. Larry had usually beaten it out of town long before this.

"Hey, Bud," he called out.

"What's goin' on, Bud?" I asked, walking through the door.

"Ah, I'm gettin' out of here," he said.

"Plans for the weekend?"

"Home tonight. Out tomorrow."

"Cool."

"Hey, did Ellen talk to you about the Vision project?"

"Uh, what Vision project?" I said, raising my eyebrows.

"Vision's got this thing they want to do—a little different than some of the stuff we've been doing. Not quite so edgy."

"I thought edgy was the whole point of the Vision."

"Well, we may have been pushing them too edgy lately."

"There's a surprise," I snorted.

"Yeah, yeah. Keith does love edgy. But this one is gonna be directed at parents who've lost a child to handguns."

"Ugh."

"Yeah, so this needs to be a little more emotional, a little more respectful, a little more sophisticated."

"Aaah-haaaaa..."

"What?"

"My role in this is coming into focus."

"Yeah, man, this is right up your alley. I really need you to help out on this one."

"How does Keith feel about my helping out on this one?"

"He'll be fine with it."

"Oh, he'll *be* fine with it—as in the future tense—as in he doesn't know yet."

"Ah, don't be like that. Keith thinks you're awesome. He'll love your help. Besides, he doesn't really have a choice. 'Cause I think you're perfect for this one."

"OK, El Jefe—if you say so."

He clicked off the light on his desk.

"Let's get out of here. We'll talk more about it on Monday."

So as I sat in the passenger seat while Alex buried the accelerator, I was thinking about what this assignment would mean. On the one hand, any assignment on The Vision was a good thing—a big, fat, awards-show fastball right down the middle. But on the other hand, there would be a high price to pay for that in terms of dealing with Keith and his happy horseshit. I was going to have to decide whether this was worth it.

But first, I had to get back to the Hansen case.

"I love that they call it 'piracy,'" I offered up, hoping to draw a return volley.

"What?"

"The whole Internet stolen-asset thing."

"It dates from real piracy, you know."

"What do you mean?"

"In legal terms, piracy is essentially the same as what Blackbeard did. *The unlawful usurpation of property* it's called."

"Why don't they just call it theft? Like grand theft auto. Why not grand theft cyber?"

"Piracy is stealing—but it isn't just stealing. It can mean plagiarism or forgery or counterfeiting, too."

"It can?"

"Yes, my little wordsmith. It can."

"Well, and did we uncover some evidence of plagiarism or forgery or counterfeiting today?"

"A little. There's a bit too much similarity between the code on Hansen's site and the code on the competitor's site."

"In the code? Not the content?"

"Yeah. Usually these cases are about more content-based issues. But this one has to do with the actual code—because the code allows certain interaction on the site. And it's proprietary."

"So Hansen needs to protect it as a competitive advantage?"

"Very good."

"Thank you, Professor."

"We'll make a lawyer out of you yet."

"And I would want that because?"

"What's wrong with being a lawyer?"

"Nothing—for you. I just don't think I'd be that good at it."

"Why? You don't think it'd be as 'creative' as what you do?"

"Easy, now. I think being a lawyer requires plenty of creativity. But it requires a lot of structure, too. Maybe a little more discipline than I'm cut out for."

"You're a pretty disciplined thinker."

"Gee, thanks."

"What?"

"Well, to some creative people, being called a disciplined thinker is worse than being called an asshole."

"But you're not one of those creative people. You are a disciplined thinker. I mean it as a compliment."

"Oh, I know you do. I am a disciplined thinker. I'm comfortable with that. I just think it hurts my persona from time to time."

"That you don't appear the wild-eyed creative radical?"

"Something like that."

"Don't worry so much, Terry. You're very good at what you do."

I smiled. "In my experience, anyone who's really good at what they do doesn't really believe they're really good at what they do."

"Oh! Pass me the phone—I've gotta call Mom."

"And tell her I'm not any good?"

"And tell her we're almost there. "

Once off the highway, the road to the Clarke residence wound through the town of Chelton, a 100-year-old fishing village that looked like the set of *Murder, She Wrote*. There were a lot of touristy shops and stuff along the main street now, but the harbor area was still a working fishing operation—big, diesel-powered trawlers chugging out to sea at dawn, returning in the late afternoon wreathed with seagulls. There were actually a couple of different harbors in the town, which served to segregate the commercial fisherman from the recreational sailors. In the smaller harbors along the coast, Pearsons and Bertrams and J-boats bobbed at their moorings waiting for the weekend.

Turning right off Main Street, Alex gunned the Jetta past the Queen Anne Inn, across the salt marsh and out toward Sewall Cove. This was the Le Mans portion of the Home-to-the-Clarke's race—lots of reverse turns and short straight-aways. Alex downshifted with a vengeance as we shot past the road to the lighthouse and leaned into the turn that led to Sewell's. Two gray, sagging boathouses stood at the corner next door to the Sewell Yacht Club where Alex had learned to sail and water ski and drink gin and tonics. A quarter mile down the road on the left was the Clarke's homestead.

We pulled slowly into the gravel drive.

"Oh, *now* you slow down," I laughed. "So you won't get busted by the 'rents?"

"Old instinct," she smiled.

Maggie and Bert Clarke were sitting in the living room, a fire in the fireplace, cheese and crackers on the coffee table, highballs in hand.

"There they are!" Bert exclaimed, rising out of his chair.

"Alex! Terry!" said Maggie, placing her drink on the table.

A flurry of hugs and kisses, and a firm, look-em-in-the-eye handshake for me from Bert followed by a trip to the bar. Alex had the requisite glass of white wine and followed her mother into the kitchen.

"Still drinking Scotch, Terry?" Bert inquired.

"As often as I can, Bert."

"Heh, heh, heh." Bert chuckled, pouring me an enormous belt. Bert wasn't shy about his booze—or much else, for that matter. Although I'm not exactly a wallflower, I envied his certainty, his conviction. I often wondered what the world looked like through a lens like that.

Bert was an attorney. Actually, to be more precise, Bert was an icon. He was a partner in the firm of Hoffman, Haversham & Clarke and was a legendary corporate lawyer and power broker. One of the things I most respected about Alex was that she had not simply waltzed in the door at H, H & C and taken some cushy gig there—although God knows, she could have. And while I was sure Bert had exerted a little influence to get Alex in the door of Hadley Storrs, she did have to pull her own weight. That was part of the reason she had immersed herself in the developing areas of Internet law—because it was a million miles from what dear old Dad did.

"How's the advertising world?" he asked, walking back under the carved wooden arch into the den.

"It's good," I began tentatively.

"Business good?"

"Yeah, we're busy."

"Busy's a good way to be. Hey, you know what ad I love? The one where the guy..." and he went on to describe some commercial he'd seen. This happened all the time, not just with Bert but with other people as well. It was the same dynamic as being a doctor at a cocktail party. Everyone wants to get an opinion, share an opinion. I suppose it's because of the mass appeal or connection of the two—everyone has their health to think about and everyone sees ads. Not everyone has their lives touched by the subordinated debt structure of a multi-national merger. I mean, there are thousands of highly capable people working in jobs like that—it's just that it's probably easier for them to delineate work and play because no one wants to talk that much about what they do.

"...ah, funny as hell. You guys do that one?"

"No, we didn't."

"Ah, well."

"How's things with you?"

"Oh good, Maggie and I came down last night."

"Still doing the 3-day-a-week thing?" Bert had begun to pull back from the practice in the past year—due largely to some pressure applied by Maggie who thought they should travel, spend some time at the beach and generally chip away at the considerable pile of gold Bert had amassed.

"Yeah, but, Jesus Terry, I gotta tell ya—it can be boring down here."

"There's days when boring sounds pretty good to me," I laughed. "Playing any golf?"

"Sure, but how much golf can you play? I'm down to a 10—how much better am I gonna get?"

"I hear ya."

"We should play again."

"Any time. That member-guest was a good time."

"Business and golf—can't you talk about anything else?" said Maggie, shaking her head as she entered the room. "Dinner is served. Terry, you come sit next to me and we'll talk about books and movies while the two lawyers talk about obscure cases and the politics of making partner."

I didn't mind a bit. Maggie was good company—well read, thoughtful, and interested in all things cultural. She was also, I was reminded as I looked down at my plate of *coq au vin*, a helluva cook. Life here at The Manse was pretty nice, actually, for a schmuck like me—a point I made to Alex as we sat on the seawall out back later that night.

"I like being here," I said. The sailboats clanged quietly off the beach and the lighthouse swept its beam over us every 30 seconds or so.

"Good. They like having you here," Alex said turning and putting her arms around me. "And so do I."

Her brown hair was blowing against my face, her nose touching mine, her brown eyes enormous, the salt air mingling with Calvin Klein's Eternity.

Yeah...this would pretty much do, I thought to myself.

I opened my mouth to kiss her—the faint taste of red wine on her tongue matched my own.

"Think those shells are sharp?" I murmured.

She smiled without letting go of the kiss.

"I don't know," she murmured back. "But I do know that you're the one who's going to find out."

CHAPTER 22

Monday morning came and I rolled into the office.

I had a lot going on. Concordia to check on, a bunch of other odds and ends to cover off on, and a solemn promise to myself to check in on Ross.

But the most interesting, promising, pressing, and anxiety-inducing item of all was the meeting with Larry about this Vision assignment. Between sparring matches with Bert Clarke, playing Book of the Month Club with Maggie Clarke, and sneaking a roll in the shells with Alex, I hadn't had much time to think about it all weekend.

But what time I'd had, had been devoted to thinking about little else.

I was going to have to do it. Of course, I'd pretty much known that on Friday when Larry first mentioned it. I mean, first off, Larry wanted me to—and for all the we're-all-in-this-together, buddy-buddy stuff, he was still my boss and could make the assignment stick.

But most of all, it had winner potential written all over it—and I needed a winner right now.

Of course, it also had Keith written all over it—and that was really what my hesitation was about. It wasn't so much that I wondered whether I should take the assignment—I was kind of just steeling myself for the experience. Which I knew would somehow, some way, at some point absolutely suck.

"Morning, Terry," called Meghan, as I strolled past her station.

"Morning, Meg. How was the weekend?"

"A blur of exotic parties and hot men. Or was it the other way around?"

"Nice."

"And you?"

"Alex's parents for the weekend."

"Lovely." She was looking at schedule for the day. "A light day, it would seem—except for this late entry." She held up a yellow sticky.

"Ten o'clock? Larry's office?" I asked.

"With...Keith?" She looked at me quizzically.

I nodded. "Project for The Vision."

"You're the boss," she said, shaking her head as if I was insane.

"On occasion."

Keith was already there when I arrived at Larry's office. Christina, Larry's stunning new Cuban assistant, looked up and smiled a smile that could light up whole neighborhoods.

It was all about the aesthetic with him. Even his women were well designed.

"Go ahead in, Terry."

"Thanks, Christina."

"Hey, Bud!" Larry called as I started across the wide stretch of white carpet between the door and the two swivel chairs in front of his sleek, glass and steel desk.

"Hey, dude" Keith chimed in, holding out a fist for me to bump. "What's goin' on?"

"Gonna find out right now, I guess," I said, trading fists with Keith as I sat down.

"Aw, this is gonna be cool, man. People who have had someone go down 'cause of a handgun," Keith nodded gravely.

"Yeah, I told you all about it on Friday," Larry said off-handedly.

"Well, you told me a little about it—gimme a little background" I said, turning to Keith.

"Well, you know, most of what we do for The Vision is to educate a mass audience," Keith began.

It was beautiful—explaining it to me like I'd never heard of this cause before. You had to admire the guy. He either had the most highly evolved sense of irony on the planet or he was just a world-class asshole.

"...but this time, they want to do an effort to talk to the people who've really suffered a loss, man—people who've felt the pain."

"You gotta talk to these people differently," Larry said. "Ya can't be in their face. Ya gotta show some empathy, some respect."

"Absolutely" I nodded, with wrinkled brow. It was true—I mean, whatever we were getting out of our efforts on behalf of The Vision, these people had had their lives ruined in many cases. "What's the message? Are they trying to bring these people together for something specific?"

"Naw, it's more of a tribute," Larry said.

"Yeah, we want them to know we're working for them, dude, working to change things. We're fighting for their cause, dude," Keith said.

"Uh...doesn't that sound a little self-serving? A campaign to these people who are wracked with grief over the loss of a child to tell them what a swell job *we're* doing?" I asked.

I mean this was pretty blatant even by Keith's standards.

"Yeah—it's a little different than that, Keith" Larry kind of smiled. "It's gotta be bigger than that. Gotta be about them— about their loved one not having died in vain or having their loss go unnoticed. We need to talk about The Vision as being a way for their loss to stand for something. A way for the loss of their loved one to create social change. It's really a legacy of sorts."

Larry had, once again, gotten to the heart of the issue.

"Oh yeah, yeah" Keith acknowledged. "That's what I mean. It's all about them, dude."

"We doin' spots?" I asked.

"The assignment's for print but I think we can look at all sorts of stuff...maybe do spots, maybe tie it to a web site..." Keith answered.

"Cool. Do we have any kind of info on how these people feel? I mean, I know they feel horrible, but I mean, specifics from Research on how they get over a thing like this, how their feelings change over time, how they feel about legislative efforts, is the killer in prison, any stuff like that?"

Larry nodded. "Yeah, you're right, even though they've all suffered the same loss, the emotions of these people aren't gonna be exactly the same."

"I don't know. I'll have to ask Paolo. He may have some stuff." Keith said.

I smiled at him. That was beautiful. How could you not know this if you were in charge of The Vision? The answer, of course, was that Keith wasn't interested in how these people felt. He was only interested in telling everyone how he felt. And how did he feel? He felt like he'd feel better if he could shock the shit out of you and win another fistful of awards.

Yeah, it's all about them, dude.

"So," I said turning back toward Larry. "You want teams on this or you want me to take a whack at it first?"

"Oh, dude, you gotta do this. No one can do this like you, dude." Keith was practically bouncing in his chair.

I felt the warm, billowing sensation of smoke being blown up my kilt.

"This's got you written all over it, man," Larry said, waving his hand dismissively. "You're perfect for this."

"OK, don't have to ask me twice," I said, raising my hands defensively. "So—we gonna work on this together?" I asked Keith.

"Aw, man, I'm buried on the 'Who's the Target Now?' part of the campaign. Ya heard about this? We're staging these guerilla demonstrations inside gun manufacturers and we're gonna do a live webcast of the whole thing. Gonna be sick!"

"Pick whoever you want," Larry said. "You can write it and then have other teams blow it out into the other media."

"Cool," I said.

It sounded like a legit opportunity. But nothing I'd heard had lessened the apprehension I always felt at the start of a Keith-driven project. Something was gonna happen—I just didn't know what yet.

"Well, we're off," I said.

The first step in this Vision thing was to spend some time with the Research folks. I knew as I sat in Larry's office that Keith wasn't going to hunt down my info on victims' families' feelings. I mean, hell, he wouldn't look it up for himself—he sure wasn't going to investigate it for me.

I put in a call to Paolo Estefan, the lead planner for The Vision.

"Hey, Terry. What's up?" he answered. He sounded a little hesitant.

"Well, I'm gonna be workin' on this new Vision assignment—the victims project?"

"Oh. Oh, sure."

"I wondered if maybe we could get together, talk a little about it?"

"Sure. Pick a time."

"How 'bout 2? This afternoon?"

"Great. I'll come to your office?"

"Or I can come to yours."

"No, I'll come up. Is...Keith..." He left the question hanging.

"Nope. Just you and me for now."

"See you at 2."

CHAPTER 23

"Have you heard about this?" Ellen was storming up the hallway outside The Hole.

"Heard about what?" I asked.

"This thing with the 'C'?" She was absolutely bug-eyed. It took a lot to rattle Ellen—she'd seen it all and then some.

"No," I laughed.

She poked her head inside The Hole and then grabbed me by the sleeve and dragged me in. She closed the door.

"You haven't heard about this fucking thing with Keith?"

"No."

"Well," she began, with a roll of her eyes and a sweep of her hand. "Stacy comes to me this morning all upset." Stacy was the young woman who coordinated all our dealings with the award-show world—entries, entry fees, keeping track of the categories, receiving notification of the winners, buying tickets to the show, etc. An absolutely critical and utterly thankless job.

"About what?"

"Apparently, The One Club called up and said they were asking each winning team to create some kind of poster or banner with the agency's name on it or some kind of message about the agency."

"Oh, yeah—didn't I see some e-mail about this last week?"

"Yeah, Keith sent it around to some people."

"And..."

"Well, somebody said we should just make a huge banner, like a medieval flag with a big red 'C' on it."

"I'm guessing that's not the part that upsets you..."

"So Keith says 'Ya know what'd be better? We'll make a big red C—but we'll paint it red with blood.'"

"What?"

"Yeah—he wants to paint it red with blood."

"Real blood?"

"Yeah."

"What, like pig's blood or something?"

"No—he wants to draw blood from the team members and use their actual blood."

"Human blood?"

"Yeah, like 'we put our blood, sweat and tears into everything we do' kinda thing."

I looked at her for a second.

"C'mon, you're making this up."

"No, I'm not!" she said, waving her arms around. "He wants Stacy to figure out how we can draw blood from all the members of The Vision team and paint the "C" with it..."

"Does Larry know about this?"

"He's on vacation."

"You're serious? Blood?"

"Absolutely! Stacy's trying to figure out if she needs to get a nurse to come in or should everyone go to a clinic or what..."

"He's finally gone off the edge."

"You gotta do something."

"Well, it is his turn to be the Awards Guru," I said. "He can do whatever he wants."

Every year, one of us was assigned or volunteered to be Stacy's supervisor on the whole awards thing—answering questions, approving entry lists, and helping to field requests from the various shows.

"Shit!" Ellen said and stormed out into the hallway.

CHAPTER 24

Run, Lola, Run may not have been the answer to the Concordia assignment, but it wasn't a bad place to start.

"Do you want to...write this?" Nicole asked when I told them about it.

"No." I said. "This is just the bare bones of the thing. Maybe you guys can take it, flesh it out, and figure out how to make it work."

"Do you have scripts already?" Mary Ann asked.

"No, I just sketched out this outline—how different spots might work together, how the thing might extend. If you think it has any merit, take it and make it your own."

"Oh, it has merit," Mary Ann jumped to add.

"Yeah, I mean, it could work, it's just that..." Nicole was always the pessimist of the duo.

"What?"

"Well, I'm not sure how you'd do direct response in that format."

Oh, Christ. Here they were without an idea to call their own and she's quibbling over logistics.

"I think it might extend," I offered. "I mean, maybe not easily but you know, remember what we're trying to do here. We're trying to sneak a branding campaign past them. If you can make it work for the branding part, we'll backfill the direct."

"OK" said Nicole. She didn't sound enthusiastic but I knew

her well enough to know that she really would try to make it work.

"Cool. Get back to you—when?" Mary Ann asked.

"Day after tomorrow is fine."

They packed up their stuff and walked out of my office. They were gone only a beat when Mary Ann stuck her head back in the door.

"Hey, Terry?"

"Yeah?"

"Thanks."

"No problem."

A couple days later, I asked everyone to meet in The Hole at 2.

"You sure they're not going to want to do it alone again?" Meghan asked. "Saving face and all that."

"Nah, they'll be fine."

"Ya think?"

"Oh yeah. Everyone's only nervous before anyone's seen anything. Once they show me and know they've got a contestant in the race, they'll be happy to show each other what they've got. In fact, they probably already have."

"C'mon."

"Oh, sure. They've already had hallway meetings where they've described their best idea to each other and talked about what they like about it. They've probably even talked about ideas that I've killed, telling each other what an asshole I am for not picking what was clearly the best idea."

"Uh, excuse me, but aren't you the one who gets paid to recognize the best idea?" Meghan said with withering sarcasm.

"Theoretically."

"I'll have them there at 2."

The troops were all there when I arrived.

"Hey Terry."

"Terry."

"Ter."

"Hey, Ter."

"Hello, gang. How we all doin'?"

"Believe we're gonna find that out right now," Mark drawled softly.

They all laughed.

"Yes you are. Shall we start?"

"Sure."

"Yeah."

"Let's get going."

And then, of course, everyone just sat there.

"OK," I laughed. "Jimmy and Ivan—how're you guys doin'?"

The second round in preparation for a presentation like this was easier in many ways because you were looking at less work, more tightly done. But it was more difficult in some ways, because now you were getting serious. It wasn't like any half-assed idea was OK. Stuff had to hang together. The trick now was you had to be serious without being unimaginative. You had to avoid what the advertising icon David Ogilvy referred to as "skating about on the slippery surface of irrelevant brilliance."

As our session went on, it was clear that there was both some progress and some skating. Jimmy and Ivan had a very interesting idea to break the commercials only on-line and only over Concordia phone lines. The commercials themselves would capitalize on the fact that they (the commercials) wouldn't be as clear on any other lines. It wasn't really what the assignment called for, but it was an interesting demonstration.

Mary Ann and Nicole had started to flesh out the "*Lola*" idea and it wasn't bad. It needed some work to figure out what to change from scenario to scenario and what to keep the same, but the general consensus in the room was that it could be cool. Mary Ann made no mention of the genesis of the idea. Nicole started to disclaim it a bit by saying how I had helped them.

"Oh no, this stuff is all yours," I jumped in. "I never said anything about this scenario or this one,"—pointing to the tissues on the table—"or this one, either. This is all you guys."

This was, of course, what a college professor had once described as a lie of omission rather than a lie of commission. A lie of commission is when you flat-out tell an untruth. A lie of omission is when you tell the truth but leave out a piece of it.

Like the piece that, yeah, this was pretty much my idea.

CHAPTER 25

I had carved myself out a couple of hours to think about The Vision thing late that afternoon. And as I sat behind my closed door starting to think about it, I started to realize that the thing that made this easy was also the thing that made this hard.

You knew that the emotion of having lost a child to a handgun—maybe even to your own handgun—was something that was painful even to contemplate much less experience. And you knew that the more you tapped into it, the more real, the more dimensional, the more debilitating you could make it sound, the more your claim that you understood how these people felt would ring true.

I mean, I knew exactly where to go with this. Larry had chosen me for a reason here and it's because he knew and I knew that I could wring tears and heartache out of this.

But even knowing all that, there came a point, the first point where you had to touch it. Had to probe that stuff with your fingers. Had to pick up the letters you had marked up, the accounts of parents' grief, the documents from a hundred civil and criminal cases, parents' pleas to juries, had to try and get inside their skin and feel the devastating, knee-buckling grief these people felt and start to work with it.

Now, I'm not saying, "Woe is me, this is too hard, I feel their loss too much." I mean I'm not quite that self-absorbed—although God knows I know people who are.

It's by way of explaining why I was procrastinating a little.

Oh, I had already explored the usual suspects of this kind of stuff. I had a couple pages of lines that touched on missed birthdays and weddings that would never happen and grandchildren who would never be born. Some of it pretty touching but still a little too Hallmark-y for this, I thought. It was clear from reading through all the background stuff that while those issues were real, the stuff that pained these parents was way smaller and more personal.

The smell of the bathroom after their daughter had washed her hair; the pile of laundry inside the teenage son's room; laughter, noise, even familiar, on-going arguments over stupid stuff—these were the things they missed.

All of which is why I sat at my laptop, clicked off the Word document that contained my lines and started cruising around The Vision website.

It was a fantastic site—beautifully designed, very interactive, and filled with information on legislation, support groups, you name it. We had designed it for them, a kid upstairs named Jules—Hawaiian kid with bleached-blonde dreads—doing most of the work, fantastic stuff. I hadn't visited the site in a while and I was reminded immediately how stunning it was. They had a lot of our stuff posted, obviously, spots and ads and such, plus all kinds of links to government sites, lists of senators, representatives, Bureau of Alcohol, Tobacco, & Firearms, etc.

Disguising my procrastination as research, I clicked my way over to our local firearm registry. There was a new link there where you could look up the entire list of firearm licenses issued in the state.

I started randomly scrolling through the list. It wasn't like I knew any of the people. I was looking at the towns, mostly—towns like Rawley and Triton and Burrill. I didn't know much about these places except that they were rural. Very rural. Farm country to the northwest of the city. Guns probably being used for plinking and scaring off coyotes and stuff. And, of course, for storing in racks in the back window of your pick-up truck.

I started to wonder—do I actually know anyone who owns a gun? I didn't think so. Who did I even know who might have a gun?

I thought for a minute.

There was a guy I used to work with, an art director. Real outdoorsy type, a regular L.L. Bean on his own time. I could definitely see him with a couple of duck guns or a deer rifle. What was his name again? Dawson, that's right, Ned Dawson. I scrolled through to the D's. Yup, sure enough, there he was—Edward C. Dawson, 14 Spoonbill Rd. Spoonbill Road? That was almost too perfect. I wondered if he had re-named the street to better fit his image.

Who else? How about Bert Clarke? Wouldn't that be a hoot? It wasn't outside the realm of possibility, though. I could see him doing a little duck hunting in the bogs off the ocean during the fall.

I scrolled back up to the C's—nothing doing. Tons of Clark's and a bunch of Clarke's but no Bertram J. Clarke of Sewell Rd.

How about Sean? I laughed to myself. I could almost see it, I thought, as I scrolled toward the H's. Not a .38 or some .9-mm Glock or anything, though. If he had a license it was to cover some pair of antique dueling pistols that the Duke of Norfolk had once used to defend his honor against the Third Earl of Devonshire or something.

Healey, Healy, Heely, Henley—nope. That was a little far-fetched, I supposed. Sean would be a pretty improbable gun owner.

Suddenly, I thought—hey, how about Keith? Wouldn't he be the least likely gun owner on Earth?

Laughing, I scrolled back toward the F's.

Fage, Famiglietti, Farlton, Farmer...

Holy shit.

Keith A. Farner, 17 Welton Rd.

Holy shit!

The guy was on the list.

Holy shit!

I looked closer. There was a statistic I hadn't noticed before—it had the date when the license was issued. And according to the state firearm registry, four months ago, Keith Farner, the King of Anti-Handgun Violence, had applied for and received a license to carry a handgun!

I just sat there with the cursor blinking next to his name like some sort of alarm going off.

Keith had a handgun.

That arrogant, condescending, cooler-than-thou, hypocritical fucking prick had a gun. I almost couldn't get my head around it.

And then I did.

I sat alone in my office and whispered quietly to the screen: "You're mine."

I smiled.

"Dude."

CHAPTER 26

The next morning, Larry called us all together in his office. Not just the CDs but also writers, art directors, every creative person on the floor.

"Thanks for comin' down. We've, uh...we've got a little problem," he began, leaning against his beautiful, hand-carved desk. "I need your help."

We all looked back at him.

"It's with Hanny..." Hanover Life Insurance was a medium-sized account based in the Midwest. We managed to do some pretty nice magazine work for them and there was always the promise that they'd acquire some other company, get bigger and, of course, spend more. It was a piece of business that we all agreed we should cultivate.

"We're not losin' it, are we?" asked Rob, the senior art director on the business.

"No, no—nothing like that," said Richard Forrester, who was the Associate Creative Director on the business.

"But we do have to put on a little dog and pony show," Larry continued.

"I thought they liked the campaign?" Rob said.

"They do, they do," Larry said, holding up both hands in reassurance. "This is kinda...something elsc."

Everyone exchanged looks.

"Well...how do I say this? It seems that we need to show a

little extra love to Mike." Mike Adamson was the client at Hanny. Young guy who gave the impression of being fairly tuned in.

"Why?" Rob asked.

Larry paused and a little smirk came over his lips.

"Why don't you tell them, Richard?"

"Uh, sure. Well. Ah, it, ah…it seems that, ah, Mike has been dating, ah…Brianna."

The room burst into gasps, laughter and a smattering of applause.

"No!"

"You're kidding!"

"C'mon!"

Brianna Breckenridge was the Account Supervisor on Hanover—and she was hotter than lava. She was tall, blond, leggy—she looked just like Kim Cattrall and, reportedly, behaved just like Cattrall's character, Samantha.

Now, dating your agency counterpart was considered an enormous conflict of interest and not particularly good form. But considering it was Brianna—well, who could blame the guy?

"Yes. However, it appears that Brianna has decided to break it off."

"Yeah?" someone said.

"So, Mike is feeling…well, a bit unloved."

"I bet!" said someone else in the back of the room.

Everyone laughed.

"So what's supposed to happen?"

"Well, he wants us to show him a complete new retail newspaper campaign by Monday."

"What?"

"What the…"

"By Monday!?!"

"He's just making us jump through hoops!"

"Uh, yeah, he is," said Larry, raising his hands to calm the tumult. "Look, the guy is pissed and not feeling too good about himself and he has to take it out on someone. And unfortunately, that someone is us."

I looked across the room at Sean who was smiling broadly. Despite his winning smile, he looked pretty ragged this morning.

"So let me get this straight," someone was saying to Larry. "We have to do a newspaper ad that will make up for the fact that Mike isn't going to be getting it from Brianna anymore?"

Larry laughed. "Well, I guess when you put it that way—yeah."

"Larry?" I said, smiling.

"Yeah?"

"I'm not sure I can come up with anything that good."

CHAPTER 27

As I headed back to my office, I looked into Stacy DiNapoli's office.

"Hey Stace..."

"Oh—hey, Terry," she answered a little distractedly.

"How's the blood count?" I smirked.

"It's unbelievable, Terry—he won't let it go."

"How do you mean?"

"Well, I started thinking about the logistics of it all and I started thinking 'How am I going to get this thing to New York?' and so I called my brother who works for the Post Office, you know, and I said what would be the best way to ship this poster that's painted with blood and..."

I started laughing.

"What?"

"Oh I bet he loved that! What'd he say?"

"He says, '*Stacy ya moron, ya can't ship somtin' painted wit blood— it's a friggin' bio-hazard. There's all kinds of friggin' regulations you gotta meet, permits ya gotta get, it's like impossible. And by da way,*' he says, '*what da fuck are you doin' paintin' stuff wit' blood anyway, whaddya got friggin' crazy people dere?*'"

"Well..."

"Yeah, tell me about it," she said, with a roll of the eyes.

"So what'd Keith say—that seems pretty cut and dried."

"He says, OK, if we can't paint it and send it, we'll bring everyone on the team to New York, draw the blood and paint it right there."

"You're kidding."

"No—and he wants to get a video crew to record it, ya know, make it like a PR event..."

I was just looking at her.

"It's unbelievable. We'll look like savages, Terry!"

I nodded.

"Savages, Terry!"

I sighed.

"Let me know what happens," I said, patting her arm. "Someone's going to stop this. Maybe The One Club will—do they know yet?"

"I'm about to call them right now."

"Let me know."

CHAPTER 28

Carrying around my newfound knowledge of Keith and his gun gave me a vaguely military, Joint Chiefs of Staff kind of feeling. It was like being in possession of a WMD. You had a pretty good idea of what it would do—the only question was deployment.

Where would be the optimum place to detonate this sucker?

I was more than willing to wait for just such a moment—because I knew that if aimed correctly, there wouldn't be much of the landscape left afterward.

How could the fucker possibly have a gun? I kept coming back to it. On the one hand, it was pretty worrisome. Was the guy really twisted enough to be packing a Glock in the office? I mean, I wasn't the biggest Keith fan, obviously, but I didn't exactly think he was a stone killer, either.

On the other hand, what kind of lunatic was he? That he would, in a position of such high visibility on this issue, deliberately put himself on the wrong side of it? Was he really that self-destructive? I mean, anyone that nuts, you want to give him a little room, you know?

But the real question was whom to tell?

Obviously, I could bandy it about the office and let people think he was a hypocritical asshole. But that was just gossip.

I could tell Vanessa—his Account Service counterpart on The Vision. Vanessa really genuinely lived this cause. She and her husband were very cause-minded—he was an attorney who pursued corporate polluters, sort of *A Civil Action* kind of guy. She would view this as an immense betrayal—and bad for business. But that would be just a personal disappointment, and Vanessa would try to deal with it privately. And she'd be right, from her point of view.

But private was *w-a-a-ay* not what I was looking for.

I could tell Larry. He'd be pretty incredulous—probably even pissed initially. But at the end of the day, he'd protect Keith. Partly because he liked Keith; the rebellious, bad-boy image appealed to Larry. And partly because Larry would circle the wagons, lest the Creative Department be found to be in any way flawed. Larry's worldview pretty much depended on his people being perfect and everyone else being incompetent. And for one of his right-hand guys to pull a stunt like this was going to put a serious hole in that theory.

But even from the first minute I began thinking about it, I knew these were just station stops on the way to what had to be my actual destination:

Dan McManus.

Other people might think Keith owning a handgun was inappropriate, ill-advised, a serious conflict of interest, maybe just downright stupid.

But as the brains, the heart, the very *soul* of The Vision, McManus wouldn't just think it was inappropriate.

He'd think Keith was the anti-Christ.

Which I thought had a nice ring to it.

CHAPTER 29

I was having lunch with Paula Hansen, my partner in crime and the guru of all things JetSouth. We tried to get together once a month or so, with no other agenda than to just catch up, talk about life, the business, the account, whatever.

It was her idea and a smart one—and yet another reason why Paula was the anti-Rob. Rob always came at everything filled with anxiety and agenda—wild-eyed, fists-raised, face florid with blood pressure. Paula was no less passionate, but much more in control. It was, among other things, what made her good.

"So, how's it going?" she asked over her salad.

"Good," I said over mine. "Busy—on Concordia, which is insane."

"As usual," she laughed.

"Yeah," I snorted. "How's Reliance treating you?"

Like me, in fact like all of us senior types, Paula had multiple account responsibilities. In addition to sharing JetSouth with me, she also ran Reliance Financial—one of the biggest mutual fund companies in the country. It was an enormous cash cow for the agency and highly visible, although the work tended to be pretty middle of the road—which only made sense for a conservative mutual fund company. Edgy, controversial, push-the-envelope, swing-for-the-fences work was not going to win over people who were looking to invest their life savings. Work like that would indicate too big an appetite for risk—especially for people who didn't even want an appetizer's worth of risk.

"They're fine. The flows are down for the month but that could be lots of factors. It's not necessarily the campaign."

"Are they suggesting it's the campaign?"

"Not really."

"Well, someone over there is always suggesting it's the campaign's fault."

She smiled.

"Someone in every client organization is always suggesting it's the campaign's fault, my friend."

"Here's to that bleak but impeccably correct observation," I said raising my glass of Pellegrino.

She clinked.

"So good news—I think there's a good opportunity coming up with JetSouth," she said as she returned to her salad.

"Yeah?"

"Yeah," she nodded enthusiastically. "You know how we're always trying to balance the draw of the destination with the experience of getting there?"

"Yes, I do. And I have the scars to prove it."

"Well, it looks like they're opening up a handful of new destinations throughout the Caribbean and Mexico—and they want to announce it in a pretty big way. Planning to put a lot of media behind it."

"TV?"

"Probably not," she said making a face. "I think what they want to do is keep running the existing TV as an umbrella and do something big in print within that context And, obviously, something great on-line."

"Print, huh?" I said. "Magazine, you think?"

"Yup."

"Hmmm."

"Yeah?" she smiled.

"I smell Pencils!"

"Told you it was good news."

"Very good."

She picked through the remains of her salad, looking thoughtful.

"Who do you think should work on it?" she asked.

"I don't know—everybody, maybe."

Paula nodded.

"Nobody likes a gang bang, but for something with this potential..." I said.

She nodded again.

"We need the best people—it's a big opportunity," she agreed.

"Huge."

She picked at her salad a little more.

"Would you ever think about some different teams?" she asked quietly.

"What do you mean?"

"You know, people that don't work on the business?"

"I guess," I said cautiously. "What're you getting at?"

"Just that it might be interesting to see what might come from a fresh perspective."

"Maybe." I paused. "Have you somehow lost faith in the teams?"

"Oh no, not at all."

"Cause, I mean Gail and Mark...Jamie and Rob...they could do something really good with this."

"No, they should all work on it. I was just wondering what it would be like if we had our dedicated teams, plus some alternative resources—all under your senior leadership of course."

I had stopped eating about halfway through this conversation—and now I was just looking at Paula.

"Who are you talking to?" I asked.

"What?"

"Who are you talking to?"

"What do you mean? You, of course."

"Me?" I said smiling. *"Dedicated teams'? 'Alternative resources'?*

'*Senior leadership*'? What the hell is all that about? What, are you reading some Tom Peters management book on the side—and it's seeping into your normal conversation?"

"What's wrong with 'senior leadership'?"

"Nothing—if you're giving a speech to some industry conference," I said. "But you're talking to me—a friend—over lunch—like normal humans. You want to talk about the teams, they all have names. They're not 'alternative resources'. They're people you know."

"Well, you're making a big fuss over nothing," she said, leaning back so the waitress could take her plate. "There's nothing wrong with saying 'senior leadership'."

"Fine, fine," I said, holding my hands up in surrender. "I'll see if I can find you some '*alternative resources*' and '*senior leadership*' to make sure we don't blow this tasty assignment. In the meantime, I'll just tell everyone what to do."

She made a face and shook her head like I didn't get it.

And we left.

CHAPTER 30

With Sean working out of Carolyn's group, he and I rarely had the opportunity to work together on anything—which we had sort of tacitly agreed was a good thing. Sean was sensitive enough about my outranking him without having to actually report to me directly.

But every now and then there was an exception.

A little while ago, a new pro bono job had come down from on high and Ellen came to talk to me about it.

"It's some political thing," she said.

"What kind of political thing?" I laughed.

"It's called the…" she consulted her notes. "The Curriculum Coalition."

"I think I've heard of this," I said.

"It's a group that wants to, and I quote, *'privatize a portion of the country's public high schools—in order to be able to better concentrate the curriculum on teaching students core skills for the global marketplace.'*"

"I have heard of this," I nodded.

"Pretty radical idea."

"What, turning half the country's public schools into, essentially, private schools? Yeah, that's radical, all right."

"Gonna piss a lot of people off, isn't it?"

"Oh yeah. Where did this come from?"

"What do you mean?"

"I mean, how did this thing land at The Crack?"

"Came straight from Justin," she said, rolling her eyes up

either toward the heavens or Justin's floor—I wasn't sure which. Although for a lot of people, the two were indistinguishable.

"This is a wildly Republican group," I said, looking over the packet she had given me.

"Yeah, so good luck getting someone on this floor to volunteer for it," she snorted.

"Oh, on the contrary," I said. "I know the very person."

Sean, predictably, given his Anglo-mania and love of the old-school ways, was that rarest of advertising birds—a Republican creative guy. He welcomed the Coalition with open arms.

"Thrilled, Your Grace," he said when Ellen and I offered it to him. "Love the Coalition's idea—any chance it could involve uniforms for the budding scholars?"

So Sean and his partner Marty (a Democrat, but willing to suspend all his principles for a chance at a good assignment) took on the job.

Turned out that Justin had taken the assignment because in addition to the politicos involved, the Curriculum Coalition included some very heavy players from the worlds of finance and industry. There were CEOs and captains of industry, private equity kings and arbitrageurs galore. And you never knew, when you were working on a high-profile public service thing like this, when you might hit the emotional hot button of a guy who might be in a position to give you his business.

At least that's how you would think of these things from a new business perspective.

And Justin rarely thought of things in any other way.

Like many freebies, there was absolutely no money and little or no time. But the boys managed to do a wonderful newspaper campaign—a sort of combination opinion-leader, white-paper, political speech thing that Sean absolutely wrote the shit out of and Marty art directed in a way that gave it gravitas and made it seem inviting at the same time—no small feat.

Given its prominence and potential, Justin himself was

our Account Guy. And when we showed him the work, he was pleased.

Sean, however, was quietly displeased because when it came time to share the stuff with Justin, Justin had asked that I bring it to him alone. He liked small meetings and didn't like to have to make nice to creative people he didn't really know.

"But he loved it, Seano," I said. "He said it would 'change the debate and raise the profile of the issue.'"

"Which is lovely," Sean said a little sadly. "But it was my profile that I was hoping to raise."

"It will, it will," I assured him. "Justin's going to show it to the two political leaders and Mike Pellison."

"*The* Mike Pellison?" Marty asked. "Computer magnate?

"The very one," I said. "He's a big believer in the cause—self-made, global titan that he is."

"Cool."

"And we have to present it ourselves to R. Sanford 'Sandy' Sanderson at Black River Partners."

"The legendary Sandy Sanderson?" Sean said, stirring out of his mild depression. "Former Secretary of Commerce? Ambassador to France? The most feared corporate raider since Gordon Gekko?"

"The very one."

"What's he got to do with this?" Marty asked.

I rubbed my right thumb and forefinger together.

"Of course."

"He's financing the media buy," I said. "So pack your bags. I think it's next Wednesday in New York."

CHAPTER 31

"What do you mean?" Alex said over the rim of her Cosmo. We were seated in a pool of blue light at the bar at Obu, a new, tragically hip Japanese place near Alex's office.

"I mean, Keith has a handgun," I replied.

"Yeah..." she said somewhat blankly, delicately picking an edamame pod out of the bowl on the bar.

I stared at her trying to figure out why she didn't seem to grasp the enormity of this.

"What? Lots of people have handguns," she said after a few seconds. "Not that that's *good*, but lots of people do..."

"Those people aren't supposed to be leading the opposition *against* handguns. Those people aren't making their living by building a reputation as a white knight, a crusader *against* handguns," I sneered.

Alex looked at me.

"I mean could you be any more hypocritical?" I pleaded.

"How do you know this again?"

"I was doing some research for this project I'm doing on The Vision..."

"The one Larry asked you to do..."

"Right...and I looked up the government's gun license mini-site and Keith's name was on it."

"Like, the *only* name on it?"

"No, it wasn't the only name on it," I said with a trace of

growing exasperation. "There's hundreds of names on it. I looked up a bunch of names, just seeing who might be there."

"Sounds like procrastination to me," Alex smiled before taking another sip of her Cosmo.

"Yeah, well, thank God for making me a procrastinator," I said. "Cause it helped me find out that Keith Farner has a *handgun.*"

"Maybe it's for research," she said, reaching for another edamame pod.

"He doesn't need to research the inner workings of hand-guns," I said, my frustration becoming more evident. "Their very existence is the problem!"

"Are you afraid he's going to shoot you?" she said laughing.

"Of course not, that's not the point…"

"Well then what *is* the point?" she sighed.

"The point is that Keith's got a gun," I said, my arms wide in explanation. "*A gun.* The King of the Anti-Handgun cause owns a handgun himself!"

"Look, Terry," Alex said placing her drink on the bar very precisely. "I know this upsets you. And I want to be understanding, really I do. But I have to say—so Keith owns a handgun. So he's a hypocrite. I've met Keith and, yeah, I think he's pretty slimy and disingenuous…the whole *'dude'* thing…but so he's a hypocrite and a self-absorbed jerk and a poser. I mean is he the first guy you've ever met in business who was a hypocrite, a self-absorbed jerk and a poser? 'Cause I meet people like that every day."

"He's gotta pay," I said.

"Pay for what?" Alex asked frustrated.

"For how he is."

"How is he?"

"He's manipulative, he's duplicitous, he's a fucking political weasel."

"So stay out of his way, if that's how he is to people."

"That's how he is to me. He's wrecking my career!" I saw the bar-tender shoot a glance down the bar.

"He's not wrecking your career, Terry. You have your accounts, Larry relies on you, other people respect you...you've said yourself, when things get hard, you're the one they turn to. Look at this thing you're writing now..."

"*Exactly!*" I said, waving my arms wildly. "*I do all the heavy lifting and he prances around and gets all the glory!*"

"Terry..." Alex said quietly.

"What?"

"You've gotta let this go."

"*Let it go?*" I practically screamed. The bartender gave another look—a little longer this time. "Are you insane? Letting it go is the *last* thing I'm thinking about."

"What exactly *are* you thinking about?"

"I'm trying to figure out what to do with this information, exactly how to reveal it. Who to tell, how to tell it—if I get the timing just right, this'll be beautiful..."

Alex was staring down, fingering the stem of her Cosmo as it dripped condensation onto the polished granite bar.

"Why are you so unhappy lately?" she said so softly I barely heard her.

"I'm not unhappy, I'm pissed. Actually, knowing this little nugget about Keith? Makes me *very* happy." I laughed cynically. "Happier than I've been in a long time."

Alex took a very long time to look up from her drink. When she did, the air seemed to have gone out of her.

"Yeah."

She shook her head wearily; small, slow shakes from side to side.

"I know it does."

CHAPTER 32

"Hey, El," I said, poking my head in Ellen's door as I passed by on my way to a meeting. A little drive-by hello. "What's up?"

She looked up with an expression of concern.

"Plenty," she said flatly.

"Why, what's going on?" I walked in and sat down.

She leaned forward in her chair and lowered her voice as she spoke.

"The bean counters are at it again," she said.

"Really?"

"Yeah," she nodded for emphasis. "I was in a meeting with them yesterday—they're up there sharpening their knives."

"Why? Did we lose something that we don't know about yet?"

"No, I think things are just flat. But expenses have gone up."

"They can't have gone up that much."

"Well," she said, smiling sardonically. "As much as I hate to agree with the money boys…expenses have gone up. A lot. You remember when we had to hire all those interactive people on Reliance Financial? To handle the overflow on the site maintenance?"

"Yeah, sorta."

"Well, we didn't get paid any more money to hire those people. We just had to add bodies at the same fee or we were going to screw up the whole account."

"'Cause we're good like that," I smiled.

"Yeah," she snorted. "Anyway, it's things like that. Situations where we had to hire extra people or upgrade technology or give someone a raise in order to keep them from leaving or whatever. You do what you have to do—and you hedge. You hope that revenue will increase over time and keep everything square. But when things are flat, well, expenses come under a lot of scrutiny."

"And the money guys start sharpening the axes."

"You got it."

"So they want people from down here?"

"Yeah."

"How many?"

"Well, they're after a dollar amount," she said. "They don't care how we get there. It could be, like, five junior people or one really senior person."

"Any names being thrown around?"

She shook her head no. "I'm meeting with Larry later to tell him about this. I'm sure there'll be a meeting to discuss it—Larry, me, you, Keith, and Carolyn and the others."

"And we'll have to offer up suggestions."

"Yup."

"And then we'll decide."

"Yup."

I stood up, late for my meeting.

"Well, look on the bright side," I said.

"What's that?"

"If we're the ones deciding?"

"Yeah?"

"Then it's not gonna be you or me."

She laughed.

"Go to your meeting, smartass."

CHAPTER 33

Wednesday morning we arrived in New York—me, Sean, Marty and our account guy *du jour* John McGinley. McGinley had, once again, been rolled out to counteract the creative guys and provide conservatism and maturity in a meeting with grown ups.

Black River Partners was located exactly where you'd expect—in an absolutely beautiful building on Park Avenue in Midtown. They had floor upon floor where all sorts of earnest, eager young men and women were grinding numbers and poring over charts and staring into computer screens and talking into headsets while trying to figure out which company, industry or even country Black River should buy, sell or liquidate.

Because our meeting was with one of the big kahunas himself, we went right to the penthouse floor—where the three founding partners and their entourages worked.

As soon as we got off the elevator, it became very clear that we were in some seriously rarefied air.

Marble floors stretched everywhere, their shine and noise dampened by the thickest, most luxurious Oriental rugs I'd ever seen. Antique tables dotted the corridors, oil paintings of historical scenes of New York shipping, mercantilism, and commerce hung above them, and everywhere you looked there was the rich, lustrous glow of oiled mahogany. It looked like an English men's club on steroids.

I didn't know if Justin had ever been here, but if he had he must have had an orgasm.

Sean nearly did.

"Oh my God, Your Excellency, I'm home at last," Sean said with a broad smile. "Do you think they might need any help here at Black River?"

"Yeah, 'help' would be the operative word, Your Grace," I said. "As in kitchen help. You'd be serving the big boys their watercress sandwiches."

"If I could do it in starched livery within these glorious walls, I'd be honored."

We announced ourselves at the reception desk where the elegant and cultured receptionist then announced us to Abigail, Sanderson's personal assistant.

"That receptionist probably makes more than I do," McGinley whispered as we followed Abigail toward the corner office.

"Guaranteed," Marty said. "And probably bought a house in the Hamptons to boot."

"I have a feeling, dear boy," Sean said "that if that woman has a house in the Hamptons, it's been in her family since the Hamptons were just a bunch of potato fields."

We were ushered into a small but magnificent conference room.

"This is Mr. Sanderson's private conference room," Abigail said, showing us in. "Make yourselves comfortable. Mr. Chadwick and Mr. Sanderson will join you shortly."

"Thanks, Abigail."

"Who's Chadwick?" I asked, after she left.

"Sanderson's keeper—right hand man," McGinley said. "Basically, he'll remind Sanderson of why we're here and why he's here, and keep the meeting going. Sanderson will probably say what he thinks, but we'll take our marching orders from Chadwick."

"Ah, the Lord High Chamberlain, as it were," Sean said with glee.

"What order do you wanna go in?" asked Marty as he unpacked our goods.

We got ourselves settled and set up and sat back to wait for Sanderson. The elegant little conference room had a wall full of books along one side and a view out onto Park Avenue on the other. The other two walls were absolutely filled with framed pictures—Sanderson with President Reagan, Sanderson with Bush 41 and Bush 43, Sanderson with Alan Greenspan, Sanderson with Tony Blair, Sanderson with Warren Buffett, Sanderson with Bill Gates, Sanderson with—well, it just went on and on. The guy had apparently met and worked with every major political and business figure of the past 40 years.

"Christ," said Marty. "The guy's like friggin' Zelig."

The reason we had time to take in Sanderson's entire photographic history was because he kept us cooling our heels for over an hour. Our meeting had been scheduled for 11, and we had been cautioned repeatedly not to be late. So we dutifully arrived at 10:45 and were set up and ready to go at 10:59.

It was now 12:15 and we hadn't seen or heard from the lovely and patrician Abigail since she deposited us in this room.

I started to wonder if maybe some of the proles downstairs were analyzing us as an investment of the great man's time—and finding us lacking.

Suddenly, the side door opened and an impeccably dressed guy in his late 30s or early 40s stepped into the room.

"Geoffrey Chadwick," he said, extending his hand to McGinley. Obviously, as hoped, Chadwick had gravitated toward the conservative adult in the room.

"If you gentlemen are all set, I'll get Mr. Sanderson," Chadwick said after all the introductions had been made.

"Ready when you are," I said.

Chadwick left and reappeared momentarily with the great Sandy Sanderson. Sanderson was in his late 60's, medium height and build, a fairly unkempt thatch of graying hair and glasses that seemed to slide down his nose every few minutes. He was wearing a pinstriped suit that by the look of it was custom tailored and must have cost about eight grand.

"Hi, Sandy Sanderson," he said in a surprisingly quiet little voice as he shook hands.

"It's an honor to meet you, Mr. Sanderson," McGinley groveled.

But I had to admit it was fairly impressive to meet a guy who was such a Wall Street Journal boldface type kind of guy.

After a couple of opening remarks from Chadwick, clearly designed to remind Sanderson that he wasn't about to hear a report on soy futures or something, we launched into our little preamble.

While Sean and Marty lifted the first boards onto the table to present, Sanderson gently pushed himself away from the table a little and lowered himself deeply into his chair—neck against the back, legs stretched out and spread, hands clasped under his chin.

As Sean began to read the first ad aloud, I looked over at Sanderson to see his reaction so far.

And saw that, as Sean read, Sanderson had dropped his right arm and was now openly scratching his balls.

I looked away—kind of out of courtesy, the way you might if you caught someone at the end of the table picking their nose or something, you know, give them a minute to pull it together.

I looked back.

He was still listening.

And he was still distractedly scratching his crotch.

I looked at Sean—who was soldiering on but I could tell by the look on his face that he saw what Sanderson was doing. And Marty looked at me with a quizzical and bemused look on his face.

The boys went through every last board, explaining the thinking, the possible extensions into other media and then McGinley laid out the basics of the media plan.

Through it all, Sanderson just kept openly scratching his nuts through the fabric of his $8,000 custom-made suit. It was unbelievable. He never stopped once—although at one point during the discussion he did change hands.

I could see why—his right hand must have been exhausted.

When we were done, Chadwick stood up and thanked us.

"Do you have any kind of executive summary for Mr. Sanderson?" he said politely.

"Yes, right here," McGinley said handing over three small bound decks. "And one for you as well—and one extra."

Sanderson stood up.

And stuck out his hand.

Lovely, I thought, steeling myself to shake it. *Just lovely.*

"Thank you," he said softly as he left the room. "Nice job."

And they closed the door behind them.

"Not a word," I said to my compadres, without even bothering to turn around. "Not a sound out of any of you until we're outside.

A quick walk around the corner and we were ensconced at the bar at Maloney & Porcelli.

Laughing our asses off.

"For the whole time," Marty was saying pounding lightly on the bar.

"That was really amazing," McGinley said, wiping the tears from his eyes.

"Yet another testament to the tremendous seriousness and significance with which the world views our labors," Sean said slightly raising his 3rd Hapsburg.

"Gentlemen," I said raising my first Scotch, "to achieving the American dream…"

"And what's that?" Marty said.

"Being so rich that you can openly scratch your balls in public and not give a shit what anyone thinks."

CHAPTER 34

"How'd the bloodbath end up?" I said to Ellen, sticking my head into her office.

"Oh my God, Terry—you won't believe it."

"It's not dead yet?"

"Dead? Holy shit, it looks like it's going to happen!"

"C'mon—what did The One Club say?"

"They think it'll be bold and edgy and cool. 'Unprecedented' they said."

"Yeah, and for a good fuckin' reason..." I snorted. "I know Larry's still away—does Justin know about this?"

"He's in Nevis."

"Of course he is," I smiled.

"But here's the thing—I found out today that this poster is going outside the hall at Lincoln Center? And in order to be visible, they're asking all the posters to be four-by-eight. Four *feet*! By eight *feet*! I went to Keith and I said do you have any idea how much blood that's gonna take?"

"Don't tell me..." I said, closing my eyes.

"'That's what'll be so cool, he says, 'like maybe the guys who did the most work will have to donate twice.' I mean, Terry, we're talking *buckets* of blood in order to paint something that big... *buckets!*"

"I gotta go. I can't talk about this anymore."

CHAPTER 35

I was coming from a meeting on JetSouth where we had been briefed on the new assignment Paula and I had discussed over lunch. It was, as promised, a magazine and interactive campaign for early next year touting new destinations. The beauty of it was that we were probably going to be able to get away with a bare minimum of rates and disclaimers and be able to focus instead on the beauty, excitement and emotional pull of the destinations themselves.

The assignment was clean, focused, and brimming with potential.

Sounded pretty damned tasty to me and I was deep in internal debate as I walked.

Who should be assigned this plum? I would deal with Paula's desire for 'alternative resources' later. Right now I needed to figure out who, of the people who worked on the business, would be right.

Maybe that was my chance to demonstrate 'senior leadership'.

There were many deserving candidates and several people who could do something really special with an assignment like this. That was the balancing act of the Creative Director job—you had a bunch of people who slogged away uncomplainingly, doing professional, creditable work on hard assignments and keeping paying clients happy...and every now and then, these people needed a real shot at something where they could stretch their wings and show what they were really capable of.

Fact was, coming through on an assignment like that was how

you made your bones in this business. It's how all of us creative big dogs had gotten to be creative big dogs in the first place. I had done it, Keith had done it, Carolyn had done it. I had done it years ago working at a place called Lonard Merchant Sawyer on an assignment for a regional bank. I had been grinding away for a year or more on rate ads, loan ads, and all the little day-to-day stuff that kept the deposits coming in. And as a result, my partner and I had been invited to throw some ideas in on a branding assignment the agency had been given.

Man, I don't think we slept for five days. We filled a room with ideas, scripts, ads, lines, you name it. And when it was our turn to present to our goateed, linen-draped creative guru, we sold hard on a big, emotional campaign we had come up with. It was a huge hit—both in the room and later at the client.

We were made guys.

On the other hand, assignments like this—big, fat fastballs right down the middle of the creative plate—were really rare.

And so you couldn't screw around.

If you were lucky enough to get one, a clean single to right wasn't gonna cut it. You had to take it out of the park, deep. The client needed something good so the communication would work and they'd fill the planes; the agency needed something great that would win awards and get us press and visibility; and, frankly, our group needed it lest we sink deeper into the perception that we were the grunts of the agency, the guys who did all the hard work and heavy lifting while others swaggered to glory.

Which was why the other side of my mental argument was to plop it right down in the laps of someone like Gail and Mark and let them work their magic. That would be a good, solid decision. They were talented, committed and would do something great, I knew. And hell, they deserved it too—they worked as hard as anyone.

From somewhere in a corner of my mind was another little voice—suggesting, politely, that maybe I should keep this assignment for myself. It wasn't an inappropriate suggestion. And it was yet another side of the Creative Director puzzle.

See, in order to get to be a Creative Director you had to demonstrate that you were a kick-ass creative person, writer, or art director. You had to have shown a great, award-winning track record of terrifically crafted work.

And then you'd be promoted to the job of Creative Director—where, essentially, you'd stop doing any work of your own and spend most of your time supervising other people's work.

My feeling was this—every now and then a CD had to take a piece of the cake for himself.

One, because it always felt good to stretch the old muscles and actually do some work. It was not only rewarding but it kept at bay any feelings of envy, jealousy, and bitterness about all the good work other people were doing. And two, because it reminded you of how friggin' hard it was to come up with terrific ideas. Someone (a writer) once said "A blank page is God's way of showing you how hard it is to be God." And let me tell you, truer words were never spoken. The work that came through my door for approval wasn't always going to be good, but someone had expended real effort to put it down on paper. So, in my opinion, doing a little of your own work from time to time helped make you more appreciative when people came in to show you work.

Suffice to say, I had a head full of conflicting thoughts as I turned the corner by the room known as Tim's House.

Tim's House had earned its name years before when there had been a young guy named Tim Brett who worked in the studio. Studio guys, especially young assistants, spend all their time mounting ads, printing out comps, building crazy shit for pitches, and generally doing all the physical scut work necessary to bring the agency's work to life. It was a great training ground, but not exactly the most skilled work in the world. As a result, young studio guys make about four cents—and rumor had it that Tim had found an abandoned storage room and was actually living out of it since he couldn't afford rent. No one had ever been able to conclusively prove it—or disprove it for that matter. And Tim had been completely non-committal on the subject. But one of the biggest clues may have been how the room became furnished. Tim may not have been paying rent anywhere, but he was obviously finding other avenues for his meager paycheck. Somehow, over time, the room had been tricked out with a massive TV from the Broadcast Production department, the latest in PS2 and XBOX hardware and perhaps the finest, most extensive collection of video games on the planet. The latest, most up-to-date versions of everything—including a collection of Japanese bootlegs that was worth a fortune. The average American teenage boy would have taken one look at the contents of Tim's House and promptly had a seizure.

Well, young Tim had long since graduated into a position that paid enough for an apartment. But his room, its name, and its contents remained, providing hours of entertainment for creative guys looking to blow off a little steam.

Larry himself was a big believer in blowing off steam with a couple rounds of Halo or some other game. The latest version of Golden Eye was a popular favorite. Larry was, in fact, not only a big believer but also a frequent participant, often playing Golden Eye for hours against young art directors and writers. (There was a theory among some of the young people in the department that the fastest way to advance your career at The Crack wasn't to do some great piece of work but to let Larry beat you at Golden Eye. I didn't think that was true. Well—I didn't think it was entirely true.)

As I rounded the corner before heading through the reception area, I heard an eruption of shouts.

I stopped and smiled.

Someone was dead. Someone else was happy.

Clarity is a beautiful thing.

CHAPTER 36

"Ter?" Meghan said from the doorway.

"Yes, my dear?"

"Larry wanted you to come down."

"Oh, uh...sure."

I bet Larry did want me to come down. And the reason he wanted me to come down, I had no doubt, was to ask me where the fuck The Vision campaign was.

Although slightly more politely.

He was right, of course. I'd been sitting on it for a while now. After a promising and ambitious start, I'd made my discovery about Keith and his off-hours hobbies and the train had gone completely off the tracks. I had spent hours and hours thinking about Keith and his handgun and what to do with this incendiary bit of information—and as a result hadn't really furthered my Vision ideas one inch.

In my mind, of course, this was a noble and worthy trade-off.

I wasn't sure Larry would agree.

"Hey, Bud," I said coming through his door with as much manufactured enthusiasm as I could muster.

Larry was turned sideways, facing his laptop.

"Bud, what's up?" he said, quickly swiping the Armani specs off his face. He was getting really good at it. It was almost like some sort of Ricky Jay card trick, a sleight-of-hand move that left you wondering whether you'd actually seen a pair of glasses a moment ago.

"What's goin' on?" I said plopping down in one of the two chairs facing his desk.

"Ah, dealin' with the bullshit," he said. "Finance boys are about to go on the warpath again."

"Yeah, I heard something about that."

"And as if that didn't suck enough," he said waving one hand in the air, "now Justin and Mike have got me on a plane every day the next two weeks."

"To where?"

"I don't know," he said. "To make a speech in New York, to do capabilities to some company in Florida, to sit on the dais at some fucking Four A's thing in Arizona. Runnin' me around to perform like I'm the organ grinder's monkey."

He threw his hands in the air in exasperation.

Larry was always indignant and outraged when Justin and Mike occasionally demanded that he go to meetings, presentations, and conferences and generally behave like the public face of the agency.

And you could see his point.

Except for the fact that attending meetings, presentations, conferences, and generally behaving like the public face of the agency was, you know, sort of, well…his job.

And if you really wanted to see what Larry thought of the situation, all you had to do was offer to go in his place. Oh, no, no, no. There would be no substitutes. For all of his protestations, there was no way he was gonna give up this 5-city traveling ego fix.

"That's a drag," I said, shaking my head. "You'll probably have a little downtime, though."

"Yeah," he snorted. "In Arizona. Where I'll probably end up having to play golf with Mike."

"Resist, at all costs," I said laughing—partly because I knew

Larry hated playing golf and partly because Mike was a legendary sandbagger and would probably take a lot of money off him.

"So, anyway..." he said leaning forward. "Weren't we supposed to see something on that Vision thing yesterday?"

"Yeah, yeah you were," I said apologetically. "But Concordia got a little nuts and JetSouth was busy—the day sort of got away."

"Ya got anything yet?" he asked.

"Yeah, some interesting ways to take it," I said, trying to sound very collaborative so it would look less like I had fucked up all on my own. "Couple rough things..."

"Well, let's get on it, huh?" he said, looking straight at me.

"Absolutely."

"I want to see stuff before I leave in a couple days."

"You got it."

He leaned back in his chair.

"This is a One Show pencil waiting to happen, Bud," he said.

I nodded.

He smiled and gave me his favorite personal blessing.

"So don't fuck it up," he smiled.

CHAPTER 37

My e-mail alert binged and I snapped off my Vision file and looked.

It was from Stacy. The subject was 'Bloody Mess'.

> *"Terry—*
>
> *Just an update on the blood poster. I tried another tack with him—I told him that once you paint the poster with the blood, the blood's going to dry brown and it won't look good. He said to contact the poster company and see if they could make the poster vinyl so the blood will look wetter longer. I think I'm going crazy...*
>
> *– S"*

So the blood will look wetter longer...

It was like working with Jeffrey Dahmer.

CHAPTER 38

"Terry? Can you open that wine?" Alex called from the living room. "The Macon-Villages? The Cotes-du-Rhone's for dinner…"

"Got it," I called back.

It was Friday night and Alex was hosting a small dinner party. She did this every couple of months. A group of eight or ten, depending on how squeezed she wanted her dinner table to be, established couples, mutual friends, assorted people from her office and usually one wild card couple.

Tonight's wild card was a beauty.

She had invited Sean and an associate from her office named Victoria Alberlin as a sort of supervised blind date.

"A flanking maneuver," he had laughed when I asked him. "An attack from an unexpected quarter."

"Yeah, well the invasion begins at 7:30 next Friday at Fort Clarke. Be there in time to get entrenched."

The small kitchen smelled amazing. Her mother's famous *coq au vin* was simmering in the oven, there was an enormous and elaborate salad chilling in the refrigerator and there were tightly wrapped packages of six different artisanal cheeses on a plate on the shelf below.

"Rather a Franco-themed dinner this evening, Al," I said as she swept into the kitchen, a massive bouquet of irises in her hand. "Hope there aren't any over-zealous patriots in the group."

"It's food, not a political statement," she snapped as she

passed behind me. "Wise *ass*." Which she punctuated with a slap on my not necessarily wise but certainly wide ass.

The buzzer blared in the hall.

"Get that, will you?" Alex said from behind a curtain of irises.

"Clarke residence…" I intoned into the speaker in my most cultured servant voice.

"Hey, Ter—let me in, will ya? This friggin' ice is drippin' everywhere…" said the voice. It was Kathleen Halsey, in many ways Alex's best friend. They had gone to college together and been close ever since. She was big, loud, and very, very funny. A lot of people felt that Kat, as she was known, was an acquired taste. That was fine with me—I had acquired the taste long ago.

We were pals.

"Yes, Miss Halsey…"

She entered the apartment like a tropical storm.

"Hey campers. Here take this bag of water, will you, Ter? Jesus, what a mess. Oh my God, it smells good in here. Ooh, look at the table. Al, you fussed…" she swept across the place, leaving a swirl of words and floral scent in her wake.

"Hi honey," she said, giving Alex a kiss on the cheek. Al was half turned from putting the irises in a vase.

"Hey, babe…thanks for bringing the ice. Terry, could you put it in that bucket?" Al said.

By the time the buzzer began to ring in earnest a half hour later, we were set—the irises divided between three vases around the room, a little John Pizzarelli spinning in the CD player and the luxurious fragrance of Rigaux candles beginning to compete with the *coq au vin*.

The guests were a varied group, as Alex had planned.

Jack Mueller, an attorney from Alex's office and his wife Audrey who I'd met before; Roz Levine, another attorney, and her boyfriend, the rhythmically-named Eduardo Mercado; Lise Johansson, a friend of Alex's from forever; Kat Halsey, already reducing everyone to tears with her stories; and one of the guests of honor, Victoria, who came as advertised—beautiful, smart, funny.

What was immediately and painfully clear as I looked around this jovial little group, was that Sean was MIA.

From across the circle, Alex looked at her watch and raised an eyebrow at me. I shrugged slightly.

"...but seriously, how much reality TV can people watch?" Audrey Mueller was saying. "Terry—you're in the business—how much longer can this go on?"

"Well, I'm not in *that* business—unfortunately..." I said.

"Why *unfortunately?*" Audrey said with disdain.

"Because if I was, we'd be having this little soiree on my private jet on the way to dinner in Paris." I said.

"Is it really that lucrative?" Jack asked.

"God, yeah..." I said. "Before reality TV, the biggest things on TV were all sitcoms—'Seinfeld', 'Friends', 'Will & Grace', 'Everybody Loves Raymond'. And the biggest problem with shows like that is the overhead. Shows like that cost millions to produce. But look at reality TV—no stars, no writers...put your money into production and you can sell commercials on 'Survivor' for the same price as 'Friends'."

"And pocket the difference," Eduardo said, raising his glass. "Capitalism at its finest."

"Exactly," I said. "So, to answer your question, Audrey—how much longer can this go on? I'd say until the producers in Hollywood all get together and say, 'Gee, I think we're making way too much money'."

Alex interrupted the group chuckle.

"Dinner is served. Look for your name card on the table,"

The group began to migrate into the next room.

"Where *is* he?" Alex hissed at me as I passed her on the way to the table.

"I'll try him again on his cell," I said turning back into the living room while pulling out my cell phone.

"Victoria doesn't deserve this—she's a nice person, she's..."

"I know, Al, I know..." I said impatiently as I punched digits.

Alex whirled around and headed for the kitchen where Kat was yelling "Oh, Mademoiselle—où est le friggin' serving spoon?"

After several tries, all of them ending with Sean's voice mail, I finally did as instructed and spoke at the tone:

"Sean. It's Terry. Where...the...fuck...*are*...you?"

And hung up.

I had no sooner snapped my phone shut than the buzzer rang.

"Excellency—is that you?" Sean's voice crackled through the speaker.

"Get up here," I said evenly and pressed the button.

I turned and caught Alex's eye through the door to the dining room. I nodded to indicate that Sean had arrived. She gave me a glare that could have etched glass.

I opened the door and Sean stepped in. One look at his grinning, disheveled figure and I realized that he was shattered.

"Which front is the attack coming from?" he smiled clapping me on the shoulder.

"Every front—Jesus, Sean, it's ten past 9...you were supposed to be here at 7:30...shit, look at you..."

"Ah yes, well, I was holding down my post at Jo Jo—but I'm afraid we were overrun...had to consume the last of our stores, lest they fall into enemy hands...nasty business," he slurred.

This was beautiful. I didn't know whether to usher him into the dinner table or boot his ass out the door. I figured the reaction was probably going to be about the same regardless.

"Is the officer's mess still open?" Sean grinned. '*Mess*' came out '*mesh*'.

"Yeah, well 'mess' would just about describe it," I said grabbing his sleeve and dragging him toward the dining room.

"Ladies and gentlemen—Sean Healy," I said as we walked into the room.

"My lords and ladies," Sean announced at the door, accompanied by a low, sweeping bow.

Out of the corner of my eye, I could see Victoria turn her graceful, swan-like, cashmere-draped neck and give Alex the most elegant "what-the-fuck?" look I'd ever seen.

I hadn't really looked at Alex. In fact, I was kind of wondering if it was possible to maintain our relationship without ever having to look at her again. I figured the expression on her face was good for the next, oh, 15 to 20 years.

Sean was introducing himself to Victoria at the other end of the table.

"My dear Miss Alberlin..." he was purring slurringly to her. I couldn't hear the rest of what was being mumbled—and I was really glad.

"Sean, let me get you a plate," Alex was saying. *And break it over your head,* her tone clearly implied.

"Tough day, Seano?" said Kat smiling broadly. She was clearly loving this.

"War is hell, my dear," Sean answered, wrinkling his brow. "The enemy's resistance was fierce..."

Kat was enjoying the spectacle and Victoria seemed to be putting up a brave front in the face of this madness. Audrey Mueller, on the other hand, looked as if she was watching a particularly grotesque episode of *'Fear Factor'*.

Which, in a way she was.

Actually—if it meant I could leave?

I would have gladly eaten a bowl of bugs.

Maybe two.

CHAPTER 39

Saturday morning dawned much too soon and every bit as ugly as I'd thought it would.

"How could he do that?" Alex asked for what must've been the 2,000[th] time. "How could he have done that?"

She was alarmingly awake, considering the late night and the amount of wine everyone had consumed—although I had noticed that consumption began to tail off not long after Sean arrived. Tough to keep slugging back the Cotes-du-Rhone with the Ghost of Rehab Future sitting at the table.

I had one arm flung over my eyes and my head turned away from the white-hot, arc-welding flame that was Alex.

"I'm going to call him," she said conclusively, turning over to reach for the phone.

"No!" I said, sitting bolt upright. "That's not a good idea."

"Why are you protecting him?" she snarled. "After what he did?"

"I'm not protecting him," I sighed. "I'm protecting you. You don't want to have that particular conversation right now—not as mad as you are, not as tired as you are-"

"I'm not tired," she snapped.

"OK."

"I'm furious!"

"Yes, I'm aware of that."

"I can't just let this pass!"

"I'm not suggesting that," I said. "Not suggesting that at all. I just think you shouldn't have that conversation at this particular moment."

She sat leaning against the headboard, arms folded across her chest, jaw set, brow furrowed, eyes black and cold. She was rage incarnate.

"When?"

"I don't know," I struggled. It didn't seem like the kind of thing you wanted to schedule like a workout or something. "This afternoon or something...I mean, you'll be calmer, you can plan out what you want to say...and he'll be even more sober."

"I doubt it."

"And I should talk to him," I said, finally putting into words the thought that had been rattling around my brain. "I should talk to him first."

"Oooh no," she began. "You'll be soft on him."

"Maybe," I said with a trace of annoyance. "But I owe it to him to broach the subject. To let him know that not even I think that was OK. Let me do that—then you can get your pound of flesh."

"I don't want a pound of flesh, you asshole," she smacked me with a small decorative pillow. "I want him to call Victoria and apologize."

"Oh boy."

"What?"

"Well, I don't think Sean thinks his performance was all that stellar. And I'm sure that a verbal beating from you would be considered the price to be paid. But calling Victoria...*whoa*."

"It would be the right thing to do."

"Perhaps," I sighed, thinking. "Actually, Sean's sense of decorum–"

"Scan's sense of decorum?"

"Allow me to rephrase. Sean's sense of courtliness might actually beat you to that."

"It better."

"What are you doing?" I asked as she got up.

"Going to the gym," she said. "You wanna come?"

"Later," I said, rolling over. "Work the heavy bag while you're there. You'll feel better."

The thump of yet another decorative pillow served as her goodbye.

CHAPTER 40

"Excellency."

I was standing in Sean's doorway, cup of coffee in one hand, folder of work under the other arm.

"Your Grace!" he said looking up from his computer screen. "To what do I owe this honor so early on this bleak Monday morning?"

"Just checkin' in, see how you're doin'"

"I'm doing lovely, thank you! And that's because I've had...'*a bottle of sunshine*' already!" he said, brandishing his empty Sun Grove OJ bottle and partially quoting their tagline. (As much as possible, we always kept a healthy supply of our clients' products on hand for the agency to use—a small but nonetheless appreciated show of good faith. Except for car accounts and banks—the liberal provision of free product seemed to end there for some reason.)

"See? I was right," I said sitting down. "I told Alex you were a closet health nut."

Sean seemed to sag in his chair a little.

"Ah, yes—dear Alex. Not #1 on her Hit Parade, I would imagine."

"No, Excellency—on the old American Bandstand rating scale of 1 to 100? I believe she'd give you about a 2..."

He winced.

"Uh, not my best effort."

"*Best* effort? It didn't look like *any* effort."

"Hm."

"I mean, that was quite a show, Your Grace—quite a show."

"I take it Ms. Alberlin was offended?"

"I actually think Ms. Alberlin was slightly amused," I said smiling. "And Ms. Halsey was *highly* amused."

"Yeah," he snorted. "She would be."

"But the lovely and talented Alex was not. In fact, if it weren't for Herculean efforts on my part, you would have had her on your doorstep with hatred in her heart by 8 a.m. Saturday morning."

He winced again. A little harder this time.

"I owe you one."

"You don't owe me anything—but you're going to owe Alex an apology. And probably an explanation. And...ah..."

"What?" he said putting his face in his hands.

"Alex wants you to call Victoria and apologize."

"I thought you said she was amused?"

"I said slightly."

"*Sean! Marty! Now!*" came a screech from next door.

"Speaking of not amused," I smirked.

Sean rolled his eyes.

"Her Highness would appear to be in residence," he said heaving himself to his feet.

"Anyway," I said. "Here's Alex's number at the office. And Victoria's. Should the mood strike you today."

"Thanks, Excellency. I will, I will." He clapped me on the shoulder. "And now, if you'll excuse me—duty calls."

I left the note with the phone numbers on his keypad and followed him out the door. Sean walked into Carolyn's floral-bedecked boudoir and sat on the love seat next to Marty. I stopped at the door.

"Morning, Carolyn," I smiled.

Carolyn snapped her fierce gaze up from the pile of layouts on the coffee table toward the door—and then instantly softened. Damn, I could never figure out how she did that. The transformation was so fast you'd think she'd get the bends or something.

"Morning, Handsome," she said with a brilliant megawatt smile.

"How's everything so far today?"

"Shitty, thanks," she said with the same high voltage smile. "But we're about to fix that."

I toasted her with my coffee cup.

"Happy fixing, guys."

As I turned and headed down the hall toward my office I heard Cruella arrive with a vengeance.

"Sean, what the *fuck*..." Carolyn said as I turned the corner.

I sighed.

Between Carolyn and me, His Excellency's day was off to a very rough start.

CHAPTER 41

"Oh, Ter?" Meghan said, standing in the doorway.

"Y-e-e-s?" I said without looking up from my laptop.

"Stacy wondered if you had a minute?"

"Stacy DiNapoli?" I asked, looking up. Stacy was standing behind Meghan smiling. "Oh, do come in, Stace..."

"Thought you'd wanna know the latest."

"Now what?" I said covering my eyes with my hands.

"Oh no, you're gonna like this—it's dead."

"Really? How? Did it bleed to death?"

"Well, everyone else involved was saying go for it—The One Club, the printer, everybody. We only needed one final approval..."

"From?"

"Lincoln Center. I just got off the phone with the guy there."

"And?"

"He asked me if I was out of my goddamned mind."

"Of course he did," I laughed.

"He said it was in violation of every single health regulation in Manhattan, probably in violation of Federal law, and was, on top of it all, he said..."

She looked down at a piece of paper she had in her hand.

"...it was an affront to the good taste, high standards, and human decency of Lincoln Center and The Metropolitan Opera."

"Perfect. You wrote it down?"

"I wanted to make sure I got it exactly right when I told Keith."

"You're learnin' kid—you're learnin'"

"Awright—gotta go. One Show still needs some reprints and credit sheets," she said heading out of my office. "At least we won't look like savages…"

"Right."

Even though we are, I thought.

CHAPTER 42

After weeks of working, endless false starts, no fewer than five internal tissue sessions, piles of rejected ideas, and barrels of midnight oil we were now reaching the homestretch of the Concordia pitch.

We had about a week to go—which sounds like a lot but isn't.

So a small group of us had gathered in The Hole to lay out the battle plan for the remaining time—myself, Gail, Ellen, Marcus who ran the art studio, Chloe who was our traffic coordinator, and Zack from broadcast.

"So the meeting is on Thursday, right?" Ellen began.

"Yes, but it's in New York—at 10," I pointed out. "So everything's gotta be done as early on Wednesday as possible."

Nods all around.

"Terry, how many total boards do you think you're gonna have?" Marcus was asking.

"God, Marcus—right now I have no idea," I said, trying to come up with some kind of ballpark figure. "I don't know...50?"

I looked at Gail questioningly.

"Yeah," she said cocking her head to one side and thinking. "With all the versions and integrated stuff. Could be 50..."

Marcus nodded and made a note.

"I'll go in shifts," he said. "Starting over the weekend. So as things are ready, you just start feeding them to us."

He smiled.

"We'll make it," he said. "We always do."

I smiled back. "Yeah... you do."

Marcus was one of the great unsung heroes of the place. A big bear of a guy, but a gentle giant—helpful, dedicated, solid. No matter what you threw at him and his boys, they seemed to be able to handle it. Whenever things were going into crisis mode, I always felt better if Marcus was in the room.

"I assume it's all hands on deck this weekend," Ellen said.

"Oh yeah," I said. "The ol' social life is going on the back burner for a few days. The teams are gonna be cranking every day from here on out."

"I'll be here this weekend," Chloe said. "I figure I'll have a small crew Saturday and Sunday—then start adding people as we get closer."

"Sounds good," Ellen said. "Chloe, why don't you coordinate with Marcus how many bodies you're each going to have."

"Sure."

"Terry, are you gonna need any other kind of support?"

"By the end of the week? I'll probably need to be on life support."

Everyone laughed.

"But please, no extraordinary measures," I said holding my hands up. "I want to go out with whatever dignity I have left."

"You work in advertising," Gail said dryly.

"Oh—that's right," I said. "I don't have any dignity."

"Seriously," Ellen said.

"Nah," I said. "Meghan'll be here. She can help out with scripts and what not."

"Good," Ellen said, making another note. "I'll have Allison and Caitlin on call, too. They could help with food and stuff."

"You ready for 5 straight days of California Pizza Kitchen?" I said to Gail.

"You know, it's the only time I eat that stuff?" she said. "My husband took me to a CPK when we were out shopping once. As soon as I ordered I started feeling all tense and anxious. I figured out it was like this Pavlovian thing. I'm always tense and anxious when I eat their stuff so my body was just reacting."

We all laughed.

I stood up.

"All right, let the tension and anxiety begin."

CHAPTER 43

Very often, part of the protocol of the pitch process is that at some point, the client offers to conduct a meeting or a conference call with the agency in the hopes of clarifying, re-directing, or otherwise guiding the agency toward the correct answer.

While I have no doubt that this offer is extended with the sincerest and most helpful of motives, I can assure you that all the agency ever gets out of this is either complete confusion or false hope.

This is due to several factors.

First, whatever the agency is sharing isn't the finished, crafted idea. This is partly because it's still the middle of the process—and in the advertising world, if it weren't for the last minute, nothing would ever get done—and partly because, as desperately as they want guidance, the agency is even more desperate to protect the 'wow!' factor. Advance buy-in on an idea is nice. But presenting is theater—and you never get a standing ovation for a performance the audience has already seen.

The second reason is that the client, as much as they're trying to help, is also trying to maintain impartiality. There are, after all, other agencies involved, each of whom is going to have their own meeting or call, and the client has to make sure that no one is given an unfair advantage.

So the agency is sharing incomplete information and asking cryptic questions, the client is sharing incomplete impressions and giving cryptic answers. And by the time all the fencing is over, the agency either believes they've absolutely cracked it or that they don't have a clue and should practically start over.

In both cases, they're wrong.

But at least the client can say they tried to help.

Concordia had announced that they would, indeed, conduct a conference call for the agency, to last no longer than 30 minutes, to further clarify the strategy and to answer any questions we might have. Anne Wheeler, Jess, Martha, and Tad would be on their end; we were allowed four people on our end.

Which meant we'd have about eight—four speaking participants, three non-speaking participants who would be there for political reasons, and one scribe.

Rob and myself were locks—we ran the business, we were running the pitch, we were obvious. I had asked Gail to sit in as well.

The final slot had turned out to be Mike Haggerty.

Rob had wanted Audrey Mathieson. She was second in command on Rob's side and would have an even better grasp on the details and minutiae than Rob did—if that was possible.

But Mike had gotten wind of the fact that we were having this call and that Anne would be on it. He felt that, as the most senior guy, Anne would appreciate his participation and presence. And that he really should be there. After all, he'd been at the briefing, he said.

Of course, this was how these things perpetuated themselves. He hadn't needed to be at the briefing any more than he needed to be on this call. He, essentially, had nothing to do with Concordia. But because this assignment was a jump ball between the roster agencies, Mike would be able to claim it as a New Business victory if we won.

So Audrey got bumped to the bench.

She would of course be in the room, raising the number of non-speaking participants to four. She would be slipping Rob notes, answers and information the whole time.

"You have reached the conference center," said the preposterously cheery disembodied voice. "There are... three callers currently on the line."

Audrey pressed the code buttons and there was a click and we lurched into Concordia-land.

"Hey guys," Rob said.

"Hello Cracknell," I heard Jess sing song.

"Hey guys," I said.

"Who've we got there?" Jess said.

"We've got myself, Terry, Gail and Mike," Rob said.

"Mike?" growled Anne's unmistakable rasp. "Mike who?"

"Hi, Anne—it's Mike Haggerty," Mike said.

"Mike Haggerty?" she barked. "What the hell are you doing on this call?"

"Uh," Mike hesitated, his ears beginning to turn pink under his prematurely grey hair. "I thought it might be good from, you know, a strategic point of view, to you know, have some..."

"Jesus Christ, we don't need any strategy review, Mike," she snarled. "The strategy is set—this call is to answer any executional questions the team might have. Period. We haven't got time to go back to the beginning to see if you think the strategy is all right."

Katherine Lyman, one of the young account crew, reached over and adjusted the volume on the speakerphone.

"So you can stay and listen if you want, Mike, but *I don't want to talk any strategy crap*." Her anger was making her voice raspier by the minute. "And Rob?"

"Yes, Anne?"

"Don't think for a minute that I'm paying whatever hourly rate you're charging to have a guy as senior as Mike Haggerty sit in this meeting and contribute *nothing*!"

She was screeching now.

When Anne had first lit into him, Haggerty had turned kind

of a pale pink. He was now well on his way to some vibrant, Lily Pulitzer shade.

Katherine reached to adjust the phone again.

I held up my hand and shook my head at her.

"Um, OK, Anne," Rob stammered.

Katherine slid a note over to me that said, *"I think there's something wrong with the speaker…she sounds raspy."*

I wrote back, *"No—that's how she sounds. That's her voice."*

"OMG," she wrote back.

"Why don't we move on to the questions," Jess said, attempting to right the ship.

"Yeah, that's a good idea," Rob said.

"Yeah, we just have a couple of things, guys," I said. "Gail and I just want to clarify that when we're thinking about the retail promotion, is it all right if some of the visual or graphic elements we use are really precursors for where we'd like the branding to go?"

"As long as it sells," Anne growled.

Mike quietly got up and left.

"Oh, absolutely," Gail chimed in. "We would never sacrifice the short-term promotion for something with a longer fuse."

"No," I reiterated—and winked at Gail.

Who made a finger-down-the-throat gesture at me.

"Good, good," Jess was saying. "As long as the retail portion pushes hard, you can start to seed some future thinking into it."

The conversation rattled on for another 15 minutes, mostly about logistics and timing and the room we'd be in next week.

"OK, then guys, see you next week," Jess said.

"Yup, thanks guys," Rob said.

The red light on the phone went out, Rob picked up the receiver and made sure they were gone.

"Oh…my…God," he said putting the receiver back.

Everybody burst out laughing and talking at once.

"Holy shit, she torched him," one of the young guys was saying.

"Wow," I said looking at Rob. "Wow."

"He's gonna kill me," Rob said lowering his head in his hands.

"Why's he gonna kill you?" Gail said.

"Yeah, you didn't do anything," I said. "Anne's the one who—"

"Shredded him!" someone said.

"Yes—shredded him," I laughed.

Everyone started picking up their stuff and heading for other meetings.

As usual, the mid-pitch conference call had given us absolutely nothing to make our job any easier.

Although this one had turned out to have above-average entertainment value.

CHAPTER 44

Friday night in the big city, the end of another fun-filled week at The Crack. So, of course, it was time to assemble a distinguished group of ad minds at Bistro Jo-Jo to review, consider and otherwise mull over the events of the week—their political significance, how the powers that be had bungled their opportunities—and generally prognosticate about the week to come.

It was like our very own Washington Week in Review.

Only with w-a-a-y more booze.

And screaming.

"*They* sent it back to us," Andy Hamilton, young art director was saying, the veins in his neck bulging just a little. "The account guys! It had never even gotten to the client and they were saying they 'had a few tweaks'! Fuckin' A!"

"Well, it's not like it wasn't going to get butchered at the client," Jen Barton, his writer partner chimed in. "I mean, the Duchess has been on a rampage lately."

"I love that you call her the Duchess," I chuckled.

"Well, it fits, right?" Jen smiled. "I mean, you've met her—the way she comes into the meeting, the way she sits at the head of the table, the way she orders her people around, nose in the air," (she did a dead on imitation), "theatrical arm movements," (again with the imitation), "I keep waiting for her to come in wearing a little tiara."

The group laughed.

"Revelry amongst the peasantry? The lords and ladies will be outraged! There will be reprisals!" came a voice from behind us.

"*Sean!*"

"*Seano!*"

"*Hey!*"

"*Seany!*"

He accepted the handshakes, back claps, and proffered cheeks of the group, then turned to me and bowed slightly.

"Excellency,"

"You Grace," I bowed. "In good spirits?"

"I am in good spirits. And in just a moment, good spirits shall be in me."

He turned toward the bar.

"Jason, my good man!" he called.

Jason was way ahead of him. He was already striding down the bar with a tall, pink, perfectly hemophiliac glass in his hand.

"A Hapsburg Prince, Guvnor?" he smiled as he placed it on the bar.

"A credit to your trade, sir!" beamed Sean. "And clairvoyant, as well!"

Jason gave a little bow of thanks and stepped over to where Mike Patsio, an art director in Caroline's group, was waiting to order two Bud Lights with nowhere near the same histrionics.

"Excellency," Sean said, turning to me and raising his Hapsburg to my Scotch. "To your continued prosperity..."

"And yours," I clinked.

"Ah," he said, taking a healthy belt. "Much too late for discussions of my prosperity, Excellency. How goes the crusade on your front? Holding fast against the infidels I trust?"

"Barely."

"And which of our esteemed clients are we currently at war with?"

"Ya know, Seano, I'm beginning to feel like it's more of a civil war, actually."

"Ah, internecine warfare. Led by Major Farner, the Desert Rat, no doubt."

"Fucking sewer rat, more like."

Sean barely avoided sputtering a fine, pink mist into the air.

"*Excellency!* How uncharacteristically unmeasured of you!"

"Yeah, well…"

"No need to apologize. Good to see you like this, the passion rising, the venom boiling. Not to mention the fact that I completely concur with your assessment of that posing, self-promoting ponce. He's a right bugger. But, what can you do?"

"Well, we'll see," I said into my Scotch.

"I detect a threat of a raid of some sort. A frontal assault? Or perhaps a more covert, guerilla-style sortie?"

"We'll see."

Sean seemed to be looking over my shoulder toward the door.

"On the subject of frontal assaults," he said quietly. "I believe I'm about to experience one."

I turned and looked toward the door. Alex's chestnut head bobbed slowly toward us, making her way through the crowd.

"Oh, yeah—I meant to mention that Al was meeting me here. We're meeting Kat and some people later. Have you two, uh, spoken this week?"

"Depends on your definition of 'spoken'," Sean said with cast down eyes. "There was an episode when I picked up the phone and listened while receiving the dressing down of a lifetime. If that's what you mean by 'spoken' then yes, Alex and I have, as you say…'spoken'."

"Looks like you're gonna speak again," I said.

Alex finally edged her way past the last of the impeccably turned out barflies and entered the little clearing we'd made for ourselves at the corner of the bar.

"Hey, Al," I said, reaching an arm around her as she kissed me hello.

"Hey hon," she said.

She reached over and put her briefcase between the brass foot-rail and the bar. She straightened up and gave her head a little toss, clearing the hair out of her face. Properly composed now, she acknowledged Sean.

"Sean," she nodded.

"Alex," he returned, raising his glass ever so slightly. The gesture seemed to irritate her.

"What can I get you, babe?"

"Chardonnay."

"Coming up."

I turned to the bar knowing I was leaving Sean to face the fire alone.

"How's goes life amongst the legal eagles?" Sean asked as winningly as humanly possible.

"Fine, thanks," Alex answered—as bloodlessly as humanly possible.

"You guys are handling that Hansen case, right?" Sean said, boldly trying to make this work. "The stolen code thing that was in The Times?"

"The code wasn't exactly stolen," Alex replied coolly. "There may have been infringement issues in the development stage."

"Ah," Sean, clearly ready to abandon this particular front and beat a hasty retreat. "Infringement. The very word."

"Here you go, Al," I said proffering the glass of chardonnay.

"Thanks, babe."

"To Friday," I said, raising my Scotch and clinking Al's glass and then Sean's. Sean offered his glass to Alex—who hesitatingly clinked his glass as though it hurt.

"How was today?" I said.

"Not bad," Alex said, running a hand through her hair. "I thought we were going to be able to schedule the IT deposition but no one could agree."

"Can't you just say 'show up'"?

"Unfortunately, no. It's not like a subpoena—you're compelled to deliver a deposition but not on a specific day. Besides, it was more us that couldn't agree on a day then the IT guys."

"Really?" I laughed. "Roger a little too busy to do his job these days?" Roger Hollowell was the partner in charge of the case and had a reputation for only being available when the credit was being passed out. Obviously, a disease that had spread beyond the advertising industry. I had spent many an evening listening to Alex's tirades about his unique combination of indifference, incompetence, and meddling.

"Yeah," she snorted. "Exactly. Whenever he can squeeze us in, I guess we'll pursue the biggest copyright case in the firm. And you, my marketing maven? Did we sell, sell, sell today?"

"Our souls. Several times over."

"Now, now."

"Ah, it was fine," I said.

"Everyone excited about the Concordia thing?"

"Yeah—excited. Wired is more like it," I kind of laughed. "And girding themselves for the days ahead."

"Yeah?"

"Yeah, that's why there are so many people here tonight—they figure they'd best enjoy themselves. It's probably their last taste of freedom for a week."

"You, too?"

"Oh, me especially."

"Poor baby."

"Gee, thanks."

"The legal biz can't be much different," Sean said, trying bravely to stay in the game.

"No—it's not," she answered efficiently.

"Yeah," I said, trying desperately to keep Sean's conversational balloon aloft. "I mean when it comes time to go to court on this Hansen thing, you guys'll be burning the midnight oil."

"Oh, absolutely," she said to me directly. "If this thing goes to trial, you might not see me for a month. But if you win, that makes your year."

"That'd be nice," I laughed, looking at Sean.

"What?" Alex asked.

"Well, winning one case might make your year, but winning this Concordia assignment will just be a day's work for us."

"C'mon, that can't be true."

"Afraid it is positively true," said Sean, looking at his feet.

"Yeah, it'll be 'Thanks very much, what have you done for me lately.'"

"Is that the industry?"

"Yeah, to a degree," I mused.

"But Cracknell has a particularly virulent strain of that disease," Sean offered.

"Oh, yeah—Justin has practically terminal ADD when it comes to chasing money. It's always on to the next thing."

"Speaking of on to the next thing," Alex said, polishing off the rest of her Chardonnay. "I told Kat we'd meet her at 7:00."

"Off we go, then," I said draining the last of my Scotch. "Let me just settle up with Jason…"

"Allow me, Your Grace," Sean said holding up a hand.

"You sure?"

"Absolutely—least I can do," he said furtively indicating Alex with his eyes.

"Well, very gracious of you, Excellency—you're a prince."

"Goodbye, Sean," Alex said—in the very definition of a perfunctory farewell.

"Excellency," I bowed.

"You Grace—enjoy the balance of your evening."

As we jockeyed our way toward the door, Alex said over her shoulder "He just wants to leave the tab open."

"C'mon, Al—give the guy a break."

"Everyone gives him a break—that's his problem."

She took a few more steps toward the door and then turned to face me.

"His *other* problem."

She turned and joined a crowd that was leaving and we spilled out into the night.

CHAPTER 45

"So where are we?" Rob was asking.

"And a happy Monday morning to you too, Rob!" I laughed.

"Seriously, where are we?" he said. "How bad is it?"

"It's not bad at all, Rob," I said. "We're looking good, I think. Been a very long but productive weekend."

We were standing in the lobby of the Creative floor where the elevator banks emptied out onto the new blond wood that Justin had so painstakingly picked out—and which contrasted so much with the mahogany, J.P. Morgan look of his own office.

"We need to get together and match everything up to the assignment grid," he said. "We need to answer every one of the squares on the assignment matrix."

"Well, I can tell you right now, Rob, that we aren't going to answer every square on the assignment matrix."

"But we have to, Terry—*we have to!*" His eyes were bugging out of his head behind his round, tortoise-shell glasses.

"No, Rob—what we have to do is deliver two or three really good campaign ideas that they can get excited about."

"But they won't get excited about anything if it doesn't conform to the matrix! It's how they're going to measure us against the other agencies! If we don't conform to the rules of the assignment, we may as well not show up!"

"Rob," I said smiling. "Will ya calm down? You haven't even seen what we have yet. We've got some really good ideas in there.

Let's look at the ideas and start to see where they'd fit in the almighty matrix and then take it from there. OK?"

"Fine, fine," he muttered.

The room we were using as the Concordia war room was a repurposed storage room in the far corner of the floor. It was long and narrow and windowless—like presenting in a submarine. But it had plenty of charcoal gray cloth wall space and most of it was taken up by sheets of layout pads pinned up with spots and print ideas and interactive screens and the rest of the surviving thoughts from the teams. To the uninvolved viewer, it probably looked like a bunch of paper randomly pinned to the wall but it actually was completely orderly in my mind—I knew the ideas we liked, the flow from one to another, how they related. It all made perfect sense to me.

Rob, on the other hand, in his advanced state of anxiety, looked at it as though it was barely controlled chaos. You could tell from the look on his face that he was an inch away from hyperventilation.

"Oh my God," he kept saying looking wildly from sheet to sheet. "Oh my God…"

"Pretty cool, huh?" said Nick Burns, a young writer who had pitched in with some of the interactive stuff. "Lotta cool ideas up here…"

"That's not what he means," I said under my breath. Gail heard me.

"Why? What does he mean?" she said, her creative Spidey-sense tingling and alerting her to the fact that creative ideas might be in danger.

"He means that it doesn't look like a presentation yet," I said, assembling a pile of scripts as I sat at the table. "It looks like a shambles, nothing's plugged into the matrix and the meeting's in 72 hours." I raised my voice slightly. "That about right, Rob?"

"Oh my God," he said.

"Here, let us take you through it, Rob—you'll feel better."

So we started in.

Rob sat at the table with his personal checklist and a printout of the almighty matrix. His young, eager-beaver staff—Audrey Mathieson, Sarah Burnett, David Rothenberg, and Hilary Spitz, surrounded him. They all sat eagerly listening and making copious notes as Gail and I walked through the stuff. It made me feel like a professor in a lecture hall instead of like someone explaining something to colleagues.

"So there are five basic approaches..." I said. "Each of them has basic merit. Three of them are particularly good. One of them is killer."

"Under each idea," Gail jumped in, "There are TV executions, some print stuff, a lot of potential interactive approaches..."

"Guys," Rob said, removing his glasses and leaning forward and putting his face in his hands. "You've got to present this the way they've asked for it—by assignment, by segment, by–"

"Oh, Rob, will you stop sitting there crying and whining like a stinkin' baby? Just listen to what we're saying!" Gail exploded.

"Yeah, Rob," I said calmly. I had the luxury of calm since Gail was already playing the role of assassin. "Go through it with us and then we'll assemble the grid."

"Matrix," Sarah corrected.

"Whatever," snapped Gail.

I sighed.

The discouraging part wasn't that this was agonizing. It's that it wasn't even real. This was just practice pain.

The real thing was going to kill us.

CHAPTER 46

It was the night before.

Time to lock and load.

"The studio wants to know when we think the last boards will be ready," Gail was saying to me.

"Tell 'em to go set up shop at the airport," I snorted.

"You're probably right," she laughed.

"Probably?" I said. "You know how much stuff there is...on top of which, Rob and the magpies haven't come by yet with the Magic Matrix to rock back and forth in their seats like autistic children and wring their hands and point out all our many failings...and on top of *that*, Larry hasn't seen any of this yet."

"Holy shit," Gail gasped. "Larry doesn't know any of this yet? You're kidding!"

"No, my friend—I am most assuredly not kidding."

"And when's that going to happen?"

I looked at my watch.

"Maybe in the next 45 minutes to an hour," I said. "We can take him through the broad strokes of what we've got together without all the other voices in the room. Give him the high level view of what we're talking about. You know what I mean?"

"Yup—I do," she said looking at me steadily and nodded seriously. The look in her eyes told me she understood—we were agreeing that if Larry came in for a look, we were going to blow him through the work in such a way that he'd be able to say he saw it, be able to recall certain inarguable elements of it, even be able to say he liked it without really understanding a fucking thing. Because if we went into too much detail, he'd feel compelled to really engage and start thinking things through, at which point he'd feel further compelled to actually do something about it. He'd start making suggestions, contributions, revisions, and changes—leading, potentially, to a complete re-working of what we had. And we sure as shit didn't have time for that kind of engagement.

Her talent aside, this was what I loved best about Gail: at moments like this, she and I could read each other's minds. We knew what had to happen in order to make the meeting, and we knew how to either eliminate or minimize anything that might get in the way.

Especially other people's opinions.

It wasn't that were didn't care what other people thought...

OK—it was *precisely* that we didn't care what other people thought.

Not at this point, anyway.

The night before a presentation was like reaching Mile 23 in a marathon. You'd lugged yourself through 23 miles, marshaled your resources, paced yourself, ignored the pain, fought through the cramps and now you just had to focus for three more miles. Tunnel vision-like focus. Zen-like focus. Unwavering cult-like focus. You didn't want any water, you didn't want any orange slices and you didn't want some asshole with a beer in his hand cheering you on by saying it was "only two more miles".

What you wanted was for everyone to shut the fuck up and get out of the way.

And having conversations with people like Rob or Larry or (God help us!) Ross at a moment like this was like having someone jump out of the crowd as you plodded past and start trying to give you directions through back alleys and side streets that weren't even part of the race course. Fatigue might make you listen for a minute and then you'd lose your focus and be unable to even finish the race the way you had intended. Or even finish the race at all. In the confusion your brain might just freeze up altogether, your limbs would stop rotating and you'd just pitch forward on the ground in a heap. At which point, people would then blame it on you for not having trained hard enough or being unable to hold up until the end.

So, were Gail and I going to shut out any further advice or suggestions?

You bet your ass.

We were going to smile and nod if necessary—because of rank or protocol or common courtesy—but we were done now. We were going to ignore every helpful rat bastard that poked his head in that room.

And it wasn't long before one did.

"What's up, dudes?" Keith said curling his head around the doorjamb like a snake. The only thing missing was the flick of a forked tongue as he appeared.

"Hey," I said, as lifelessly and uninvitingly as possible.

Gail was even better, ignoring him completely and continuing to pin tissues in place on the wall with cold precision.

"Lotta work, man," he said, inviting himself in. "Lotta work."

He was walking slowly along the wall, hands behind his back, occasionally tilting his head back to read a line or a script through his hipper-than-thou reading glasses, like he was strolling around a fucking museum.

"I've seen something like this before," he clucked, tapping one of the Run, Lola, Run boards with a knuckle. "I forget what it was for…it was better than this, though…" He continued down the wall.

Gail gave me a look that clearly indicated I was about to witness a positively medieval disemboweling if I didn't step in.

"Yeah, well, we've got other stuff," I said, looking at him kind of curiously. "That's not even what we're trying to sell."

"Cool, what're you trying to sell?" he said, suddenly scanning the wall in search of something else to find lacking.

"You know, Keith," I said as calmly as possible. "We're waiting for Larry and the account guys. You can walk through all this later, but we're kinda jamming to get ready for them…"

"Oh, sure, dude," he said, hands up, palms out in a kind of no-harm-no-foul gesture. "That's cool."

He bounced toward the door.

"Hey, dude…" he called to someone passing in the hall, already on to his next encounter, Tourette-like.

"What a fucking asshole!" Gail whispered savagely as soon as he was out the door.

"Yeah, that was a big fuckin' help," I responded as I looked over the wall. "What the hell was that all about?"

"'*It was better than this, though*'" she said, in imitation. "What a friggin' jerk!"

"Yeah, well," I sighed. "Maybe it isn't the greatest thing ever."

"Of course, it's not," she said, jamming a pushpin through a tissue and into the wall so hard the point must have appeared in the next room. "That's not the point! You would come in here at the last minute and start shitting on what we're doing? Without any knowledge at all of what's going on?"

"You would if you were Keith," I sighed. "Which thank the good Lord you are not. So c'mon—let's focus. Where are we?"

The room was now an accelerating beehive of activity. There were writers, art directors, production people, and traffic people all hustling in and out of the room as they chased down the particular parts of the presentation puzzle for which they were responsible. As a result, there were no fewer than 5 different conversations going at any given moment in different parts of the room.

"Where are we printing to?" one of the art directors called out.

"TV boards go to Sleepy, print boards go to Dopey." (The

printers in the studio having been named after the Seven
Dwarfs.)

"Overflow goes to Grumpy."

"Account service wants to know what typeface we're
using…"

"Avenir condensed."

"What's Account Service doing with a typeface?"

"That's not 'Suburban Blender'—that's the guerilla idea for
'Lola'."

"They're doing the leave behind."

"Leave behind? Christ, we don't have anything to leave yet!"

"Shit!"

"What?"

"Someone check the announcer copy."

"Whaddaya need?"

"Make sure the call to action is consistent!"

"Velcro on the boards?"

"Velcro on the boards."

"What template are we using for TV boards?"

"#2!"

"Are we squeezing the Avenir?"

"Squeeze this."

"Ha!"

"Who's printing to Doc?"

"I was…"

"Doc is down."

"Scripts on the front of the boards or the back?"

"Uh…

"Pizza or Chinese?"

"Pizza."

"Pizza."

"Chinese."

"Give me a total board count when you can."

"Round edges or square?"

"Does it come with salad?"

"What's all this shit?"

"All that shit's dead…"

"Dead?"

"Chinese."

"Hey wait a minute—my spot's dead?"

"Are we getting beer?"

"NO!"

"Still waiting on that script call…"

"Broadcast has to still spec the boards."

"Hey, where's my–"

"Why are we spec-ing? We don't need estimates…"

"Script call, please?"

"Print 'em on the front, tape 'em on the back."

"Terry! Terry!"

I turned toward the door—Meghan was standing there craning her neck to find me in the blur, waving her hand and motioning me over. With her was Christina, Larry's assistant. I made my way over to the door and we stepped outside into the relative calm and privacy of the hallway.

"What's up, Meg?" I asked, running my hands over my already tired eyes.

"Uh, Christina needs to talk to you."

"Is Larry coming?" I asked.

"Larry says if you really need him, to call him on his cell."

"He's leaving?"

"Tonight's his massage…" Christina said quietly, stepping aside as a young guy from the studio turned the corner with an armload of foam core presentation board.

I smiled.

I looked at Meghan. She smiled.

I looked at Christina.

She smiled—but with her eyes cast down in embarrassment.

"Beautiful."

"I know."

"Perfect."

"He really meant that you could call him," she said. "Really."

"I know he did," I said, reaching out to touch her arm reassuringly. "It's fine. It's just..."

Three women from production swept past us into the room.

"The deck is never gonna make FedEx, so call Curb-to-Curb couriers," one of them was saying.

"It's just that his timing is so perfect," I laughed.

"I know," Christina laughed. "I know. Is there anything I can do?"

"Run."

"See you," she said, half raising a hand in a sort of goodbye wave. "Good luck."

"Thanks, Christina, have a good night."

"What can I do, Terry?" Meghan asked, genuine concern in her voice.

"Uh...nothing, kid...nothing right now. Are they getting food?"

"Yeah—Stephanie and Angela just went to get it."

I nodded.

"I'm at my desk—just yell," she said as she headed off down the hall.

When I stepped back into the room, it actually took me a minute to re-adjust to the scene. Even stepping out of it for a couple of minutes made you forget the speed and the noise inside.

"More Velcro!"

"Fuck the Velcro—use pushpins for now!"

"Why is Dopey printing so light?"

"You want the outdoor in environment or just boarded?"

"Wrong ending! Wrong ending!"

"Gail!"

"Terry!"

"Dave!"

"Angela!"

"C'mon guys—we've got the same swipe on two different campaigns…"

"Where's the radio?"

"We didn't do radio."

"Food's here!"

"Chinese? I thought we were getting pizza?"

"This is the logo treatment, people—use this as the model!"

"Terry!"

"Yeah?"

"Rob's coming in 10…"

"Great."

"Where's the beer?"

"*No beer*—not till we're done."

"It'll be morning!"

"Whatsa matter—you don't like beer with your Cheerios?"

"Why is this mounted? Who's mounting?"

"Where are the writers?"

"Stop mounting!"

"Wrong template!"

"Nobody mount anything!"

"Or anyone…"

"No, no, no—no black and white visuals!"

"Where does print go?"

"For what?"

"Get the writers to check their own scripts!"

"Sleepy is down!"

"Go to Grumpy!"

"I thought we were getting pizza?"

"Shit!"

"What?"

"Who got sesame noodles on the scripts?"

"*Hi*, guys," I heard through the racket. It was the ever cheerful, ever optimistic voice of Audrey Mathieson. "Wow, it's a lot of stuff!"

Turning toward the door, I saw Rob and his entourage had arrived. Audrey was smiling. Sarah, David, and Hilary looked pleasantly blank. Rob, as always, looked as though he were suffering from irritable bowel syndrome.

"Hey guys," I called. "Come on in. Welcome to the show."

The account guys started pulling out seats at the table, which were easy to find since no one else in the entire room was sitting. In fact, no one else in the entire room had stopped moving for about two hours.

Rob sat down as if in a trance. His eyes were focused on the wall of work—which he seemed to be scanning in a state of near panic.

"Let us get some of this cleared away," I said. "Then we can take you through it and it starts to take shape."

"Should we put the matrix up on the other wall?" Audrey asked.

"The Matrix?" asked Adrian, a young art director who was helping out. "Who did a campaign based on 'The Matrix'?"

"Not that kind of matrix," Gail said.

"Let's put it up and see how we stand," said Audrey.

"Fine," I said, flatly.

I was sitting facing the wall with all the work on it. It was the first time I had really looked at the wall in the past couple of hours—and I had to say I was actually hit with a bolt of optimism. It was looking pretty good. The 4-5 directions were all there, all taking visible shape. They looked cohesive, different from each other and fairly well integrated.

I didn't know if it was going to change advertising history.

But it sure looked like a meeting.

I gave the wall one last scan and kind of nodded quietly to myself.

And then turned around—into a withering hail of pessimism bullets from Rob.

"Oh my God, we're dead," he was saying to no one and everyone. "We are so dead. Oh my God, we're going to get fired. Tomorrow. I'm going to lose my job tomorrow."

The entire bustle of progress in the room screeched to a halt and everyone turned and looked at Rob.

"Easy, buddy, easy," I started.

"How can you say *easy?*" he practically screamed. "Look at the matrix—we're supposed to have DR spots and mail programs and integrated programs for sales support! All coming off of the launch spot in each campaign! Look at the matrix! Look at it!"

"Why don't you look at *that* wall for a while, Rob?" Gail said, her arm pointing like a spear at the wall of work. "Look at that wall and see what it is that all these people have been doing the past few weeks!"

"They haven't been answering the assignment, that's what they've been doing!!" he threatened in what would have been a scream if fear and anger hadn't combined to constrict his throat to the diameter of a coffee stirrer. Instead, his voice squeaked out and made him sound more scared than scary.

"Rob, Rob," I said. "Let us take you through the stuff and then, together, we can take a look at where it all fits in the mighty matrix." As the words were leaving my mouth, I started to realize that I had spoken that exact same sentence to Rob every other day for weeks now, and we were no closer to actually going through that exercise than we were when I first said it.

"It's not gonna fit, it's not gonna fit," he said—literally beginning to rock back and forth in his chair.

Gail looked at me.

I gave her a theatrical "See?" expression to remind her that I had predicted spontaneous onset autism.

Audrey, Sarah, David, and Hilary were all dutifully taking notes—which was interesting, given what was going on. I couldn't imagine what they could possibly be writing. They were responsible for writing meeting reports after meetings—but I couldn't quite see the report for this one saying "Creative Department presented campaign; Account Director suffered complete nervous collapse."

"Look," I said, for what I silently promised myself would be the final time I would ever say this. "Let's go through the work, OK? Then, if we want, we can all break down and cry. But if we're all going to burst into uncontrollable sobs, could we at least do it about something we've actually *seen*—instead of something we're only imagining?"

I stepped around the table to the wall.

"All right—here's where we're gonna start…"

It took a while.

I was stumbling through some of it, ideas I knew but was now seeing in finished form for the first time, reading scripts that until now had only been hypothetical, trying out some explanations of my own, wondering in my mind if things were in the right order, asking Gail for some explanations of certain elements.

Tomorrow, fueled by what I assumed would be a heady cocktail of familiarity, fear and adrenaline, it would go a lot faster.

When I was through, I looked at the group.

"There it is," I said. "They gotta like something up there. How could they not?"

Silence from across the table.

"I mean, guys—come on—the Digital Summit campaign," I pointed to it on the wall "would be unbelievable."

"It would be pretty amazing," said Audrey in a flash of enthusiasm—which was quieted by one look at Rob.

"It's not in the matrix," Rob said, his voice constricted by his anxiety.

"Well. Some of it is, Rob," I answered. "Look—this print is actually the acquisition print. And these spots here? Can be the DR stuff. And this over here–"

"It isn't what they're looking for!"

By this point, a lot of eyes in the room were furtively looking at me. The room was still full of people coming and going, putting the presentation together. Studio people, production people, creatives who had humped to get the work that was on the wall actually on the wall—they were all kind of looking at me out of the corners of their eyes as they slowly and quietly continued working.

I had been standing in front of the wall, pointing to some of the pieces. I slowly lowered my hand and stood, hands by my side, for a long minute—looking at Rob.

"Get out," I said flatly.

All activity in the room ceased.

"What?" he answered.

"I said get out," I said again.

"Terry, we need to go through the-"

"Get the fuck out," I said pointing at the door.

"C'mon, guys," Audrey said.

"No, I mean it, Rob," I continued, ignoring Audrey's attempt to broker peace. "I'm not kidding. Get out. This is the work we're showing tomorrow. These are the pieces that are going to be up on boards tomorrow morning in that conference room. I will get you copies of them to go over tonight if you want to familiarize yourself. But I can't listen to this anymore. We have too much work to do to get *these* ideas ready much less to try to track down some other ideas that you think would better fill out your precious matrix. We've all been working way too hard on this and we all still have a whole night's worth of work left to do. And it would really help things if you would take your matrix and your anxiety and your pessimism and get...the...fuck...out."

He sat staring at me.

"NOW!!"

He actually jumped.

And he actually left.

The room slowly came back to life and wound back up again and people went back to work.

Audrey and the crew still sat, unsure of what to do. David was still dutifully taking notes. I was tempted to offer to spell "fuck" for him, just so he'd get it right. After a few minutes they gathered up their stuff and left. Audrey lingered at the door for just a second.

"There's..." she started cautiously, probably scared to ignite another shit storm. "There's...a lot of really good things here, guys..."

"Thanks, Audrey," Gail said for us all.

Over the next few hours, it all started to come together. By the time I left, the wall was covered with shiny presentation boards, all the pieces were mounted in their full-color glory, logos in place, copy in place, visuals checked and double-checked.

It sure looked like a presentation to me.

"Go home," I said to Gail as I passed by her on my way out. "Get some sleep."

"I just want to make sure it all goes in the bags."

"See you at the airport in a few hours."

"Right."

"Thanks, guys!" I called to the room. "You were awesome as usual!"

"Night, Terry!"

"See ya, Terry!"

"Thanks!"

"Bye, Ter."

"Knock 'em dead!"

"Kick some ass tomorrow!"

"Thanks!"

In the cab on the way home, I rubbed my eyes and leaned my head back against the seat. Part of me thought we'd be OK, but I was also very in touch with my inner Rob, who kept reminding me that we were going to get slaughtered. I just kept trying to focus on how good some of the ideas actually were. It made me feel a little better.

It had been a hell of a night.

And amidst all of the images of the work and Rob and the matrix and the questions and my anger and the rest, there was one question that kept surfacing in my swirling brain.

What the hell was Keith doing poking his nose into a Concordia meeting?

CHAPTER 47

The cab ride to the airport the next day was 30 of the most sur-real minutes of my life. I was awake, I was pretty sure. But I had settled into a kind of catatonic state. I could see the world through the cab window but I wasn't at all convinced that it was real.

I got out at the curb and went through the revolving door.

The noise level and bustle of the terminal roused me from my coma—at least a little. I found the gate information on the screen, went through the metal detectors and wandered down the blindingly fluorescent hallway toward Gate 37. I stopped in front of the Starbucks for a long moment and then decided that the feeling of the coffee in my brain wasn't going to be worth the feeling of the coffee in my stomach.

I kept walking down the corridor, which eventually spilled out into the big, round area that contained Gates 35 through 40. Making my way through the throngs of fellow business travelers, I stepped into the small seating area in front of Gate 37 and was greeted by Rob.

Who looked positively psychotic.

"Terry, Terry," he said. His head and hands were shaking so wildly he looked like he was dancing. "I've got it."

"Got what?"

"I know what we'll do, I know what we'll do*!*"

"Easy, Rob," I said calmly. Having already passed through the panic stage myself, I was feeling fairly calm. I was experiencing the acceptance of the terminally ill. I figured my emotional phases today were going to be like Kübler-Ross's stages of grief.

Especially the part where everything culminated with acceptance of impending death.

"No, no. I've got it all figured out," he said.

Gail suddenly arrived and joined us.

"What's going on?" she asked, instantly sensing that there was madness afoot.

"Rob knows what we should do."

"What?" She said turning to him.

"Well, when we get there, we'll have about 45 minutes before we're on. So instead of going to the meeting room, we'll go find Anne in her office...and just tell her we're not ready."

Gail looked at me, expressionless.

I looked at Rob.

"Are you insane?" I said quietly.

"No, listen to me, it's the only way. We'll just be honest with her. We're not ready and could we have a few more days."

"I can't listen to this," Gail said storming off.

"Rob, will you listen to yourself? I mean why would we even go? Why would we do this?"

"Because it'll appeal to her human side."

"Rob—she doesn't have a human side."

"It's the only way, Terry. She'll listen to us. She'll give us the time—and in a couple days we could finish the assignment."

"OK, Rob. Listen to me. Get hold of yourself."

"But..."

"No. If we go down there and tell her we're not ready, she'll fire us. Right there, on the spot. Guaranteed. 100%. She might even call security and have us escorted from the building. If we show 'em what we've got, at least we've got a 50-50 chance of surviving. I mean, it's not much, but I like my odds better."

Gail came back with a coffee.

"But we didn't do the assignment!" Rob pleaded.

"Will you stop with the 'we didn't do the assignment?'" Gail said. "We did the assignment—just not the way you would've."

It was my turn to walk away now. Kind of a tag-team thing. But I really couldn't handle this. I just had to keep focused, keep moving forward, just come out the other end of this no matter the outcome.

They called the flight and I walked down the jet way and found my seat. Rob was sitting directly behind me. As we took off, I concentrated on the newspaper, reading stories about local politics just to keep myself from engaging reality for a few more minutes.

"Folks, I'm gonna put the seat belt sign on here...some aircraft ahead of us have reported some bumpy air up ahead..."

"Maybe that's it," I heard Rob muttering aloud behind me. "Maybe the plane'll go down."

"What're you, an asshole?" the guy next to him said.

Rob was making friends wherever he went this morning.

But his wish wasn't granted and we arrived right on time. Gail and I headed straight for the baggage claim to grab the portfolios. Rob trailed behind, talking on his cell phone. I wondered if he was calling Anne and putting Operation Panic Button into action.

Forty-five tense, silent minutes later, we arrived at the front door of Concordia. It was a completely nondescript building in Midtown, faceless and anonymous-looking. Which was perfect for them. It had absolutely no architectural point of view whatsoever and so was sure not to offend anyone.

We checked in at the vast security desk and headed up to the conference room.

Inside the room, Gail and I went to work pulling the boards out of the bag and arranging them in order.

"Do you want to do the alternate video-phone spot?" She asked.

"Let's have it in the pile and we'll see how things are going."

"I have a feeling we're going to have to be pretty fluid about this," she said.

"Ya think?" I laughed.

"Mor-ning, morning Cracknell," sing-songed Jessica Moore as she sailed through the door. She was cheery as usual—and, also as usual, she looked like some sort of unmade gypsy's bed. Layers of long, flowing knit vests and cardigans and swishing pant legs, her ash-grey hair billowing around her as she came. "Almost ready?"

"Good morning, Jess," said Rob. "Yeah, we're...I guess."

Christ, he sounded like Eeyore.

"Morning, Jess," I said shaking hands. "How've you been?"

"Ah, this process is killing me. Killing me. Meeting after meeting with all these agencies, and then we've got to do it all again in two weeks. She's got us crazy."

"Tell me about it," I smiled.

"Right, right," she snorted and began to arrange her stuff on the table.

Anna Rosso walked in and wordlessly slid her stuff onto the table. Anna was legendary for not being a morning person—and while it was going on 10, that was considered the crack of dawn here at Concordia. The privatization of the telephone industry had changed many things, but Concordia's work ethic wasn't one of them. It remained pure public utility. Anna was working on a large Starbucks but it didn't seem to have had its desired effect yet.

She looked slit-eyed and mean.

Perfect. Just what we needed.

The other acolytes drifted in—Martha, Tad, a couple of others. They didn't really matter. And you could tell by their manner and demeanor that they *knew* they didn't matter. Anne would make this decision—and she'd make it quickly and loudly and abrasively. She might take a little input from Jessica, but this was gonna be her call.

"Morning," croaked a voice coming through the doorway. "Are we ready here or what?"

Anne stomped into the room like a dockworker and flopped down in a chair next to Jess.

"Let's get started—we've got a lot to cover I'm sure," she rasped. "Rob? Anything you want to say?"

For a second, I thought Rob might burst into tears and throw himself on the mercy of the court. But the look I gave him assured him that if he delivered anything but the standard introduction I would go for his throat.

"No, uh...yeah, yeah. We're, uh, excited to be here today to talk about this first round of this assignment. And we..."

"Oh for Crissakes, Rob," Anne bawled. "Don't give me all that canned crap. Ya got somethin' to say about the work or not?"

"Uh, I'll just turn it over to...Terry. And Gail."

Who will assure that we all die, his eyes were saying.

"Thanks for that rousing introduction, Rob..." I smiled.

There was a small, collective chuckle from the other side of the table.

"Well, we are excited to be here today," I began. "We've taken a few looks at the assignment and I think some of them are very different. I think we've answered the assignment in a couple of unexpected ways. So without further ado—let's dive right in."

We were off and running.

I showed them the first few boards like we had planned—the more obvious concepts to begin, easing them into it, giving them safe ground to stand on. The Suburban Blender thing, as mundane as it was, was a clear answer to the assignment. You could see them nodding to it, foreheads furrowed as they checked off their mental lists.

"But let me show you another way to think about this," I segued into the next bunch of boards.

Out came 'Lola'. The hardest part was explaining the film— they had clearly never heard of it, much less seen it. But that was fine. I had expected that. I just wanted them to get the feeling that this was something that would make them seem cool as a company.

"I know it sounds a little edgy, a little avant-garde, maybe a little artsy for you," I said. "But let me show you how this would work..."

The repetitive scenarios were a little tough to follow, but I kept hammering home how much functionality we were demonstrating.

"So for this one woman, we're showing voice, data, business apps, rich media..." I was throwing every piece of jargon I could at them. I figured that even if they didn't understand the creative device, at least they could hear their products and services shining through.

They were leaning in—a good sign.

"And not only that, we're mirroring life, showing that not only does Concordia offer a tremendous array of products and services, they understand what contemporary life is like," I said.

I paused and gave a quick look around the table.

And started to have a glimmer of hope.

They were nodding in that *"gee, there's an interesting insight"* way that clients all too rarely exhibit. If I could keep this on the high conceptual level, we might never have to descend into the checklist for the dreaded 'assignment'. Of course, this would be a sleight-of-hand trick that David Copperfield would envy. But I didn't have a lot of choice, so I plowed on.

"Making that kind of connection is so much more important than just demonstrating product," I pleaded with as much sincerity as I could muster. "If you can demonstrate a product or service in a bigger, richer, more emotional cultural context? Whew! Game over."

I paused.

"Let me show you the ultimate example of that..."

Gail was way ahead of me. The two heavy retail demonstration campaigns had been pushed to the side. The Digital Summit campaign had jumped to the head of the line. As she handed the boards to me, I was already thinking of my summation. *Just show them this and get out on a high note.*

"To state the obvious, you are in the communications business. And the power, the real power of communication isn't *how* messages are transmitted..."

I let it sink in for a second.

"It's—what *are* those messages?"

I launched into the pitch.

"Not since the Cold War ended has communication been so important an issue. In those days, the lack of meaningful communication between the East and the West fueled the rise of hostility.

"And we stand ready for it to happen again."

"But this time, the lines are not so cleanly drawn. There's no Us and Them. In today's world there's Us and Them...and Them and Them and Them and the Other Them. Never before in history have there been so many opposing views."

The looks on their faces were telling me that, while they were appreciative of my little socio-political lecture, they were wondering what in the name of ringtones this had to do with them.

"And so, we need to bring differing points of view together; to encourage people to put aside their political baggage, to get people, even for a moment, to stop grinding their own individual axes, and participate in dialogue about peace. But we need a channel to bring them together. And we need an outside agent to bring them together.

"And Concordia...will be that agent."

The curiosity on their faces was just what I was looking for.

"Here's the idea: Concordia sets up a safe, hack-proof, dedicated, locked-down digital connection. You set up a worldwide, digital conference call for a specific date and time. And you invite all the world's leaders to participate—Obama, Brown, Sarkozy, etc., etc. The invitation would be in the form of a commercial which would run in all the major countries—and would look like this:"

Gail turned the concept board around. It was massive—pictures of world leaders, flags of the different countries, and portraits of kids.

"The spot opens on the face of a little girl' I explained. "She speaks to the camera. Other boys and girls each follow her delivering a line or two to the camera. The copy goes like this:

> *'Dear President Obama...*
>
> *On Wednesday, October 15th, you are invited to be part of a historic moment.*
>
> *At 10 a.m., Washington time, you are invited to participate in a worldwide conference call with Prime Minister Brown, Prime Minister Harper, President Sarkozy, President Putin, President Peres, Chancellor Merkel. President Napolitano, President Zapatero, Prime Minister Aso, President Musharraf, President Jintao, President Patil, President Karzai, President Kim Jong.*
>
> *14 leaders.*
>
> *From 14 different nations.*
>
> *To discuss peace in our world.*
>
> *It's only a beginning.*
>
> *And not everything will be solved.*
>
> *But it is a beginning we all need to make.*
>
> *So please, Mr. President.*
>
> *Please call.*
>
> *Please call.*

Please call.

Please...

The commercial would end quietly with the Concordia logo fading up over black."

"We would run this spot in each country," Gail jumped in, "Changing the name of the President or Prime Minister, with children from that country, speaking, obviously, in the native language,"

"Now, with the international component, it would be expensive to produce," I admitted. "But let me tell you where you actually save money—media coverage. You only have to run this once, and every news program, talk show, and weekly analysis will be re-running it ten times a day! Brokaw, Brown, Cooper, Matthews, Stephanopulos...they'll all be salivating over this. The YouTube views *alone* will be in the millions. The blogosphere will be on fire with this."

I paused.

"And even if not one leader accepts, think what Concordia will look like," I pleaded. "You're not the phone company anymore—you're a force for good in the world. Who'd wanna just be the phone company when you can be that?"

Gail and I stopped and looked at each other.

There was silence in the room.

A lot of it.

I looked over at Rob. He was still as a stone, not even looking at the clients but looking straight ahead at a point on the far wall, his eyes like glass. I was pretty sure he was astroprojecting.

I looked at the underlings. The way this was technically supposed to work was that the clients would now make comments in order of rank—the most junior people would start and they would work their way up to Jess and then Anne. I have no idea where this corporate tradition came from but it was annoying in the extreme. And no one seemed to be eager to jump into the breach. Anna seemed to be just feeling the first effects of the mammoth cup of coffee she had brought in. Tad was quietly shuffling papers. Martha and the others were just staring at the huge concept board we had unveiled.

You could practically hear the clock ticking.

"Brilliant," Jessica said softly.

"Yeah?" I said, not really believing what I was hearing.

"Absolutely," she continued, warming to the subject.

Rob seemed to rouse, coming back to us from far, far away.

"It's big and bold and cultural...don't you think, Anne?" Jess said, turning to her right.

We all turned and looked at Anne.

Who sat there expressionless for what seemed like an hour.

It was like lying on the floor of the Coliseum, leather breast-plate covered with blood and sand, the other guy's sword at your throat, waiting for Caligula to give you the thumbs up or thumbs down.

Anne swiveled her head, sweeping the board with the gaze through her gigantic magnifying lenses.

"It's great," she said in that industrial-grade sandpaper voice. "Nice work."

This was unbelievable.

Maybe we were going to live after all. At least for a few more minutes. It was always possible that one of the lackeys could bring up the dreaded 'assignment', producing a matrix and showing exactly what we had not delivered. I could see in his eyes that Rob was thinking the same thing. He was clearly suffering from total emotional schizophrenia, see-sawing wildly back and forth between optimism and visions of his own death.

"Like to get a sense of the costs on that one," Anne growled. "I know it will be expensive and that's fine. If we do it right, it might be worth the money. But I'd like to have a better sense of some of the production issues before we go forward."

Go forward?

Go forward?

My God, we were going to get away with it.

"And on that other campaign—the Run Lulu thing?"

"Lola" Rob interjected.

"Whatever," Anne snapped. "There's some promise there, too. See what you can do to simplify that one—like to see it again."

She looked at her watch.

"All right, we're running behind. Anyone have anything else?" she asked, acknowledging the presence of her own troops for the very first time.

"No, no…"

"I agree with what's been said so far."

"No, it looks good to me…"

Anne was already on her feet before they had finished their obsequious babbling.

"Good job, guys, thanks for the hard work," Anne croaked as she headed for the door and was gone.

I turned to Gail.

"Pack this shit up and let's get the hell out of here!" I whispered.

"W-a-a-ay ahead of you," she countered, already a blur of activity.

With our portfolios under our arms, we headed out the door. Jessica was standing out in the hall.

"Great job, Cracknell, great job!"

"Thanks Jess," I said. "Thanks for the support—as always."

"That was one of the best we've seen—really terrific."

"Hey, Jess," Gail interrupted. "Do you think you could ship this stuff back?"

"Ab-solutely," Jessica answered with an extravagant sweep of her arm. "Leave it right here and I'll have Maria ship to you overnight."

"Thanks, Jess," Gail answered. "That's great."

"We'll talk in the next day or two. Have a good trip b-a-a-a-ck," she called as she billowed her way down the hall.

Rob turned to me and there were, honest to God, tears in his eyes.

"Terry, I was wrong," he said.

"Yeah, you were," I laughed.

"I was wrong about it all—that was brilliant, just brilliant. They loved us! Oh my God, oh my God..." He was turning in little circles, around and around, like some sort of crazed wind-up toy.

"Easy, Rob, easy," I said. "Let's just get outside."

"I don't know how we did that."

Gail caught my eye and made a face.

"We?" she grimaced.

"Yeah, whatever," I said. I started down the dark, mahogany hall under the gaze of the somber portraits of past Concordia CEOs.

They'd probably seen weirder meetings than this one.

But not many.

CHAPTER 48

The cab ride to the airport was the polar opposite of that morning's ride to Concordia. The three of us were talking a mile a minute, recounting every excruciating moment of the meeting, Gail and I laughing (now!) at the tension of it all, Rob punctuating each remembrance with "Oh my God, Oh my God!", none of us believing that we had survived.

"Well, guys," I said, shaking my head. "We did great. Who knows what will happen, but at least we can look each other in the eye and say we did a great job."

"Can look Justin in the eye and say we did a great job," Rob said with emphasis.

"Good point."

"Did you call Larry?" Gail asked.

"I'll call him when we get to the airport."

"Can you imagine if he had been there?"

"Oh my God," Rob said—with a hint of this morning's terror creeping back into his voice. "Can you imagine?"

"He would have burst into flames. The tension in that room? He would have gone up like a pile of dry leaves," I said.

"I almost did," Rob said, somewhat sheepishly.

"Yeah," said Gail, turning in the middle seat to address him fully. "What the hell was that Zen trance you went into there for most of the meeting?"

Rob, to his credit, laughed.

"I mean," Gail continued, "Did you even see what we were doing? Were you even aware of which boards were up?"

"Yeah, brother, if you were in your happy place it sure is a long, long ways away," I said laughing.

"Delta?" the driver asked, rapping on the milky Plexiglas to get our attention. "Delta?"

"Yes, Delta," Rob answered, snapping to attention, ever-mindful of who the authority figure was in any given situation—in this case, an anonymous cab driver playing what sounded like Ukrainian Calypso music in the front seat. "Thank you. Sorry."

Rob sat back in his seat.

Suddenly he leaned forward again.

"We had a really great meeting today," he explained to the cabbie. "Really great. So we're a little excited."

He leaned back again.

"Really great," he said again, to no one in particular.

I looked at Gail.

She was sitting in the middle of the back seat—which she always actually preferred. She said it was because it gave her a view of the horizon and minimized motion sickness, which she was prone to, especially in lurching NYC cabs. Why anyone susceptible to motion sickness would ever get into the advertising business was beyond me—especially the creative end, where the turbulence and rocking of daily events was enough to make a veteran sea captain puke.

Gail was looking straight ahead, at the precious horizon no doubt, with a look of pure contentment on her face. She seemed to be radiating happiness and satisfaction—a state of being that Gail, with her continuing self-analysis and critical worldview, was almost never in.

We pulled up in front of the terminal and Rob paid the cabbie, tipping him so lavishly that the guy got out of the cab to help with our bags, even though we didn't have any.

Inside, our euphoria wasn't dampened even when we discovered that our flight was going to be delayed.

"How long?" I asked the woman at the gate.

She punched a few keys on the keyboard and made a face.

"Looks like it's going to be at least two hours," she said.

"Perfect," I said, and she looked at me as if I were insane.

I turned to Gail and Rob.

"My friends, Justin Cracknell would like to buy you a drink."

We headed across to the sports bar across the hall and found space at the corner of the bar. We were halfway through our first cocktail, still commiserating happily when Rob's phone rang.

"It's Jess," he said, looking down.

"Hi Jess," he said answering it.

We both looked at him.

"What?" he whispered.

Now we were really looking at him, our eyes wide, our minds spinning with the virtually endless list of possibilities good and bad that could have occurred.

"What?" he said, his voice rising. "Really?"

Gail was now waving her hands at him, begging for explanation.

"OK," he said—now smiling broadly. "We'll talk in the morning. Thanks, Jess!"

In one motion he snapped his phone shut and leapt off the barstool.

"*We won!*" he screamed.

"*What!?!*" Gail and I said at the same time.

"They saw the last group after we left and didn't see anything they liked and so they decided to vote right then and there...*and we won!*"

Rob started doing this mad little jig right there in the All-American Sports Bar.

"*We won! We won! We won, we won, we won!*" he sang.

I turned to find the bartender.

He was right in front of me—already handing over another round.

"I don't know what was on the other end of that phone," he said with a small smile. "But from the sound of it, I figured you were going to want these..."

"You figured right, my friend."

"And I also figured I'll just keep 'em coming?" he said with a smile.

"You are a wise man, my friend, a wise man," I laughed.

The three of us clinked glasses and I took a long pull on my drink.

The advertising gods rarely smile down on us hacks.

But when they do—goddam, it's sweet.

CHAPTER 49

The next morning, I was sitting in my office, bleary-eyed, awaiting the arrival of the rest of the Concordia brain trust so we could start to discuss how to move forward, make changes, get costs to Anne, all the next steps.

The fact that we were even alive to discuss next steps at all was a continuing miracle to me. Thirty-six hours earlier, I had been sitting right here, equally bleary although for different reasons, wondering how we were going to get everything together, if it it was any good at all, if the agency was going to get fired, if I was going to get fired, or if I was going to kill Rob and go to prison.

And then get fired.

Instead, we had triumphed. We had won the project.

And celebrated by partying like rock stars.

Which was why I sat here feeling happy, fulfilled and like crap all at once.

Gail wandered in with her partner Mark.

"Markus, my hero!" I said, holding out my hand for a fist bump.

"Nah, man—you," he said.

"Do you believe this?" I asked.

"I know," she laughed slumping into a chair and swinging her long legs over the arm.

Gail hung over was an infrequent sight at best but all the signs were there today—hair loosely pulled back in a butterfly clip, glasses instead of her usual contacts, an especially world-weary expression, and an absolutely massive iced Americano from Starbucks. "I can't believe we're even going to have this conversation."

"Hey, guys! Congratulations!" chimed Audrey, bursting through the door with two other young account folks I didn't even know. "I heard it went *awesome* yesterday!"

"Yeah," snorted Gail. "Awesome."

"In the end, yeah," I smiled. "Little tense up till then..."

"I can imagine," Audrey answered, eager for the details that would give her an emotional share in this latest triumph. "Rob said you were great!"

"I was petrified. I don't know if that looks anything like greatness."

"There they are," Rob said as he came through the door. "The heroes."

I smiled.

Gail rolled her head over to her right shoulder and looked at me blankly. Now I knew she was hung-over. Ordinarily, she would have ripped into Rob like a shark on a scuba diver over that one.

"Unbelievable performance yesterday," he said, applauding lightly. "Unbelievable."

"Rob, stop," Gail moaned. "Just... stop."

"Well, it's nice we're getting to talk about this stuff," I offered, trying to get us back on track. "Where do we begin?"

"Well, first off," Rob began "Jess called this morning and said that was one of the best meetings she's ever been in. Said we 'blew her away'. Brilliant, she said."

"Well, she did help our cause," I said. "That was a pretty big break with protocol yesterday, giving her opinion first. Bold move. We might not be alive if we'd had to endure Anna and Tad and everybody's weaseling comments first."

"Anna that lizard," Gail said, her eyes closed. "She's probably just waking up now, still sitting in that room wondering where everyone went. Freak."

"Yeah," I smiled. "She's nowhere near as perky as you."

Without opening her eyes, Gail slowly gave me the finger while everyone else laughed.

"Oh, I'm sorry—I was looking for a Concordia meeting," a voice said from the doorway. "But this couldn't be it. There's way too much laughter."

I looked up to see Zack standing in the door.

"Hey, bud," I said smiling. "Join the party."

"Are we actually talking about this?" he asked, arranging himself on the floor since there were no seats left.

"Everyone has the same reaction," I laughed. "But yeah— looks like it's gonna happen."

"Sweet."

"Should we start with Digital Summit?" Rob asked. "That's probably the nightmare one..."

"You know, it's not as bad as you might think," Zack said. "The thing that makes it expensive is that it's actually 14 or 15 spots—one for each country. But the individual spots themselves are actually cheap."

"How can this be cheap?" Rob asked.

"Well, if you really think about the spots, it's just one location—you're shooting the kids tight or with the background out of focus so if you got a playground or something that offered enough different visual context you can knock it all off at one location. Multiple set-ups, which takes time, but it's only one location."

"Wow," I said. "The good news continues."

"Now," Zack said, "as it's boarded, you're talking about ten-plus kids. So that's ten on-camera principals—so what you're saving in production, you're gonna pay in talent residuals. But if you could cut it to say five, six kids and repeat some of them in the spot, now you're talkin'."

Zack looked over at the by now nearly comatose Gail.

"Will five or six offend your creative sensibility there, Smiley?"

"Right now, everything offends me," she groaned. "But that sounds fine. Mark?"

"That's cool. Terry?"

"Yeah, I think we can make it work with fewer kids," I nodded. "Let's take a look at it."

"Rob, are they really gonna do 14 of these?" Zack asked.

"Well, we have to give them numbers on what that would cost, how we'd do it. Then they'll decide."

"Even though each of these is, by itself, not a bank breaker, fourteen of them is gonna be a big number," I said.

"Oh yeah," Zack nodded.

"Would you have the same director do them all?" I asked. "Or would you hire local in all the countries?"

"Well, obviously, I'd want to keep the same shooter if we can," Zack answered. "Keeps the look and the performances consistent and it gives us much more control. Much easier from a production standpoint."

"It's all about you, isn't it?" Gail said, having roused herself slightly.

"Only when it's not about you, darlin'," Zack smiled broadly.

"But if we had to, we could hire local, right?" Rob asked.

"Well, yeah, I suppose," Zack said.

"Who do you figure is the best director in Afghanistan?" I smiled.

Everyone laughed.

"You know..." Audrey said tentatively. She had been sitting and listening quietly along with the other account folks, scribbling notes and making to-do lists for Rob.

"Yeah?" Zack said.

"Um, some of these countries that we're talking about, um... aren't going to let us in," she said quietly.

"Like?" Zack said—you could sense the producer in him coming out. Rising to the challenge, willing to not only try the impossible but to accomplish it—the sort of *'oh yeah? Well watch this!'* DNA that all great producers have.

"Well," Audrey said, "Afghanistan is Muslim and has essentially broken off diplomatic relations with the US. And North Korea is even worse…"

"Good point," I said. "I want to shoot these spots—not *get* shot while shooting these spots."

"OK, well that saves us some dough," Zack said.

"Would we still include those countries' leaders in our other scripts?" Rob asked.

"Oh for God's sake," Gail spit out.

"Of course, we would," I said. "We might even be able to do some sort of press story about the fact that we weren't allowed to shoot there—being all the more evidence of why this call needs to happen."

"OK, OK, I'm just asking," Rob said.

"So, next steps?"

"I can put together some rough numbers," Zack said—and then looked hard at Rob. "But they are *not* to be shared with the client. It'll just give us an idea of what we're dealing with. I repeat—*not* to be shared."

"Got it," Rob nodded.

"Did I mention *not* to be shared?" Zack said.

"As in *not* to be shared," Gail said eyes squeezed shut.

"I got it, I got it," Rob said, raising his hands in mock self-defense. "*Not* to be shared."

"Then I think the next step would be to sit with you and Gail and think about directors…" Zack concluded.

"Any thoughts?" I said. "Gail?"

"I think I'll go home," she moaned.

"Zack?"

"Oh, I don't know—there's a bunch of guys…" he said. "Given

that it's all casting and performance, you might want to think about feature guys as well as commercial directors."

"Yeah," I mused. "Given the nature of it, you might get someone interested…"

The conversation petered out. The group stood up, gathering their notepads and papers.

"OK, thanks everyone," I said. "Exciting."

"Great!"

"Thanks."

"See ya."

"This is gonna be awesome!" Audrey said.

They all filed out, leaving me and the supine, barely conscious form of Gail.

"Gail?" I said quietly.

"Yes?" she said as if it hurt.

"Go home."

"Thank you."

She didn't move.

"Am I moving yet?" she asked.

CHAPTER 50

"You lookin' for me?" I said leaning through Larry's door.

(*Poof!* went the glasses.)

"Hey, bud," he said turning away from his laptop. "Yeah, I was."

"Cool," I said. "I wanted to fill you in more on the Concordia meeting."

I had called him from the airport right after we got the news—and right before I had slipped into Dewar's-induced oblivion.

"Yeah, nice going," he said. "Anything else happen? Since then?"

"No, not so far. But they want us to go ahead with numbers and schedules and everything."

"No shit?" he said shaking his head. "You know, every now and then...even guys like this do the right thing."

"Yeah," I laughed. "The planets finally align, huh?"

"Dudes! What's shaking?"

Keith bounced into the room and reached over me to fist bump Larry. As he leaned over me, I had a golden opportunity to punch him right in the balls.

Which I somehow resisted.

"What's goin' on?" he said slumping down in the chair opposite me.

"Just talkin' about the Concordia meeting the other day," Larry said, indicating me with a nod of his head.

"Yeah, I heard it was cool, dude."

"Yeah," I said cautiously. "It was."

"So'd they buy something?"

"Looks like they might have."

"Cool," he said nodding thoughtfully.

I nodded.

"Now that we won, think you can take another whack at the work?"

"Uh, why would we want to do that?" I said even more cautiously.

"I don't know—chance to do something great," he said—shooting a look at Larry like what he was saying was so obvious only a dolt wouldn't agree.

"Keith," I laughed "You don't even know what we did...how do you know we didn't already do something great?"

"Yeah, it's pretty good, bud," Larry chimed in, looking at Keith.

"Yeah, something about world leaders," Keith said dismissively.

"Yeah—something like that," I said.

"Hey—I don't know," he said shrugging. "Just a thought. A little more time, couple new teams, might come up with something even better."

"Your teams," I said. I was practically baring my teeth at this point.

"Well, sure—I got a coupla guys with some time."

He suddenly looked at his watch and jumped up.

"Think about it, dude," he said clapping me on the shoulder. "Gotta go to a Vision meeting. Later, dudes."

He bounced out of the room.

I looked at Larry.

"Is it me?"

"What?"

"Is it just me or was that an amazingly asshole performance?" I said pointing to the chair that the asshole had just vacated.

"Ah, don't worry about it," Larry said, waving his hand.

"I mean, you and I are sitting here talking about how great everything went, and then he comes in and trashes our whole effort," I said, my voice rising. *"He doesn't even know what that fucking campaign looks like!!"*

"I know, I know."

"But he's in here automatically assuming that if you gave it to a couple of his arrogant, self-absorbed pricks they'd come up with something better."

"Don't let him get to you."

"Fucking A, Larry!"

"Ah…" He waved his hand again.

I stood up.

"Hey, one other thing," Larry said.

"Sure," I said with a notable lack of enthusiasm.

"I need somebody to go to this dinner tomorrow night."

"What dinner?"

"It's with the guys from Hanover."

"Is that still going on? The whole thing with Brianna?"

"Yeah," he laughed. "A little. It's calmed down—but we're still trying to show Mike the love."

"And how do you propose that I'm going to show him the love?"

"Well, he and his team are in town for meetings all day tomorrow. The account team is taking them out for dinner and it'd be great if I could send a really senior creative guy with them. Just to show interest and commitment."

"But not you," I laughed.

"I got something else."

"Great—I'll see if Keith's free."

"C'mon," he said, a little more seriously this time. "You know I can't send Keith to a thing like that."

"Why the fuck not?"

"Because he'll act like an asshole."

"Oh, *really?*"

"He'll start questioning the work we're doing, try to sell some idea he pulled out of his ass—he'll be like putting out the fire with gasoline."

"Gee—that'd be a goddam shame."

"OK, look," Larry said leaning forward. "It's bad timing asking you this—after Keith just...but I need you to do this. I really do."

I sighed.

"Fine."

"It won't be that bad," he said brightening. "It's at..."

He ruffled through a couple of pieces of paper—and, against all odds, put on his glasses.

"...Sandoval. You been there?"

"No. Supposed to be great."

"C'mon, it'll be all right," he said. "Mike's not a bad guy, you can talk to him. And order a couple bottles of great wine and bring me the bill."

"All right," I said heading for the door. "But you owe me."

"Hey Terry," he said as I reached the doorway.

I stopped and turned.

"Nice job on Concordia."

"Thanks."

"Don't let Keith get to you."

"Sure."

Fucking Keith.

Should have punched him in the balls when I had the chance.

CHAPTER 51

"So I talked to Zack this morning," I said. I was doing a little update with Rob over the phone. "The numbers don't seem too bad."

"No?" he said.

"Well," I said, "It ain't free—but they could be worse."

"Two point what?" Rob asked, guessing pretty accurately the range we were in.

"Well, it could be 2.3," I said. "But it could end up under two depending on residuals and who actually shoots it."

"Under two would be unbelievable. What about the foreign budgets?"

"Still working on that—have we figured out how to off-load some of this cost to their foreign budgets?"

"Well, it wouldn't be foreign budgets, really," he answered. "They don't really have foreign budgets. They have strategic alliances and long-term tactical partnerships that could absorb some of the cost..."

"Yeah, whatever, Rob—have we made any headway in exploring how their "long-term tactical partnerships" are gonna help foot the bill for this sucker?"

"Getting there," Rob said.

"Well, that's important, because the budgets on that could tank the rest. You know?"

"Oh, I know...I know..." He suddenly sounded a little distracted.

"OK," I said. "You sound like you gotta go."

"Just got pinged by Jessica—I'll call you back."

"Cool."

CHAPTER 52

Sandoval was, in fact, an amazing restaurant. And once my rage had subsided, I realized that maybe a night out at a place like this would do me good. Sort of my own little celebration for the Concordia win.

Only with food, this time.

I arrived just after the rest of the Hanover crowd got there—there was a small knot of them near the bar when I got there, all waiting to be herded to the private room Amanda Miller had reserved.

Amanda had been tapped as the successor to the lovely Brianna when things hit the fan. Amanda was ambitious, very smart, and the perfect person to guide a troubled client relationship back on track. She was also not unattractive herself—short black hair, dazzling green eyes and a body that spoke for the miles and miles of running she put in each week.

But as good-looking as Amanda was, she was no Brianna.

Brianna could make a man break out in a sweat.

We were led down a small hallway and through a gauzy curtain into a room that looked like something out of Jerusalem circa the Crusades. Archways and large couches and minaret-shaped windows and window seats ringed the room. In the center was a long refectory table set up for our large party.

I sat across the table from Amanda and our client Mike, in between a young woman from Hanover named Emily something-

or-other, and a young account guy from The Crack named Preston Davenport—an eager beaver if ever there was one.

I picked up my menu from the table and noticed that it was a custom menu, specially made for tonight's group. It even had Hanover's logo printed at the top of the page, a majestic elk looking out over what I imagined was a valley full of safe, well-insured dream homes and college educations, and retirements that were well on their way to being paid for—courtesy of the wise, long-term advice of the advisors at Hanover.

Everyone was chatting quietly—the cocktails had just arrived and not kicked in yet—about odds and ends.

This group had been together all day talking business, so the chance to make meaningless chit-chat about anything but business was welcome.

Mike was telling a story about when he first got into marketing and some lunatic boss he had. He was a good guy, Mike was, despite all the craziness of recent events.

As we all laughed at the story's conclusion, I felt a nudge at my elbow.

It was Preston.

"What's up, Pres?" I said smiling.

"What are you gonna have?" he said to me, a little awkwardly.

I always forgot that, for someone like Preston, sitting with someone as far up the food chain from him as I was could make him nervous.

"You know, I don't know, Pres," I said, trying to seem as collegial as possible. "Everything looks pretty good."

"I know, it's hard to decide," he said, warming up a little.

"You know what I'm thinking, though?" I said. "They've got that venison special. I'm thinking of that—something a little different."

He seemed to get momentarily uncomfortable again.

"I was thinking of that," he said. "At first."

"And then?"

"I don't know."

"Animal rights concerns? Bambi maybe?"

He looked embarrassed.

"No, nothing like that."

"What?" I smiled.

He leaned in.

"I just thought it might seem inappropriate," he whispered.

"Inappropriate? How?"

He looked around a little furtively. And then put his hands on either side of his head with his fingers splayed out, like antlers.

I looked at him and shrugged.

"I'm sorry. I don't get it, Pres."

He pointed to the menu. Not to the selections, but to the Hanover logo.

Oh dear God.

"You don't want to order the venison because you're afraid it'll look like you're eating their logo?"

He nodded.

The poor kid.

"They'll think you love the brand so much you can't get enough of it," I said, clapping him on the shoulder in reassurance. "Don't worry about it. C'mon, I'll get it too."

"Thanks, Terry," he said sheepishly. "But I'm going to get the chicken just to be safe."

"That's fine, Pres—whatever makes you comfortable."

My Dewar's arrived and I took a big belt.

Scared they'd think he was eating their logo.

Jesus, this business was enough to drive people fucking crazy.

CHAPTER 53

My phone chirped and I looked at the display.

R D'Angelo ext. 8655

"What'd Jess want?" I asked, picking up.

"Something about schedules."

"For this? We haven't even figured out if we can afford it yet..."

"Yeah, I know. It was for this and our existing scope of work."

"What, the on-going stuff?"

"Yeah—probably wanting to make sure this project doesn't mean a slow-down or problems with the stuff they've already got us doing. You know how they are about resources and band-width."

"True—always got to be on the lookout for ways in which we're going to screw up."

"Yeah. I don't know."

"We getting together tomorrow to recap where we're at?"

"Yeah—11. Your office?"

"Or yours. Doesn't matter."

"We'll come down there."

"See ya then."

CHAPTER 54

"I just can never get over what those things sound like," Gail was saying.

We were gathered, where else, at the bar at Jo Jo—Gail, Mark, Sean, a couple others and myself. I was sipping a Scotch, Gail had a veritable bowl of the house red (a mourvedre I knew to be excellent) and Sean, of course, was deep into his continuing research on the Hapsburg Empire.

We were discussing pharmaceutical advertising—a category none of us had really worked in but which amazed us for its completely matter-of-fact discussion of what sounded like absolutely horrific side effects.

"Oh, isn't it unbelievable?" Sean said. "I saw one last night for some product—the names themselves are unpronounceable—but it's for hair growth in men. And at the end of the spot the announcer says, calm as you please '...*women who are pregnant should not handle broken tablets because of the possibility of a specific birth defect.*' I'm sitting there thinking to myself, 'a woman just handling a broken tablet could produce birth defects? And I'm supposed to put it in my mouth? And swallow it? Daily?"

We were all laughing.

"Christ, if the hair loss gets that bad, I'll shave myself bald like a tonsured monk—and go on living a deformity-free life thank you very much," he sputtered. "These people are mad!"

"I know, I know," I laughed. "There was one on the other night for some remedy or other—again, I don't even remember what it was for—but one of the potential side effects was '...*possible rectal bleeding.*'"

Everybody guffawed.

"I've seen that one! I've seen that one!" Sean was shouting.

"'*Rectal bleeding?*'" I said. "What, in public? Uncontrolled, sudden, spontaneous, spur-of-the-moment rectal bleeding?"

Sean was pounding on the bar, trying not to spit a mouthful of Hapsburg Prince onto Jason, who was delivering him a fresh one.

"I mean, I don't know what these poor people are trying to cure, but, holy shit, if that's the side effect?" I said. "I'll take my chances with the disease!"

"And the names?" Gail chimed in. "That's got to be a whole industry of its own, coming up with those names."

"Tripecia, Lipocia, Rialis, Magnecia..." Sean said.

"The names all sound like the names of pop singers," Mark said laughing. "'Opening for Beyonce tonight, will you please give a warm welcome to...Tripecia!'"

"Singing her new hit song 'Spontaneous Rectal Bleeding'!" I said. "'Give it up for Tripecia!'"

We all laughed again.

Sean was wiping his eyes as he started getting his hysteria under control.

"Ah, shit," he said, catching his breath. "I don't know what I'm laughing at—that's probably the next stop for me."

"For all of us," said Gail, shaking her head and still laughing.

"Maybe that whole industry is a cure in itself," I said.

"For what?" Mark said.

"For our side of the industry," I said.

"Could be," Sean said. "It's not like our business doesn't sometimes have rectal bleeding as a side effect."

CHAPTER 55

Entourage chimed at me from the screen and I could see that there was a meeting change. Quickly retrieving it, I saw that Rob had just cancelled the Concordia re-group that was due to take place in my office in about a half an hour.

"Meg?" I called

"No, I don't know why he's canceling—but I'm on it..."

Gail poked her head in.

"Why is Rob canceling?"

"No clue—Meghan's trying to find out right now."

"They're killing everything," Gail said.

"What?" I sneered. "Are you crazy? They're not killing anything. Rob's probably got some ridiculous call he's gotta get on or something."

"I don't like it."

"Well, of course you don't like it—you're the World's Most Suspicious Woman."

"And I'm usually right."

"No—you're not," I said.

Yeah, you are, I thought, turning back to my screen. And it was true. Gail had an amazing sixth sense when it came to deceit, deception and duplicity in all its forms. I was hoping against hope that she was wrong on this one.

But I wasn't counting on it.

"Teresa doesn't know why, either," called Meghan, on the line with her counterpart, Rob's assistant. "He cancelled it himself."

I picked up the phone and dialed.

"Are you alone?" Rob said, bypassing any of the traditional phone greetings.

"Yeah, why?"

"I'll be right down."

I hung up. And started calculating the various levels of disaster that could be coming through my door momentarily.

Had we lost the business? Impossible—we'd just won a shoot-out against all the other agencies.

Had we lost the campaign? Entirely possible—but since we'd won, there had to be something on the table that they liked enough to pick us. Even if it didn't turn out to be the thing we liked.

Had we lost part of the campaign? That'd be more than par for the course—they loved it, loved it, loved it, but wanted to change enough of it to wreck it.

Maybe it was just the money. Not that money woes would be any small thing, but at least that you could work through.

Maybe it was–

"Hey," said Rob as he swept into my office and closed the door behind him. The look on his face was concerned but not nearly as concerned as I thought it should be. In fact, his face was a strange combination of concern and satisfaction. This was the thing with people like Rob who spend every waking minute thinking that something bad is going to happen. When it does, it's strangely satisfying. They feel a huge level of justification.

"How bad is it?" I asked, cutting to the chase.

"Bad."

"Jesus Christ, how can it be bad? We just won a shoot-out among all the agencies less than a week ago—how can Anne kill us after that?"

"It's not Anne," he said ominously.

"Who?" I said. "Not Jess? She loves us right now."

"The trouble isn't in Marketing."

"What?" The thought that we could have trouble outside the Marketing Department hadn't even occurred to me. For the most part, we were invisible outside Marketing. As long as we didn't screw up on a colossal scale, the mucky-mucks didn't really pay much attention to the likes of us.

"It's DelNardo..."

"The CEO of the company has a problem with us?"

"Well, not with us—but he has a problem."

I looked at him, eyebrows up, arms spread wide, a face full of anticipation.

"He's out."

"What?!" I practically screamed.

"He's out," Rob continued, head in his hands. He suddenly sat bolt upright. "But no one knows this yet—no one. Strictly confidential."

"Why is he out?" I asked in bewilderment.

"Turns out he lied on his resume," Rob said shaking his head.

"Lied on his resume?" I sputtered. "Who gives a shit? He's been CEO for like 4 years? Now they find this out?"

"Yeah, exactly," Rob said. "It's a political hit job. Performance has been down a little, we've been talking about that, right?"

"For the whole industry, though."

"Right, but, you know, there've been forces at work behind the scenes, people on the board, others who see that as a reason for change."

"Then fine, make a change—but what's all this resume bullshit?"

"Well, the performance thing is a little hard to pin," Rob continued. "Some of his enemies have been trying to make it stick for two quarters now, but DelNardo's smart. He's managed to spin the numbers and the story pretty well."

"So they don't think they can get him on the actual numbers."

"Well, they think they can, but they think it will take time, based on how aggressive he's been at defending the performance."

"Because a lot of the performance is subjective."

"Oh, yeah. I mean, the numbers are what they are, but they can be manipulated a hundred ways. I mean if new subscribers go up and they put everyone's focus on those numbers, it can mask the fact that revenue from existing customers is going down. Or if they add a huge number of new handsets it can look great—even though the promotion they ran to get those new handsets is actually gonna lose them money in the long run."

"So they're gonna go for an emotional lightning rod."

"Yup."

"Something public, visceral..."

"And above all, quick."

"But," I said scratching my head. "Why the resume? That seems kinda lightweight, doesn't it? Is that really enough to put him down?"

"Actually, yeah, it is. And, uh, we're probably the reason why."

"We're the reason why? Why is this our fault?"

"Because, uh..." Rob said shaking his head at what was apparently going to be a sweet bit of irony. "Aside from all the product stuff, what's the corporate message we're running right now?"

I sagged in my chair.

"Oh my God..."

"Yeah."

"'The Pledge' campaign..." I rubbed my eyes with my right hand.

"Exactly," he smiled. "A campaign telling consumers that, in all our dealings, we will be open, candid, transparent. From their bills to their service to the quality of the phone service staff, they will be treated with a spirit of openness not to be found at any other carrier. A campaign telling every customer that 'all your transactions with Concordia will be marked by honesty–'"

"–sincerity, and integrity. That's my pledge." I finished the sentence for him. Which I could do easily. Because I had written those very words.

"And who is it that personally delivers those heartfelt words at the end of each spot?"

"That would be Larry DelNardo."

"Yes, yes it would."

"He's dead."

"Yes."

"And so are we."

"Well, no," Rob said, somewhat reassuringly. "We're not going to get fired."

"No?"

"Oh no," he said. "Anne says we're fine—we just have to ride it out along with them. She's sure that this won't have any effect on 'her agencies', as she put it."

I sighed.

Cracknell, Burroughs might not be dead. But I knew what was.

"Digital Summit is dead, isn't it?"

"Ah..." Rob looked down at his hands. "It's not dead..."

"Yeah, it is."

"It's just gonna be on hold," he said quietly. "Anne just feels that there's no way we can launch such a high profile, corporate statement when the leadership of the company is in such flux."

I nodded.

"But there is a bunch of interim stuff they're gonna want to do," Rob said, much too enthusiastically for me to handle.

I held up one hand.

"What?" he blinked.

"Let's talk about that another time...OK?" I said quietly.

"Uh, yeah...sure," Rob nodded. My disappointment and despair must have been particularly evident since even Rob could see it. "Tomorrow or something."

"Yeah," I said quietly.

He got up to leave.

"I'm gonna need to tell people," I said.

"Can you wait until tomorrow? It'll all be out in the morning."

"Yeah."

"You want this open or closed?" he said, hand on the door.

"Close it."

As the door clicked softly shut, I turned and looked out the window to the river beyond the apartment buildings.

I understood.

I really did.

Anne was doing the right thing.

But knowing that didn't make me any less homicidal.

Shit.

Gail's radar had been right once again. They were, essentially, killing everything. Because by the time they came back to it they would either be bored with it or the new management would see this great campaign as merely another piece of flotsam from the wreck of the previous guy and sweep it aside in favor of anything new.

I'd played long enough to know how the game is played.

I sat that way for a long time, looking out at the small sailboats with their clean, trim white sails tacking into the wind. I was trying hard to keep my mind blank—and to resist the overpowering urge to smash everything in my office.

They say that advertising is a young man's game. And most people interpret that to mean that only young guys have the attitude, the rebelliousness, and the skill to come up with great ideas.

But that's not it at all.

Experienced people have just as many great ideas. Maybe more. In fact, the veterans actually have better ideas because they've learned discipline. They don't come at you with an undifferentiated bag of crap. They've thrown the clunkers out already—if they even bothered to write them down in the first place.

No, what makes advertising a young man's game is that only when you're young are you naïve enough to be so relentlessly optimistic. To be able to show up, each time, convinced that it's going to go great this time.

It's like Charlie Brown believing that this time he's really going to kick that football.

But hell, even Charlie Brown has to be talked into trying to kick it every time.

Young ad guys?

They would go knock on Lucy's door, bring her outside and hand her the ball.

Landing flat on your ass has very little appeal to begin with.

And as you get older, it has even less.

CHAPTER 56

"Meg," I said walking into my office the next morning. "Can I get the teams together in The Hole this morning?"

"The Concordia teams?"

"Yeah—give 'em the happy news."

"Sure," she smiled, grabbing a pad. "Any particular time?"

"Nah—I only need them for about ten, maybe 15 minutes."

She consulted her computer screen for a minute.

"I can get you The Hole at 10:30," she said scanning the options. "Or Empire at 9:45 if you want to do it sooner..."

"Empire? Oh, good God no," I said. "That's for celebratory announcements. The Hole is fine."

"You want everyone, right?"

"As many as I can get," I said. "If someone has a conflict or something, it's OK."

"Should they bring anything with them?"

"Yeah," I snorted. "Their sense of humor. Goin' for coffee—need one?"

"I'm good."

A little while later, I gathered everyone and took them through the politics and intrigue of what was suddenly going on in our world.

"The upshot, guys," I sighed "is that Digital Summit—as well as the other worthy contenders—have been cryogenically frozen in the hope we'll be able to thaw them out at some future date when we have a cure for what ails them."

There was a collective groan.

"Great," moaned Nick Burns, the young writer who had worked so hard on Digital Summit. "I work my ass off on this thing, they actually buy it—and now I'm fuckin' Walt Disney."

"Well, look on the bright side, Nick," I said. "You're not Ted Williams. When we thaw you out, at least you'll be in one piece."

He laughed, but he didn't seem convinced he was any better off.

"How long do you think it'll be before we can thaw them out?" It was Mark, Gail's partner on Digital Summit.

"No idea, Mark," I shrugged. "Soon as possible, I guess. Why?"

"Well, Gail and I were talking about the fact that..." he hesitated.

"Yeah?"

"Well, The Show is tomorrow night," he began quietly. "Which means that it'll only be like six or eight months until we'd have to enter for next year's Show."

They were right. I had forgotten that The Show, the annual local advertising award show, was the next night.

"And it'll practically take that much time to get this done— even if we *weren't* being put on hold," Gail finished.

"You're depressing me," I said.

"Well..." Gail said.

"No, you're right," I said. "You're right. Depressing, but right."

"I mean, this would probably kick ass, but we've gotta do it in order to be able to enter it," Mark concluded.

"OK, let's see what we can do," I said. "I'll get Stacy to see if they've announced next year's deadline yet. And we'll start working against that."

"Cool."

"Everybody going tomorrow night?" I asked.

"Yeah."

"Oh yeah."

"Absolutely."

"No doubt."

"Any predictions?" I asked.

"Yeah," said Chris Hillman, a young writer.

"Really?" I turned. "What?"

"I'm gonna be really shitfaced."

I laughed.

"And the Gold for Best Public Puking goes to..." someone said, as they all filed out the door.

CHAPTER 57

While every industry has its own conventions and forms of recognition, advertising has to be, by far, the most self-congratulatory industry on the planet. There are hundreds of shows, celebrations, achievement nights, and top-ten lists. It's gotten so bad that I read recently that someone was proposing (in all seriousness, no less) that there be an award for best award show.

In the wide-ranging pantheon of award shows, there are three basic kinds:

There are the internationally based international shows: Cannes, D&AD in London, and the London International Advertising Awards.

There are the American-based international shows: The One Show, the ANDYs, the Clios, The New York Art Director's Club awards, and the Communication Arts annual, affectionately known as CA.

And then there are the local or regional shows. Every major advertising city in the country has one. And while they may lack the stature and the prestige of the other shows, they have one distinct advantage:

Everyone can attend.

The general rule of thumb with the national and international shows is that if you've won (which they're not supposed to tell you but somehow manage to always leak out in advance), you can attend the show. The agency will pay for your ticket, fly you out there, put you up overnight and, as long as you don't party like Keith Richards, pay for your celebratory bar bill.

But unless you've won, forget it—you're not going anywhere. Read about it in ADWEEK.

Not so for the local show. For that, they walk the whole place over to Memorial Auditorium to applaud, scream, shout and carry on whenever we win and whine, boo and generally complain when anyone else does. Then the whole mad, swirling entourage troops over to some carefully selected hipster joint to party deep into the morning.

Once again, the day was upon us.

Up at The Crack, the place was abuzz by late afternoon. In Account Service, the ladies' room was filled with young AEs attempting casually constructed up-do's at the mirrors; in Broadcast, young producers were slipping on suit jackets for the first time since their weddings; and the Creative Department, as always, was divided between people dressing as if they were going to the Oscars and those choosing ripped jeans and faded T-shirts so as to show the proper creative disdain for convention.

I myself went for the obligatory black suit and French blue shirt. Hey, in my position, I was considered management. Best to look the part.

"Headin' over?" I said, poking my head in Gail's office.

"Yeah, you wanna go?" she said shutting down her laptop.

"So what's your guess?" she asked when we were out on the street.

"For Best of Show? Hard to say...Rothman, Simon did that nice campaign for Techtronic..." I said.

"Yeah, that stuff was nice—beautifully art directed."

"Yeah—very tasty."

"Michelle Higgins," Gail said, indicating the art director who had designed the campaign.

"At her very best," I nodded in agreement.

"How about those spots from LMB?" she asked.

"The stuff for the hospital?"

"Yeah—pretty good…"

"True—should win something," I nodded in agreement. "But if you were going to predict a big winner, it might be our friend down the hall."

"Keith?"

"Tough to beat The Vision as an awards opportunity…"

"Yeah," she said quietly. "I had kinda thought that they might clean up."

"Could be a big night for Captain Cause Marketing."

Ten minutes into the show, it was worse than I could have possibly imagined.

The rout was on almost immediately. The Vision was winning everything in sight.

"The Gold in Newspaper Less than a Page goes to…Cracknell, Burroughs for The Vision—Keith Farner Creative Director…"

I wasn't even listening as they announced the creative team that had actually done the work, the writer and art director who had worked weekends, stayed late and generally busted their ass to do something this good.

All I could hear was Keith's name reverberating through the hall and as they announced it again and again. He was sitting a row in front of me and one seat to my right. So not only was I treated to the hallucination of his name filling every molecule of space in the room, I had to watch him bobbing up and down like some crazed jack-in-the-box with every trip to the stage.

"The Gold, the Silver, AND the Bronze in Magazine all belong to Cracknell, Burroughs for The Vision…come on up Keith Farner, Jeremy Richardson, David Martin, Ian Grady…

I felt like I was going mad. A feeling that my own three modest wins did nothing to soothe. The longer the massacre went on, the more obvious the ultimate outcome became in my head.

Like the Oscars, where the individual categories like cinematography and best supporting actress lead up to the night's definitive prize of Best Picture, so did this show lead up to the *ne plus ultra* of Best of Show.

The winner was considered King of the Ad World.

And I had little doubt that I was about to witness the coronation.

When they finally announced it, I got up and headed toward the door. The crowd was cheering, the emcee was reading off the names of everyone who had contributed to the campaign—a seemingly endless list of writers, art directors, producers and others. I turned at the top of the aisle and looked back at the stage. It was a maelstrom of bodies, everyone high-fiving, hugging, pumping their fists in the air.

I watched for a minute, arms crossed over my chest.

Suddenly, I remembered.

I couldn't believe I hadn't thought of it through the whole long, excruciating show.

I had him.

And it was time to take the son of a bitch down.

CHAPTER 58

The after party this year was at Mockba—a brand new, so-hip-it-hurts place in an abandoned warehouse. It specialized in obscure, imported Russian vodkas.

In addition to its status as a shrine to niche vodkas, Mockba was a triumph of lighting. The farther reaches of the room were practically opaque, they were so dark, which meant that the objects and figures in the foreground jumped out at you as if they had been painted on black velvet. The hard surfaces of the place were stark and sleek, the metal railings and table legs finished in a flat matte finish. In an oasis of light along one wall was the bar—where row upon row of the precious bottles glowed.

The waitresses had begun to circulate. They wore dark grey, skin-tight Danskin bodysuits with spectacularly low scoop-necks. It looked like a casting call for *"Catwoman"*.

Except they had much better dialogue.

"Can I get you a drink?" one of them purred.

"Yes," I said. "I will have a very large vodka martini."

"Straight up or rocks?"

"Oh, I think it's a night for straight up."

"Any particular vodka?" she smiled.

"What do you recommend?"

"I like the Petroshnikov. It's from a small distillery in the Ukraine. It's a little unusual."

"Perfect. I'm feeling a little unusual."

She smirked and disappeared into the dark.

All around me the place was filling up with happy revelers. The noise level was climbing and somewhere in the darkest nether reaches of the room a DJ had began to pump music into the room.

"Congratulations, Terry!" said a perky young thing in a black dress. She worked in Account Service, I thought. No clue on her name.

"Thanks!" I smiled. It took me a moment to remember that, yes; I had indeed won three prizes tonight. Nothing wrong with that. I had looked around and seen more than a few of my contemporaries in the crowd tonight winning nothing. In fact, squeezing out wins in three different categories given the few legitimate opportunities I'd gotten was actually pretty fuckin' good. But being congratulated on those wins in the face of the Vision's avalanche—it was like being complimented on the lovely candle you're holding, while the guy standing next to you is holding the sun.

"Excellency!"

"Ah, Your Grace," I responded instinctively, before I even turned and discovered Sean at my left. "Just the person I wanted to see."

"Happy to be of service."

The waitress arrived with my drink.

"Ah, a fortifying flagon—my dear, ask the innkeeper if he feels up to assembling another one of those."

The waitress eyed him with a mixture of amusement and caution. It was a look Sean got a lot.

"I'm sure *she'll* be happy to..." she said.

"My apologies to the lady..." Sean bowed to her as she left for the bar.

We stood surveying the room. Like me, Sean had opted for the black suit, pairing his with a gray shirt. As he looked out over the crowd he also wore a look of bemusement, as if the whole thing were being staged for him. He had this small, tight smile and a twinkle in his eye. Despite the twinkle, there was something faraway in his gaze.

"And what did you think of our little show this evening?" Sean said out of the side of his mouth.

"I thought it was fucking fantastic," I snapped. "I can hardly wait for the little prince to arrive."

"And join the revels..."

"Oh, I'm quite sure he'll be the center of the revels," I said. "Probably come in on a sedan chair being fanned by Larry and Justin to the cheers of the adoring hoards."

"How vivid, Excellency," Sean smiled, turning to face me. "You must be a writer."

"On occasion."

"I must say I would love to see that spectacle."

"Stand right here and you probably will."

His drink arrived. He bowed to the waitress and took his drink.

"Excellency," he said raising his glass. "To your rage—long may it smolder..."

"Thanks," I snorted and took a sip of the Ukraine's finest.

"My Liege—would you pardon me while I go attempt to curry favor with Carolyn?" he said, indicating with his head where she stood with a small knot of people from her group. "A brief genuflection, a kiss of the ring and perhaps I can live another day..."

"To your continued survival, Your Grace," I said raising my glass to him.

"And yours," he said, bowing as he turned to go.

As Sean went off to dance the political tango, I headed into the crowd on another vector. Familiar faces surrounded me, although none I particularly cared about talking to. People were celebrating with abandon—partly because they had picked up awards themselves tonight, partly because they worked at the agency that had declared itself King of the Creative Hill, and partly because they were young and hip and good looking and who wouldn't want to celebrate that?

I slugged down the last of my Ukrainian prescription and thought it might be a good moment to hit the men's room. On the way back out, I also thought it might be a good moment to call Alex.

"Hey!" she answered, her tone indicating that her caller ID was functioning properly.

"Hey," I answered back unimaginatively.

"So how was it?"

"The Coronation of Keith the First—Ruler of the Ad Kingdom," I spat into the phone.

"Yeah?"

"The Vision won everything in sight—including Best of Show. Dozens of awards. I'm surprised they didn't give him the Thurlow Award just for good measure."

"What's the Thurlow Award?"

"For Lifetime Achievement in the industry. You have to be retired to be eligible."

"How did you do?" she asked quietly.

"Ah, I won three."

"That's great, Terry," she said. "Why wouldn't you tell me that news first?"

"Cause it doesn't matter. Whatever tiny little success I had tonight will be overshadowed, obliterated by that asshole and his freebie account."

"You're driving yourself crazy. You know that, don't you?"

"I'm going crazy, yes, but it's not me that's doing it. It's *him! And his posing and grandstanding and everyone else buying into his bullshit! It's how unfair this all is! How I don't get the opportunities but then get tagged with not winning awards!*"

"But you did win tonight," she corrected.

"*And I'm being further driven crazy by the fact that you don't seem get any of this!*"

"Terry, I know this is hard—but you've got to get past this..."

"You have no idea how I feel about this."

"Yes, I do."

"No, you don't—because if you did you wouldn't be telling me to just 'get past this' like it was some headache or fatigue or something. *This is the center of my life and it just sucks!*"

I was practically screaming.

Actually I was screaming.

"Listen, you go to the party and I'll talk to you tomorrow when you're calmer."

"Fine."

"Good night."

I snapped my phone shut.

Fucking A, how did she not see this? How did she not understand that I was on the brink of homicide here? Godammit, her lack of understanding just pissed me off.

I had been wrong. This had not been a good time to call Alex.

I probably needed to disappear, since further contact with humans ran the risk of more eruptions like this one. But I decided on another drink instead and headed to the bar.

A fresh Petroshnikov in hand, I headed into the maelstrom of the party.

Against the black velvet background, the party now swirled in full, colorful relief. The music didn't so much play as thump in your chest—a tribute to the enormous subwoofer lurking somewhere in the darkness.

"Ter-*ry*!" a voice bellowed over the crowd.

I scanned the writhing mass of bodies on the dance floor. Out of the middle of it was coming the disheveled, goofily smiling figure of Chris Hillman, the young writer who had predicted his own drunkenness yesterday. And boy, had he been right. He had won his first award tonight, and was celebrating as if it would be his last.

"Terry...Terry, man," he practically panted, giving me the obligatory gangsta fist grab and chest bump.

"What's up, Chris...congrats, man."

"Thanks, man," he beamed. "I didn't think that could win."

"You didn't? I did."

"That's why you're the *m-a-a-n*...cause you *know*, man, you *know* these things..."

"Nah, I just thought it was nice work. Nice work always has a chance."

"Thanks, man, thanks..."

I clapped him on his upper arm—carefully. Didn't want him to go over.

"Enjoy, Chris!"

I turned and headed toward a small group bunched around a banquette in the far corner. I could see Paula Hanlon, Zack, and Mike Shaw, another producer, all standing together.

I walked up, exchanged kisses on the cheek with Paula, handshakes with Zack and Mike.

"How's it goin', guys?" I said.

"Wasn't that awesome tonight?" Paula said. She had no more to do with The Vision than I did, but she was a relentless cheerleader for what she perceived to be the party line of the agency.

"Yeah...it was great," I answered.

"It was, wasn't it?" she continued, all smiles and glittering eyes.

"Yep. Great." I shot a look at Zack. Zack felt almost as little love for Keith as me. He had worked on many a project with Keith and they almost always came to blows. Largely because Zack was good, smart, and had an opinion about things—which almost invariably got him booted off any Keith project. The only opinion Keith was ever interested in was his own.

Zack rolled his eyes.

Suddenly, I felt a hand at the small of my back.

I turned slightly to my left and found Carolyn standing at my shoulder.

"Hey, honey" she said—leaning over to kiss me on the cheek.

"Hey, Car—how are ya?" I said leaning into the kiss.

"Great—just great," she said holding her martini glass out so I could clink it with mine.

"What have ya got going there?" I said, indicating her glass.

"Something...ov," she shrugged.

"You're not that particular tonight?"

"Long as it works," she smiled.

Carolyn was wearing one of her trademark Sex and The City rigs tonight—a black, spaghetti strap number that I was sure cost more than her assistant made in a year. But, as I took it in, she actually looked pretty good. It suddenly struck me that this was her natural *milieu*. She looked completely out of place during the day amidst the jeans and the cargo shorts of the creative floor. But here, she not only looked like she belonged—she looked perfect. Maybe it was the addition of the martini glass. Or maybe it was the addition of two martinis to my system.

"We're heading to the bar," Zack interrupted. "Guys need anything?"

"Nah, I'm good," I answered. "Carolyn?"

She shook her head.

Zack and Mike headed to the bar. Paula had turned to talk to one of her "direct reports".

"So how are you tonight, sweetie?" she said quietly. The hand that had begun in the small of my back had now migrated all the way around to my right side. Carolyn used it to pull me closer as she spoke.

"I'm fine," I said taking another sip of Petroshnikov.

"C'mon, Ter—quite a show tonight?"

"Yeah—pretty impressive."

"He's nowhere near as good as you are, you know..."

"Oh, I think he's quite a bit better, don't you think?"

"No," she purred. "I don't."

When Carolyn had put her arm around me, she had slipped it between my left arm and my body. As she kept pulling me closer, it was slowly raising my left arm up until it really had no place else to go but around her shoulders.

Which were bare.

And warm.

And very, very soft.

Which took me a little by surprise. Based on her persona, I had pretty much always assumed that Carolyn felt like flint.

"And why is that?"

"Because you're talented and he's just ambitious and ruthless."

I smiled.

Carolyn reached up with her glass and touched her index finger to my lips.

"And before you say anything...yes—I would know all about that."

She removed her finger and—without ever loosening her hold on me or taking her eyes off mine—took a long sip of her martini-OV.

Cruella de Vil appeared to have stayed home tonight.

CHAPTER 59

Ah, shit.

Without even opening my eyes, I knew this was bad.

Catastrophically bad.

Classically bad.

Maybe worst of all, clichely bad.

There was a constant, dull pain emanating from the base of my skull. My stomach felt like it was manufacturing concrete.

The room smelled unfamiliar, the sheets felt unfamiliar, even the street sounds outside were unfamiliar.

Ah, shit.

I slowly opened my eyes. From my vantage point on the bed, I could see my clothes scattered on the floor. My pants hung by one leg from the arm of a chair. Hanging off the pant leg and lying on top of my suit jacket on the floor were several pieces of very expensive-looking, plum-colored lingerie.

Ah, shit.

As part of my aching brain began to register that lovely tableau, the rest of it began to register the fact that as I lay there on my stomach, my legs were intertwined with someone else's.

I knew they weren't Alex's.

Ah, shit.

They weren't even Carolyn's.

"Hey," said a quiet voice from across the pillow. "Remember me?"

I turned my head very slowly to my left. It probably looked

like I was doing it for dramatic effect but it was simply because I was afraid that a sudden, painful move of my head would probably make me throw up.

There, inches away, was the beautiful, tousled, brunette head and coal-eyed face of Genevieve Reade.

"Hello, Gen," I said, mustering as much of a suave smile as I could. "And how are you this morning?"

"Not good."

"Why?"

"You hurt me," she said.

Ah, *shit!*

"Uh, what? How?"

"With that crazy vodka. Are you on their payroll or something?"

"I might be now," I said, closing my eyes and burrowing my head into the pillow. It was very soft. I seemed to remember a conversation in between the gymnastics last night about sheets. If I recalled correctly, these were Sferra sheets—1,020 thread count Egyptian cotton. Gen worked in Consumer Insight and was our resident Cultural Analyst. It was her job to have her finger on the pulse of certain consumer groups and the trends, preferences, and proclivities of those groups.

Her specialty was the Luxury Sector.

"Nice sheets," I mumbled into the pillow.

"Aren't they great?" she answered, turning over on her back as she did.

"Must be expensive."

"About $1,500 for the set."

What was left of my brain couldn't begin to compute this.

"You spent $1,500 on sheets?"

"Of course not," she said with a smile. "Cracknell, Burroughs did."

"Research?"

"Of course."

Out of my left eye I could see that she had her arms up and the backs of her hands resting over her eyes.

"Ow," she said quietly.

She let her hands slip over her head and onto the pillow above. Moving her arms back like that raised her chest up a little and made her breasts strain at the luxurious softness of the Sferra sheet.

I closed my eye—trying to suppress the wrestling match that was beginning between my hangover and my libido. My hangover had a big lead in points, but I had a feeling that my libido could pin it at any moment.

"I think I gotta go…" I said, trying to make it sound as if I didn't want to.

Gen rolled over to face me, her hands now clasped together under her left cheek.

"Yeah—me, too. I've got a flight to Dallas in a few hours."

"What's in Dallas?" I asked.

"Groups of 18-25 year-old guys. We're trying to find out why they're not watching as much TV anymore."

"Any theories?"

"Oh, we know exactly why they're not watching TV…"

"Why?"

"Cause they're all playing video games and watching on-line porn."

I started laughing. Which made my head hurt.

A lot.

"Seriously—we know exactly why they aren't watching. It's just a question of having some concrete data and then trying to find a diplomatic way of telling that to clients."

I smiled.

She smiled back.

"Hope your day's OK today, Terry," she said gently.

"Thanks."

"I'll be thinking of you."

There was a long pause.

And then she reached out to me. I stretched my arms out to her and we held each other for a long minute.

On the one hand, it felt wonderful. She was beautiful and soft and warm and understanding.

On the other hand, nothing seemed to feel right because she was taller and curved differently and was just very, very powerfully not Alex.

Nine hours ago, with a head full of rage and Petroshnikov, I had been completely focused on the beauty and the understanding.

Now, as I prepared to roll out of her bed, I couldn't see anything beyond the powerfully not Alex part.

Ah, shit.

CHAPTER 60

Outside on the sidewalk, I buttoned my suit jacket. It was wrinkled, but way less wrinkled than my shirt, which looked positively indecent. I gave my hair a little smoothing down.

Gen had offered a shower, but I claimed I was late. I probably should've gone for the shower but at the moment, I just needed to get as far away from here as humanly possible as fast as humanly possible.

I wasn't even sure if I would go into work today. First, because of the unbearable basking that would be going on. Even the thought of it ratcheted my nausea up a level.

Then, this episode with Gen Reade—holy shit.

Maybe all that information and indecision swirling in my head was why I made my next catastrophic mistake.

I stepped off the sidewalk and raised my arm to hail a cab. There were a few dotting the pack of cars coming down Broad Street.

Suddenly, from the opposite side of the street, a cab lurched across three lanes of traffic in a swirl of squealing tires and blaring horns and skidded to a stop in front of me.

Jesus, did this guy really need a fare that badly?

I stepped over and opened the door.

Before I even had it fully-opened, a voice said

"Good morning, Sunshine!"

Startled, I snapped into a crouch and looked into the backseat.

And there, surrounded by a briefcase, a canvas tote and a plastic bag full of newspapers was none other than Kat Halsey.

Oh...my...God.

"I looked over and thought 'There's a boy in need of a ride'— so I told my man here to get his ass over here and getcha," she laughed.

"Uh, thanks, uh, Kat," I stammered.

"Here—hop in."

I probably should have just started running. I still had that option for a few seconds more. I could just slam the door shut and bolt down the sidewalk. Claim insanity later.

But I didn't.

I just got in, slowly, distractedly. I felt like I was starting to become separated from my body, as if I was somehow spiritually removing myself from the scene.

"I'm just headed downtown for a meeting and I can take you...Jesus, Terry. What the hell happened to you?"

She had finally taken in my full visual magnificence.

"Long night."

"Yeah, I guess. Christ, Ter, you look like you got hit by a train."

"Yeah."

She paused a long second.

"Where are you coming from?"

"Friend's place."

She was staring at me.

"Yeah?"

"Yeah," I said, leaning my head in my right hand. "A buddy of mine."

She was still staring.

"Award show last night. Kind of a tough night."

"I can see that..."

She turned and looked straight ahead. We rode quietly for a minute before Kat turned back to me.

"Let me ask you a question," she said.

"Sure," I said, head back, eyes closed.

"Your 'buddy' always wear Obsession?" she asked. "Or just when he's with you?"

I didn't answer. There was no need to. No need for any more questions, either. So Kat and I sat in silence.

When the cab reached Commercial Crossing, Kat paid for her trip and said nothing to the driver about what to do with me.

She got out of the cab, collecting her many belongings and leaned into the cab.

"You know, I never had you pegged as an asshole," she said shaking her head in mild disbelief.

And slammed the door.

The cabbie turned slightly to look at me.

"Where you wanna go?" he asked, his Russian accent vaguely discernible.

The truth was I had no idea.

CHAPTER 61

It was the day after The Day After and I was lying in bed trying to muster the reserves to get up. My physical hangover was long gone thanks to the prodigious amounts of Advil and water I'd been forcing for over 24 hours now.

But the emotional pain was nowhere near abating. If anything, it was getting worse.

I had come nowhere near going into the office yesterday. Once I'd stumbled out of the Death Cab and crawled up the stairs to my apartment, I quickly took to my bed like some consumption-ridden Jane Austen heroine and pretty much remained there until now; rousing myself only to medicate and hydrate.

I had also roused myself twice to call Alex. Once at the office in the early afternoon as was our custom—checking in, seeing how the day was going, discussing any evening plans. Got her voicemail, which presented its own set of problems. Specifically, how to leave a message that didn't fully reveal my behavior in case Kat hadn't gotten to her yet but not sounding too casual and cavalier in case Kat had. The effort of that pretty much did me in for the rest of the afternoon. I made a second attempt, at home, around seven. Voicemail again and I tried to leave an equally nondescript and diplomatic message as the one I'd left at the office.

I got no response to either one.

Paralyzed as I felt, I knew that I really did have to get up. My Treo had buzzed several times last night and, checking e-mail, I'd seen that there was another status meeting on Concordia, a review of some work on the airline biz and a very interesting request from Glynis in Justin's office asking me to "pop by" around 2.

I swung my legs over the side of the bed, moaning as my feet hit the floor and levered me up.

I was off.

An hour and a half later I walked into my office. Meghan looked up as I passed by her.

"It lives," she said.

"Sort of."

As I plunked down in my chair she appeared in the doorway and leaned against the doorjamb.

"Feeling better?" she smiled.

"On some fronts," I said, scanning my eyes quickly over the Entourage screen. "How was it here yesterday?"

"You don't want to know."

"I bet I don't. What's up for today?"

"Nothing really—the stuff that's on your calendar is all. Rob's being nudgy about briefing teams for this new interim work. But that's about it."

"Yup."

"You OK?" she asked.

"Yah, why?" I looked up. "Kinda hurtin' yesterday, but I'm OK today."

"Ya sure everything's all right?"

"Yeah, sure."

"OK," she shrugged and turned out of the doorway. "Just seem a little quiet."

"I'm fine."

"You know," she began, turning back into the doorway. "Uh, there was a little rumor going around about you yesterday."

"What?" I snapped.

"Just a little whisper that, ah, you might have, ah, gone home with, ah, Carolyn…"

"Not true."

"Yeah?"

"Absolutely false," I nodded firmly. "We had a drink together at Mockba, a few of us left together to go to Division Street after that and as far as I know she left on her own from there."

Unlike myself, I stopped short of adding.

"I *told* them that," she said, with obvious relief. "I said that would be the *last* thing you'd do. Aside from her being a tramp and a viper, there is the issue of a certain Miss Alex..."

"Yes," I sighed. "There certainly is."

Meghan left and I begun to burrow into the day.

Rob and crew had nothing new to report on the Concordia front. Well, they had nothing good to report, anyway. Digital Summit was still languishing in purgatory and would be for the foreseeable future. Instead, we had a wagonload of new, crappy interim assignments—price-off promotions and rebate programs and BOGOs (Buy One Get One, for those of you playing along at home) for handsets and you name it. Instead of doing something big, visible, groundbreaking and reputation making, it looked like we were all going to die in a hail of bright red starbursts and screaming prices.

The airline stuff was a piece of cake—thank God. My day seemed to be looking up.

Well, my workday, anyway. The specter of a conversation with Alex at the end of the day loomed over everything. I was trying to block it out or at least compartmentalize it by staying busy.

Two o'clock arrived and I headed up to Justin's office.

"Hey, Glynis," I said as I arrived in the waiting area.

"Hi, Terry," she smiled. "He's ready for you. Go ahead in."

I walked in to Justin's movie set of an office. He was sitting in one of the wing chairs, a fistful of memos in his lap, his tortoise half-glasses perched on the tip of his nose, immaculate in his Turnbull & Asser shirt and Gieves & Hawke suit.

"Terry, Terry, come in," he said to me, tilting his head slightly so as to look at me over his glasses.

"Afternoon, Justin," I said shaking his hand as he rose from the chair.

"Have a seat," he motioned to the couch under the painting of the Cotswold's.

I sat.

He arranged himself on the other end of the couch, smoothly folding his reading glasses and slipping them into the breast pocket of his suit, one bow extending outside the pocket.

"How are you, my boy?" he said.

"Fine," I answered. "Busy."

"Good, good," he smiled.

He paused sort of nodding to himself about what he'd just said.

"Quite a show the other night..." he said looking up.

"Yeah, amazing," I said.

"You did well," he said, extending his hand toward me, palm up.

"Yeah, I was happy," I lied. "There's some stuff we're working on right now that I think could win big in next year's show, some stuff for Concordia that could be–"

"Good, good," he nodded. "That's fine."

Okaaaay, I thought. *And what is it that you would like to talk about?*

"The agency did very well, the other night," he said. "Extremely well. Best we've ever done, in fact."

I nodded. Although I wasn't sure I liked where this was heading.

"And while there were lots of contributions, yours included, the impetus for our unparalleled success really came from one particular quarter. And so, Terry, we're feeling that we want to recognize and reward that contribution. In a significant way."

Tell me this isn't happening. Not today. Tell me this isn't happening today.

"And so, we're going to elevate Keith—to the new position of Executive Creative Director. He'll now officially be Larry's #2.

The group Creative Directors will now report to Keith, rather than directly to Larry. Carolyn, Alan, Diego from Design, Lindsay from Interactive..."

He paused.

"And me," I said flatly.

"Yes, Terry," he said quietly. "And you."

I looked at him. Crossed my arms over my chest and looked away. I had a lot of emotions filling up my head today—most of them surrounding Alex. Remorse, regret, guilt, fear.

Suddenly, though, they were all being elbowed aside by rage.

"Terry, I know this isn't easy for you to hear," he said. "It's why I wanted to tell you myself."

"I appreciate that."

"And in no way does this diminish all your contributions to the agency or the extremely important role you play here," he said. "But I think that in the best interests of the agency–"

"The best interests of the agency?" I snapped. Rage had apparently managed to elbow decorum out of the way, as well.

"Yes," he said evenly. "I believe Keith will do whatever it takes, whatever is required to push the agency forward."

"And I won't?"

"As I say, this in no way diminishes your contribution."

"Like hell it doesn't!"

"No, it doesn't—but Keith's accomplishments and creative leadership are worthy of recognition."

"Because he cleaned up at the Show?" I said. "He *should* clean up at the Show for Crissakes! The only thing he really works on is a Public Service account!"

"The Vision pays us," he said calmly.

"You know what I mean—it's an awards freebie, a lob."

"Terry, in fairness—you can't deny the landslide of awards— and the publicity it gets us," he said. "The success of The Vision is appealing to new clients. And, frankly, Keith's success allows us to market him in a way that will attract new business."

"As opposed to my measly handful of awards? On the toughest accounts in the place?"

He didn't say anything.

"You think Concordia doesn't win because I'm not good enough?" I leaned forward. "Fine—let's swap accounts and see how much different it is."

"That's not the point, Terry."

"I work on the toughest stuff in the place, Justin."

"As I said, your contribution–"

"Stuff that doesn't win a lot of awards because it's hard and complicated and run by clients that don't get it."

He just sat.

"So I'm really sorry that Concordia didn't bring home a bunch of awards. But you know what it does do, all that hard, ugly, gnarly business with no glory opportunities for anyone?"

He just stared.

"It makes you a lot of money, Justin," I spat. "A lot of money."

"All right, that's enough," he said. "As I said, I believe this move is in the best interests of the agency."

"Keith will do what's in the best interest of the agency as long as that's what's in the best interest of Keith," I snarled. "As soon as those two aren't the same thing, you can bet your ass which one he's going to choose."

"Careful, Terry," Justin said, a little steel creeping into his up to now compassionate tone.

I sat back in my seat.

I was done.

In more ways than one.

"I need you to make this work," he said looking steadily at me.

"Fine."

"I mean it, Terry," he said. "A lot of people are going to be looking at you to see how you react to this. So however you may feel inside, I'm asking you to be outwardly supportive of this."

"Yeah, sure. I'll do my best."

He paused and looked at me for several seconds.

"Be sure that you do."

"This won't be public for a couple of weeks," he finally said, stirring off the couch. "So keep it confidential until then. But as I say, I wanted you to hear it from me."

"Who else knows?" I said standing up.

"Keith, of course," he said. "Larry, Ross, Mike…and now you."

He extended his hand. We shook.

"I'll do my best."

"I know you will."

I'll do my best, all right, I thought, as I walked into the hall. *Do my best to kill that motherfucker.*

My hand was completely forced now. I had two weeks to get to McManus and blow the bastard up. I had to find out if he was going to be in the agency in the next week or ten days. Of course, I was going to have to be a little more stealthy—having just sworn Justin my allegiance to his heinous plan.

But that was just a detail. I could figure that out.

As my mind became more pragmatic and practical about what to do next, my rage began to subside. Which cracked the wall of my compartmentalized dike and allowed all the other emotions to flood back in.

I wasn't sure it was a good trade.

At least rage had a sharp, single-minded focus.

The regret and remorse and the rest was just an amorphous cloud of pain.

Jesus Christ, what was I gonna say to Alex?

CHAPTER 62

I pounded off the elevator and all the way down to my office.

"Meghan, come here," I snapped as I passed by her desk.

I flung my legal pad onto my desk, hurling my pen after it.

"Well, yes sir, Mr. Bossy Pants," Meghan said as she sashayed through the door. But one look at my face and she stopped.

"What? What is it?"

"I need to know if Dan McManus is going to be at the agency in the next two weeks." I practically spat it out.

"Who?"

"Dan McManus! The founder of The Vision!"

"Uh, yeah, I'm sorry, sure—I'll find out," she said making a note on her pad.

"And if he is, then I want to meet with him." I was pacing now. "Cup of coffee in the morning, a drink at the end of the day, something."

"I'll see what I can find out." She turned to go and then turned back. "Everything OK?"

"No," I said. "Everything is *not* OK."

She turned to leave.

"And Meghan?"

"Yeah?"

"Keep this quiet, huh?"

"Sure."

And she left.

I sat down at my laptop and opened up a blank Word page. I

needed to write out what I would say to McManus—really needed to think it through, script it out. I was only gonna get one shot at this and I had to make it count. It had to be a bull's-eye.

Dan, when you started The Vision, even before it was called The Vision...

"Terry?" Meghan said from the doorway.

"Yeah, Meg?" I said without looking up.

"He'll be here a week from Thursday."

Now I looked up.

"Really?"

"Yeah." She consulted her notepad. "He's coming in the night before, having breakfast with Justin early Thursday morning, and then meeting with The Vision team all day Thursday. His assistant says he could meet for a drink that Wednesday night or at the end of the day Thursday before he flies out."

"OK...great," I answered, starting to think about the best scenario.

"You don't have to decide right now," Meghan said. "She said both times are open right now—she'll keep them that way and call if she gets pressure on them. Said to call whenever you decide."

"Good, good. Thanks Meg." I turned back to my screen.

Meghan walked out. And immediately returned.

"OK, I'm sorry, maybe it's none of my business but what the hell is going on here?"

I looked up at Meghan. She had a right to know.

"Close the door," I said.

When I'd told her the glad tidings, she was initially angry. A few F-bombs, a couple goddammits. But by the time I was finished she just stood up, walked over and gave me a hug.

When she opened the door to leave, she revealed an ashen-faced Larry standing outside.

"Hey, Bud," he said with a combination of guilt, sympathy, depression, and lack of energy that made me ache. I'd only had two conversations about this mess so far and already I didn't want to talk about it anymore. In fact, I didn't want to talk, period.

"I guess you heard," he said sitting down.

"Yeah," I said. "I fucking heard."

"There was nothing I could do," he said spreading his hands in front of him.

"I didn't say there was."

"Justin just..." He shrugged.

I just looked at him.

"I mean, you know how he is with these things."

I wasn't even making the pretense of conversation anymore. If Larry wanted the blanks in the conversation filled in, he was gonna have to fill them in himself. Between his natural hyperactivity and the anxiety he had to be feeling talking to me, I was pretty sure he would.

"I mean, the press and the buzz from the Show the other night," he said. "It was everywhere, ya know?"

I just kept looking.

He was up now, walking around, running a hand through his thinning hair. It was like he was trying to explain it to himself as much as to me.

"I mean, you know how Justin is—man, he gets a taste of that, he's like a fuckin' crack addict, man. He's gotta have more," he said, hands spread wide again.

He paused—probably waiting for me to let him off the conversational hook. He shuffled his feet a little and started in again.

"I mean, he's looking for a way to keep the buzz going, a way to up it, to look like we have all this momentum," he said, as he walked in tight little circles across the desk from me.

He looked at me again.

Nothing.

"So clients will think we're a hot agency," he continued. "We'll get invited to more pitches. And you know, it's all about new business with him..."

He looked at me again.

More nothing.

He kept looking at me. There are only so many balls you can hit over the net when they don't come back. Eventually you run out of balls.

And he had.

He sighed.

"And he looks at promoting Keith as the way to do all that."

He sat down.

"Well, what's a few crushed souls when Budweiser might call, right?" I said, finally letting him off the hook.

He smiled ruefully.

"Try Mad Mark's Furniture. They called this morning."

"Even better."

"You gonna be OK?"

"Yeah, I guess," I shrugged without conviction. "What choice do I have?"

He got up to go.

"Hang in there," he said—and pointed at me. "I'm there for you."

"Thanks, Larry."

He left.

There for me.

Boy, what a relief. I was safe now.

CHAPTER 63

It was 7:00 when I leaned on the buzzer at Alex's apartment.

I wasn't sure why I had come.

Well, I was pretty sure of why I had come, just unsure how I had worked up the nerve. It may have been that in some remote, deluded remnant of my shattered brain I actually believed it was all going to be OK.

Or it might have been the instinct to seek her out when things had not gone exactly my way at work.

Or it might just have been a long dormant suicidal impulse deciding that today was a particularly good day to come to life.

In any event, I pressed the buzzer.

There was, what seemed to me anyway, an excruciatingly long wait.

And then the door buzzed.

When I got to the landing, I saw that Alex's door was open a crack. I pushed through into the hall.

Alex wasn't there.

But my leather overnight bag was. It sat full of all my 'boy-friend-in-residence' stuff. Including my blue button-down Oxford that Alex regularly wore as pajamas.

Ah.

So.

I knew where I stood. So much for the part of my brain that thought things were going to be OK.

In a bizarre way, it was almost a relief. Having to cop to what

I'd done was going to be awful. Having to actually be the one who delivered the news was more than I could imagine.

I sighed.

And turned the corner into the living room.

Alex was sitting in one of the wing chairs her mother had given her—legs crossed at the knees, hands on the arms of the chair, black cashmere sweater, white high-collared shirt underneath, her dark hair swept back on one side. She looked perfectly calm—and perfectly beautiful.

"Hi," I said softly.

"How could you?" she said quietly.

I sat slowly down on the love seat facing her.

"Alex, I'm so sorry."

"How could you?" she said again.

Not yelling. Just quietly.

It was worse than yelling.

"Alex, I..."

"I love you, Terry," she said. "And maybe even more important, I trusted you. I trusted you because you were a good person. You were decent and honest. And above all, you were kind. And so I felt I could give you my heart."

For the first time there was a little catch in her voice.

"And you've broken it."

"Alex, please..."

"But even more than being sad?" she said, sniffing once and composing herself. "As bad as I feel? You know what's worse? I'm ashamed of you. I'm ashamed of you. Because you're better than this—much better. Or at least you used to be."

"I know," I said my head hanging down. "I know."

"The Terry Wilson I fell in love with would never have done this."

She sniffed a little.

"*Never!*" she said.

I just hung my head. I wondered how much longer it would be before pain just began oozing out of my pores.

"You want to know when I fell in love with you?" she asked.

Without looking up, I just raised my left hand in a feeble 'stop'.

"I'll tell you exactly when," she continued. "We had been dating for a couple of months and we went to my parents for dinner. It was the first time they'd met you. And my father was giving you a lot of shit about being in advertising."

"I remember," I said weakly.

"He was testing you. The way he does, sometimes. And he was dumping on advertising as a profession. He said something to you about 'selling diapers and hemorrhoid cream and erection pills—what kind of life is that?'"

I nodded.

"And—I'll never forget it—I looked at you out of the corner of my eye. And you looked down at your plate with this crooked little smile—and then you looked at him and you said 'Well, Bert—I like to think my life has a little more depth and complexity than just what I do for a living. I feel like it's what I do, but not necessarily who I am. Besides—those companies all have lawyers, too, you know.'"

I sighed.

"And my mother leaned back in her chair a little and shot Dad a look, kind of like, 'Ha, top that!' And he looked at you for a minute—and then he kind of smiled and nodded his head. And right there, you were his guy. And I fell completely in love with you."

I was past agony.

"And do you know why?" she continued. "Do you know why I fell in love with you right then? Not because you'd impressed my Daddy. I fell in love with you because you had the courage to stand up for yourself. And because you really believed what you said to him. You really believed that you were more than just your job. You really knew who you were."

I was fighting tears, a few of them escaping and falling into the tan and navy florals of the Oriental rug.

"And I loved that Terry Wilson more than anything," she said. "More than anything."

Her voice sounded confident but her face was streaked with tears as she spoke.

"And I don't know where that Terry Wilson went."

I shuddered with a sob.

"Neither do I," I said, barely audible.

"I know you don't," she said quietly. "And that might be the saddest part of all. But you're not the man I fell in love with."

I looked up.

"And that's why you need to go."

I stood up.

"Alex," I said with whatever strength I had left. "I am so sorry."

But she was done.

And said nothing.

It was only about 8:30 by the time I walked into my apartment.

I didn't turn on a single light.

I went straight to the bedroom.

I dropped my bag on the floor next to the bed.

And lay down on the bed.

I don't cry much.

But I couldn't cry much more than I did then.

CHAPTER 64

It was Saturday morning.

I was lying in bed.

I had managed to sleepwalk through the past few days, partly because I didn't know what else to do—and partly because I figured if I could just get to the weekend, I could hole up at home, stop resisting the siren song of depression, give in and fully embrace my despair.

Which was all I had planned for the day.

The phone rang.

I ignored it. It wasn't part of the despair-embracing plan.

A few minutes later it rang again.

Probably somebody wanting me to do something.

No, thank you, I thought.

Again, a few minutes later.

I was sticking with the plan.

A few minutes went by and I began to trust the silence. I had just shifted onto my left side and pulled the covers tightly to my chin when my Treo began to vibrate insistently on the bedside table.

Enough already.

I hoisted myself up on my left elbow and reached for it.

I checked the Caller ID. Not familiar—but...

I pressed 'Answer'.

"Hello?" I said, my voice gravelly.

"Uh, Terry?" said a guy's voice.

I cleared my throat a little.

"Yeah, this is Terry."

"Terry, it's Kevin Madden," he said. "Sean's cousin?"

"Oh, hey Kevin. How're you doin'?"

"Um, not very good...actually," Kevin said, his voice catching.

"Why? What's up?" I said hoisting myself further up on my elbow.

There was a long pause.

And when Kevin spoke again, he was barely getting the words out.

"Sean's dead, Terry."

CHAPTER 65

Mercy Hospital was across town from my apartment, maybe a half hour trip.

I made it in 15 minutes.

All Kevin had told me was that Sean had suffered some kind of head injury. He had told me that he and a small group of guys were gathered there. Sean's parents hadn't arrived yet but were due within a couple of hours.

I walked into the emergency room and looked around. Kevin was standing up the corridor a little ways and we walked toward each other, meeting halfway, hugging and breaking into tears.

"What happened?" I said through my tears, holding Kevin by the shoulders.

"We're not really sure," Kevin said shaking his head. "One of the other people in the building found him."

"In the apartment?"

"In the hallway," he said, removing his hands from my shoulders and wiping his eyes.

"Just lying in the hallway?"

He shook his head as he tried to dry his eyes.

"Foot of the stairs," he said. "The EMTs said it looked like he probably fell."

"Oh my God," I closed my eyes.

"Were you with him last night?" Kevin asked.

I shook my head.

"I talked to him at the end of the day," Kevin said. "Said he was going to Jo Jo and then to some party."

"He wanted me to come with him, but I..." I said, starting to sob. "Oh my God, Kevin...it was because..."

"No, no—don't do that to yourself, Terry, don't do that..."

"But if I'd...I could've...Alex and I..."

"No," Kevin said, looking me straight in the eyes. "You couldn't have."

I looked at him through my tears.

"You couldn't have changed anything," he said. "Believe me...I know...."

"Was anybody with him?"

"Billy Hutchins said he talked to him on the cell around ten."

"Where was he then?"

"Don't know. He'd left Jo Jo by then, though."

"How do you know?"

"I called Jason, you know, to let him know...and he said Sean'd been there for a couple hours but left around 9-9:30 with a bunch of people from your office."

"Did he say how he was at that point?"

"No...he didn't."

I nodded.

A nurse approached us from down the hall, I assumed from the room where Sean was.

"Kevin?" she said gently.

"Yuh," he answered turning around.

"Have you talked to the parents again?" she asked quietly.

"Yeah, I did." Kevin let out a big breath. "They should be here..." He looked at his watch. "Maybe 45 minutes?"

"That's fine, that's fine," she said touching him on the arm. "There's no rush. We're just changing shifts—but I won't leave until they arrive."

"You don't have to do that, Jean."

"Don't worry about it," she said. "I'll be at the nurses' station. You just come get me when they get here."

Kevin nodded.

"Nice of her," I said watching her go.

"She was here when they brought him in," he said. "She said they tried everything, but…"

I looked away, down toward the entrance to the ER. A couple of EMTs were talking to the duty nurse, an older guy was shuffling by in his hospital Johnny pushing a wheeled IV rack as he went, a young kid was walking slowly toward the door flanked by his mother and a doctor—the kid had his arm in a sling and appeared to be wearing a brand new cast.

"Where're the other guys?" I said, turning back to Kevin.

"They left," he said. "Actually, I told them I thought it'd be better if there weren't too many people around when Peter and Fran arrive. Make it easier on them."

"That's true," I nodded. It was a wise suggestion.

"But you can stay if…" he said, clearly trying not to be rude.

"No, no—I think you're right about that," I said. "I'll take off, too. Is there anything I can do? To help you?"

"If there's some people you think oughta know, it would help if you made some calls," he said.

"Sure, no problem," I said. "I'll get on the phone as soon as I get home."

"Thanks, Terry."

I nodded.

"And thanks for coming—it was good to have someone…you know…"

"Yeah, I know."

I gave him a bear hug and turned and walked down the corridor and out the ER entrance. An ambulance sat idling in the circular drive while the two EMTs sat in the front seat doing paperwork, two nurses walked by with trays from Donny's Donuts across the street chatting as they went, the cars on Elm St. were passing by on their way to Home Depot and soccer games and haircuts and errands and I could hear Li'l Wayne playing from a car in the parking lot.

Everyone else seemed to be going about their normal Saturday morning routine.

I wasn't sure what normal was anymore.

CHAPTER 66

Sean was from Crofton, a leafy, affluent town about an hour and a half west of the city. The trip there would be a long, straight, all-highway drive—tailor made for conversation.

Or introspection.

I had called Alex to tell her about Sean, she hadn't been there, so I had left a message. Not the most elegant way to deliver that news, but it was about all I could handle. Just preparing to call her had pretty much taken it out of me for the day. I had thought about calling her back to see if she was going to the funeral and whether she wanted to drive out with me.

But I didn't have anywhere near those kind of emotional resources.

I left the tollbooth and accelerated onto the highway, and instinctively reached for the CD player. But sorting out what I wanted to hear was more than I had energy for.

My head was full of all the obvious and clichéd thoughts: when Sean and I had met, college days, first days in the work world, high hilarity with girlfriends, the at-work collaboration, the after-work commiseration, all the good memories from the superficial, booze-fueled past.

I smiled. The right piece of music and you could practically see it as one of our famous mood videos.

"Heart strings stretched tighter than mainstays," Sean had once said about a video I had done for some client.

But, I quickly realized that those thoughts were just the eager ones in the front row of my emotional classroom. The good doobies, the ones waving their arms and saying, *"Call on me! Call on me!"*

Sitting sullenly in the back of the room were the bad boys of the class—and they were just looking at me, arms folded defiantly across their chests.

"What're you smilin' about?" their expressions seemed to demand.

"Where were you, asshole?" they seemed to be asking.

"Yeah, what the hell were *you* doin'?"

"Nice, man...really nice."

There didn't seem to be enough air in the car and my chest felt tight and shallow.

The trip didn't take anywhere near as long as I would have liked. Somewhere in the back of my brain lurked the hope that if I could just keep driving and never arrive, none of this would actually take place.

The parking lot at St. Matthews was filling up when I pulled in. The lot was to the right of the huge, stone cathedral, a spider's web of walkways leading to the various entrances. Small groups of people were making their way toward the front of the church. I didn't recognize anyone yet. Probably cousins and family friends. Sean had a large, close, extended family.

Sean, of course, would have leapt at the opportunity to point out to me what a lovely oxymoron "close extended family" was.

Well, in any case, it was going to be a tough day for Sean's oxymoronic family.

I found a spot in the shade and slid the car into park, took my jacket off the hook in the back seat, slipped it on and checked my reflection in the window. I took a deep breath. My respiratory system still didn't seem to be fully functional.

I headed toward the church.

A prep-school friend of Sean's was walking up the walk from

the street. I had met him a few times over the years at football games and birthday parties for Sean.

"Hey," he said extending his hand.

"Hey—I'm Terry Wilson." There was no way he would remember my name. And I sure didn't remember his.

"Andy, Terry. Andy Sullivan. This is my wife Maureen."

"Hey, Maureen."

"Hi. Nice to..." she trailed off.

"Yeah," I said.

We all nodded awkwardly and they walked off toward the church. From my right, four guys were approaching out of the parking lot. They were his four best friends from Crofton. 'The Light Brigade' as he referred to them.

"Hey, Terry," one of them said.

"Hey, Mark," I said shaking his hand.

"Terry."

"Ter."

"Hey, man."

Handshakes all around. Quiet, unenthusiastic handshakes, all traces of their trademark cocky, cavalier bonhomie vanished.

"Unbelievable," one of them said.

"Yeah."

"Unbelievable," another one repeated.

Followed by pained, impenetrable silence and a lot of foot shuffling.

"Yeah, well, see ya inside," I said, clapping Mark on the bicep.

"Yeah."

The crowd was thickening now, people moving from all sides of the church in twos and threes, dark-clothed figures moving solemnly through the dappled light as the breeze ruffled the trees.

There was a bottleneck as they all reached the stone steps of the church and I joined the milling crowd. Slowly, ploddingly, we covered the ten granite steps to the wide stone landing. There, the crowd divided a little and dispersed through the three magnificent carved, wooden doors. As people spread out across the stone expanse in front of the doors, it cleared the way for me to see...

Alex.

She was standing off to the left, scanning the crowd as they assembled and began to climb the stairs. She hadn't seen me yet. She was wearing the sleek, black Armani suit she reserved for court dates. It made her look much taller than I knew she was. Her chestnut hair was lifting slightly in the breeze. The thin, black frames of her glasses completed what I had once referred to as her 'legal sexpot' look.

I fought my way to the left side, cutting across the flow of bodies. I was almost through the column when the slight commotion I was causing drew her attention.

I stepped into the clear space in front of her and stood looking at her, my hands at my sides.

She looked at me.

I opened my mouth to say...God only knew what.

It didn't matter.

I never got it out.

As soon as I opened my mouth, I had to close it to stifle a sob.

And then her arms were around me and I was sobbing out loud and her hair was clinging to the wetness on my face and my chest was heaving with the effort and people were looking at us furtively and she was holding me tighter and it was everything I could do to hang on.

"Let's go in," she said patting my back. "Let's go in."

Inside the church, Sean's family had filled the first five pews on both sides—not counting the empty two at the front for his parents and the pallbearers. Alex and I found a spot about halfway up the church on the right and slid in. My eyes were still bleary and I felt shaky but stabilizing. Next to me, Alex held my hand while she studied the program.

"A Celebration of the Life of Sean Brendan Healy", it said on the front in italicized Gothic type.

Somehow, 'celebration' seemed inappropriate to me. Too many celebrations were maybe why we were sitting here.

I looked down at Alex's hand in mine and noticed, not for the first time, what beautiful hands she had. They were small but perfectly proportioned, with graceful fingers and elegantly manicured nails. The clear polish she had chosen for today (she usually tended toward deep shades of red) had an understated gleam. But for all their beauty and grace, her hands weren't dainty. They looked strong and sure. On her wrist, she was wearing the Patek Phillipe Bert had given her when she graduated from law school. She had told me that he had actually given her a larger, more expensive one but she felt it was too big for her wrist and together they went and picked out this slightly smaller-faced one.

I didn't see people turn down an opportunity for excess very often. She was like that with everything, though. She had a tremendous sense of herself and confidence in being who she was. She drew a lot of strength from it. As she had pointed out a few days ago, I used to have something like that. I was beginning to wonder if it was a skill you could re-learn.

There was a little rustle of activity in the back of the church and I knew that Sean had arrived. It was, he would have been quick to point out, the first time he'd ever been on time for anything.

The organist eased into the entrance hymn; there was a stir as the congregation rose and the eight cousins serving as pallbearers began to quietly roll Sean down the aisle.

"Be not afraid," the vocalist sang. *"I go before you always..."*

I turned slightly sideways in the pew as they passed. The dark-suited young guys guided the casket with their inside hands, the outside hand bent behind their backs in a vaguely military attitude.

"...come follow me...and I will give you rest..."

The only one I knew well was Kevin.

He looked horrendous.

The procession rolled slowly past, followed by Sean's parents. His father, Peter, was positively gray, his face a grim, stone mask as he supported his wife, Frances. Fran, as she was known, wore a small, resigned smile and seemed almost serene as she walked down the aisle to bury her only child.

It was simultaneously reassuring and completely unnerving.

"My dear friends," the priest said, once everyone was settled. "We are gathered here today to give thanks for the gift of Sean's life and to try, in our small, human way, to console our beloved friends Fran and Peter..."

Father Delancey was Sean's second cousin on his mother's side. He had presided over weddings, baptisms and funerals for the Healy clan for years. He was tall, thin, and balding and wore rimless glasses with thick lenses that magnified his eyes and gave him a slightly startled look.

"To prepare ourselves to celebrate these sacred mysteries, let us call to mind our sins," he said in the familiar opening to the Mass.

The rite of Christian burial is filled with reassurance, hope and denial. Except for a few references and readings, it is the basic Mass—and so, despite the magnitude of the occasion, the ritual has a feeling of everyday normalcy about it. I leaned into the worn smoothness of the pew and let the familiar words and cadences flow over me.

"Remember your servant, Sean, whom you have taken from this life," Father Delancey prayed, arms spread wide over the altar.

It was really the perfect description.

Sean had been taken.

But not recently.

Not four days ago in that emergency room.

He had been taken gradually, over years. Taken a little each day—some days more than others, I supposed. Taken by whatever

those demons were that haunted him so, shrieking in the darkness behind his twinkling eyes and infectious smile. Taken by
weakness and opportunity and a lifestyle that fed the demons
and made it all so easy.

And he had been taken right in front of my eyes. While I
watched. Hell, while I helped. Did I not see it? Did I see it and
not want to admit it? Not want to admit what it said about Sean?
What it said about me? Tough to look back and say, with any certainty the exact moment your subconscious decided which way
to steer.

All I knew was that I saw it pretty well now.

The view from here was pretty fucking good.

"We bless Sean, in the name of the Father, and the Son and
the Holy Spirit," Father Delancey said, in the timeless concluding
ritual of the funeral. Showering the casket with Holy Water he
said, "May banns of angels greet you and with Lazarus, who once
was poor, may you have eternal rest."

Father Delancey handed the Holy Water spritzer to an altar
boy and turned to address the congregation.

"Would you please be seated," he said.

Once everyone was settled, he continued.

"Peter and Fran have asked that anyone who would like to
speak about Sean have a chance to come up and share a story,
a memory, a thought about how Sean may have touched you.
There's no order to it—but Peter and Fran would appreciate you
sharing in this ceremony in this way."

He turned toward the altar—and then turned back, with a
small, knowing smile.

"And seeing as how we're telling stories—I know Sean would
have loved it, too."

There was a long silent pause as people shuffled their feet and
suppressed their tears.

Slowly and quietly, Kevin stood up from the front pew and

approached the pulpit. He settled himself and then looked up at the congregation.

"For those of you who don't know me, I'm Kevin Madden and I was Sean's first cousin," he began.

His voice quavered as he recalled growing up with Sean, stories of their high school escapades, and even a few confessional revelations about heretofore-unknown bad behavior.

"Sorry about that one, Aunt Franny," he said when the congregation chuckled at one particularly good revelation.

"Sean wasn't just family," Kevin said, concluding his remarks. "He was my best friend."

He struggled for composure.

"And I'll miss him," he squeaked.

Head down, his face red and contorted as he fought back his tears, he walked slowly back to his place.

One by one, a handful of other cousins and family members got up to speak. There was a lot of overlap in the stories and the emotions—but it was all heartfelt and real.

As I listened to one of Sean's younger cousins, I felt a nudge. I turned to find Alex looking straight at me.

"Do you know what you're going to say?" she asked.

"Me?"

"Of course."

"Oh, no—this is just for family..."

"He loved you, Terry."

I turned back and looked straight ahead.

"And if you don't do it, you'll wish you did," she whispered.

Cousin Mary Ellen something-or-other was finishing up. She came back down the center aisle clutching a handkerchief over her mouth and took her seat across from me.

There was a long pause.

It seemed that everyone with something to say had spoken. Up on the altar, Fr. Delancey gathered his robes in preparation to get up.

I took a deep breath and stood.

Fr. Delancey saw me and sat back in his seat.

I stepped out into the aisle and walked slowly toward the altar. My only thought was not to stare at Sean's casket. Other than that, I was blank.

I stepped up onto the red-carpeted altar and walked across to the pulpit. Arriving at the lectern, I gripped its dark wooden sides and looked out at the congregation. The place was even more packed than I thought, people standing in the back and partway up the side aisles.

I adjusted the thin arm of the microphone and took yet another in a long series of shallow and unsatisfying breaths.

"Good morning. I'm Terry Wilson. And I've known Sean for a very long time. We actually went to the same college. And we've worked together off and on for almost ten years. You know, in thinking about Sean over the past few days, I was thinking that for as long as I've known Sean, I, uh, hardly ever called him Sean...we always addressed each other as 'Your Excellency' and 'Your Grace'. I don't remember exactly when it started—although I do know Sean started it."

I looked up.

"There's a shock, huh?"

There was a small ripple of laughter.

"But that was always our greeting. Didn't matter where we were or even who was around. We'd be in business meetings with clients, strangers around—Sean would walk in and we'd bow to each other—'Your Excellency'. 'Your Grace'. It happened when I showed up to interview for my first job. He was already working at Lewis, Childs. I showed up and was waiting in the lobby when all of a sudden he came walking through with another guy—on his way to some meeting. He looked over and saw me sitting there—he stopped and..."

I turned slightly sideways and acted out Sean's distinctive body language.

"E-e-e-xcellency!" I said in pretty dead-on imitation, eliciting another ripple of laughter.

"Your Grace" I simulated a little bow of my own. "The receptionist thought we were insane. But we spoke to each other that way all the time, that crazy language. '*Splicing the main brace*' and '*battling the Boer*'' and meeting for '*a tureen of the loud mouth soup*'. It was like a kind of code. I know a lot of you speak it fluently."

I looked at the faces in the front pew.

"Kevin. Tim." They smiled in response.

"But that was how it was with Sean. You could never meet and just say, "Hey, how's it goin'?" That was ordinary, that was for everyone. And I think more than anything else, Sean didn't want to be everyone. Sean loved the exclusive sense of clubbiness. You know, he took great pride in the fact that he could identify almost every English regimental tie and its origins. I once stood in front of a rack at Brooks Brothers with him and he went right down the line—the First Fusiliers, the Queen's Guard, the 4th Grenadiers. And I think our jargon, that crazy, formal lingo, that's...well, it's like our club tie. It was always what signified that we were part of the same group."

I could feel something giving way inside.

"Because you didn't just have a friendship with Sean—you shared an alternate reality. Whenever I saw him, even if it was just in the hall at the office, it was as if we slipped through some portal into another dimension. The way we spoke, the things we talked about, the movies we quoted, our view of the world—even the smallest exchange was something special to be shared. And that sense of sharing, of shared connection, of camaraderie...Sean loved that more than anything."

I paused, trying to figure out where I was going from here.

"Most of all, he loved the connection to his family."

I looked at the two stricken figures in the first pew.

"Peter. Fran. He loved you so much. I'm sure you know that. Talked about you all the time...and there was a lot to talk about.

All the trips to Turks and Caicos...diving with you Peter...the dinners at Cote d'Azure."

I smiled at Fran.

"The *'quarterly ceilidh'*, he called it..."

I shifted my gaze to Peter.

"Peter, your annual phone call at the stroke of midnight every New Year's Eve...I don't know how many times, all the different places we were when that call arrived. I'll still never figure out how you found us every year..."

He smiled as if it hurt.

Where was all this coming from? I hadn't thought about some of this stuff in years. Until it came out of my mouth, I wasn't sure that I knew some of it at all.

"And sharing books with you both—the endless biographies and histories with you, Fran."

I smiled at her.

"I once told Sean that I never knew there had been that many books written on Winston Churchill."

She smiled back as the congregation laughed quietly.

"And Peter—the Patrick O'Brien stuff with you. I don't know if you've read every one—but I know Sean has. He was so disappointed when *"Master & Commander"* came out on film. He couldn't figure out why they would combine three stories—he wanted them to make 23 movies, one for each book. He brought his whole collection into the office and started handing them out to people who had seen the movie, trying to turn everyone else into fans. 'Literary imperialism,' he called it.

I paused.

"But that was the thing with Sean—he shared something special with all of us. Each of us had some special connection to him: a book, a shared trip, a line from a movie, a joke, a favorite drink, a funny expression. Sean had a way to connect with each of us and make us feel special, make us feel unique. Make us feel loved. And in the end..."

I let out a big breath.

"...in the end, I was so busy enjoying the way he made me feel, that I forgot to worry about how he felt."

I paused.

"I failed him. I wasn't there for him. I don't think I could have stopped what happened. But I could have made sure he knew I loved him."

Sigh.

"Because I did."

I stepped away from the lectern and walked slowly to the center aisle. When I reached the casket I stopped and made a small bow.

"Goodbye...Your Excellency."

CHAPTER 67

The next days were a blur.

Actually, that's not really accurate. A blur would indicate that something was happening but at such a great rate of speed it was hard to follow.

Whereas I couldn't swear that the first few days following the funeral actually even took place at all.

Apparently, at some point, I had a couple of calls with people at the office—trying, lamely, to help direct and approve some Concordia stuff. My comments and advice were so obtuse and useless, Meghan instructed people not to call me or take calls from me until further notice.

Bed had been my main base of operations for about the past 72 hours. I had drifted in and out of sleep, watched some TV, listened to my iPod, made the horrendous mistake of finding one of Sean's all-time Top 5 movies *"The Man Who Would Be King"* on some movie channel and watching the whole thing through teary eyes, reciting lines aloud along with Sean Connery and Michael Caine; there was a pizza box on the floor, the shades hadn't been raised in days, my clock had been stashed in a drawer and after enduring hours of vibrations from incoming e-mails I had finally buried my Treo in the hamper.

As I shoved the Treo deep into the tangle of shirts and pants, I got a huge hit of Gen Reade's leftover "Obsession" wafting from the suit I had yet to clean.

It was enough to undo me.

And it did.

Everything seemed to lead by the shortest and fastest possible route to agony.

The only thing that was really keeping me going was the way Alex had behaved at Sean's funeral. I knew that reconciliation was a miracle away and that, knowing Alex, her behavior at the funeral was just her being kind and supportive to someone in need. The fact that the someone in question was me was just my dumb luck.

Still.

If that thin, almost nonexistent shred of optimism was the only flotsam available for me to hold onto to keep from going under, well then I was going to hang on like Leo DiCaprio until my cold, hard fingers were finally pried loose and I sank like a stone.

I was watching *Pardon the Interruption* on ESPN (my only indication that it must be late afternoon) when the phone rang.

I looked.

It was Meghan.

"Hey," I said picking up the receiver and hitting Mute on the remote.

"Hey," she said. "How, ah, how're you doin'?"

"All right," I said. "Not great."

"Yeah. We ever gonna see you again?"

"Probably."

"Couple people asked."

"Soon."

"Um, well, the real reason I'm calling?"

"Yeah?"

"Do you still want to meet with Dan McManus tomorrow night? His office called—wants to know if you're still on."

I rolled back onto the pillows and closed my eyes.

"Ter?"

I had forgotten all about this.

"Ter, you still there?"

"Yeah," I sighed. "Yeah, I'm still here."

"You wanna think about it a little?" she said. "I mean I can probably hold them off for a little. But they're kinda gonna want to know tonight."

I rubbed my eyes for a second and then looked up at the ceiling.

"You still want to meet with him?"

I stared at the ceiling for a long minute.

"No," I said.

There was a long pause on the other end.

"Are you sure?" Meghan said finally.

"Tell them I'll catch him next time."

"You're really sure?"

"Yeah," I said. "Yeah, I'm sure."

"All right," she said softly. "Let me know what I can do, OK?"

"Sure."

"Anything, you know?"

"Sure, Meg, I know. Thanks."

I leaned over to hang up and then rolled back onto the pillows again.

It was over.

I wasn't fighting it anymore. It wasn't a fight worth winning. Looking at it from here on the far side of all that had happened, I saw, at last, that it wasn't even a fight worth having. My preoccupation, my obsession, my fixation with Keith and his hypocrisy had now cost me more than any victory could possibly give back.

And I was done.

And as I lay there, a thought suddenly occurred to me.

As if all the other transgressions I had committed recently weren't enough, I had also committed perhaps the cardinal sin of branding.

I had let my competition define me.

We're constantly telling clients that they have to sharply define their brand, articulate it very clearly. Not just because of the obvious benefits but because if you don't strongly and unmistakably define your brand you leave yourself vulnerable to having your competitors define your brand—for their own advantage. If they stand for quality, they'll make you stand for cheap. If they stand for value, they'll make you stand for overpriced. If they stand for modern and innovative, they'll make you stand for old and outmoded. If they stand for sexy, they'll make you stand for dowdy.

And if you're not careful, you'll have to live with the results.

In the world of branding, it's the one thing you're never supposed to allow to happen.

And it was exactly what I'd done.

Now, in cases where a brand finds itself in this fix, I knew from experience exactly what steps to take. I'd stood in countless conference rooms during countless new business pitches and told them:

"Every brand, no matter how much crisis it's in, still has the core things that made it great," I would say as passionately as I could. "The essential DNA of the brand, the things that drew people to it in the first place. So we need to reach inside the brand, rediscover its strengths and bring out the greatness within."

Well, if ever there was a time to reach inside and discover if the Terry Wilson brand had any greatness left within—it was now.

CHAPTER 68

I woke up the next morning feeling so energized, I wondered if I had somehow been doing blow in my sleep.

I jumped out of bed and the rush of adrenalin after days of lethargy made me so dizzy I had to sit back down momentarily.

But it was OK.

I knew what I was doing.

First, into the shower. I actually hadn't showered since the funeral and between the passage of time, the days in bed, and the night sweats brought on by anxiety, I figured I was going to need a squeegee. Maybe sandpaper. As the water flowed over me, I turned the temperature up until it was as hot as I could stand it. I started to have this feeling that I was scrubbing off not only the sweat and the dirt but layers of depression, self-absorption and misguided obsession as well.

As that image took hold in my mind, man, I scrubbed like Lady Macbeth in there.

Next, the closet. I scanned the hangers and grabbed a gray suit and a black dress shirt. A little formal for daytime—unless you were going on an interview.

But I was.

Kinda.

I looked at my watch.

7:30. Perfect.

I thought about driving but I didn't want to get hung up

trying to park. Downtown could be tough. So I grabbed a cab outside my building.

"100 State," I said through the milky Plexiglas.

We lurched into traffic and I began to visualize the scene in my mind. Trying to roughly choreograph how I'd enter, what I'd say, all of it. As presentations go, this one needed major work. I only had the roughest possible outline in my head—even though I'd been thinking about it half the night.

State St. was the financial heart of the city. A row of office towers stretching toward the harbor, housing virtually every big-time law firm, investment house, policy think tank and power broker the city had to offer. Hoffman, Haversham & Clarke— Bert Clarke's firm—took up most of the glimmering tower that loomed over the West corner of State. On the other end of the street was 100—a slightly shorter, slightly older, but also impressive building that housed Hadley Storrs.

"$12.50," said the cabbie.

I gave him fifteen and jumped out.

I walked into the lobby of 100 State and it was bustling. People strode across the marble lobby toward the elevator banks, a small knot of people were signing in at the security desk, guys with carts were rolling platters of bagels and huge urns of coffee and assorted other breakfast delights across the shiny marble floors heading for conference rooms upstairs: another day of commerce and industry was leaping to life.

I looked at my watch again—8:05.

Great.

I knew Alex liked to get in anywhere from 8:15 to 8:30. It was a half hour to 45 minutes before the office was officially open but Alex liked the 45 minutes or so it gave her to get settled, catch up on a few e-mails and generally be fully prepared when the day began.

My plan—if you could call the vague and loose collection of points I wanted to make a plan—was to wait until I was sure

Alex was ensconced upstairs, call up, have the security guards announce me and then get upstairs to see her and make an impassioned plea to the jury.

At least that was Plan A.

As I was going through Plan A in my head, I turned and looked down one of the banks of elevators...just as Alex entered the bank through the opposite side of the lobby.

Our eyes met instantly and she stopped dead in her tracks.

OK, then.

Time for Plan B.

Which was unfortunate, because Plan B didn't exist.

I forced myself out of my semi-frozen state and walked to the security desk, which sat at the mouth of the elevator bank.

"Can I help you?" the pleasant guard said.

"He's with me, Gordon," Alex said, now standing a few feet away.

"Oh sure, Ms. Clarke," Gordon smiled, handing me my visitor badge. "You going up to 15?"

"Yeah," she said. "Thanks, Gordon."

"Thanks, Gordon," I added.

Alex and I walked into the elevator bank. There was a large group of people waiting.

"What are you doing here?" she said softly. She didn't sound angry—but she didn't sound happy either.

"I wanted to talk with you," I answered *sotto voce.*

"This isn't a good time," she said, looking up at the elevator numbers. "I've got a meeting at 9:30 and I want to go over-"

There was a loud ding as an elevator arrived.

The mob moved toward the opening door like sheep. We followed at a slight distance. When the last person had wedged herself in, we were shut out. As the door closed, there was another ding and the car next to us opened its door.

We walked in.

"Really, Terry, I know you want to talk and I understand,

but I've got this meeting and..." she reached out and pressed the button for 15.

It lit up.

"OK, then," I said staring at the lit little '15' on the button.

I turned and faced Alex.

"15 reasons why I want another chance," I said. "And I'll be done before you get off..."

The doors slid closed.

I knelt down.

"#1—I'm sorry. More than you can possibly imagine."

There was a ding as we reached the second floor.

"2," I said still on my knees. "I've never been so sorry for anything in my entire life. The thought of it makes me sick."

She was just looking at me.

There was another ding as the 3rd floor registered.

And the doors slid open. With her head down, a woman in a maintenance uniform pushed a small cart filled with cleaning products through the door. She was all the way into the cab before she realized that I was kneeling in there. She stopped dead. But it was too late. You could see her assess the fact that it'd be a bigger deal to leave than to stay. She reached over and pushed 4.

I stood up and sidled over beside Alex.

"3," I said quietly. "I'm an idiot. An absolute idiot. How I could do anything like that to you is unbelievable. It's just..."

I hung my head.

DING!

The doors slid open and the woman and her cart went through that door like she'd been shot out of a cannon. The doors slowly started to close.

"4," I said quickly. "I'm lost. You said so yourself. I don't know how I got so lost but I did. And I'm just starting to come out of the woods now—and realizing just how deep in the woods I've been. And it scares the shit out of me."

DING!

"5. I'm here. I'm still here. In spite of everything, the original Terry Wilson? The one you fell in love with at your parents' dinner table? Is still in here, somewhere. I'll find him—I promise. I have to. Not just for you but for me."

DING!

"6. No one knows me like you do. No one else knows that I go to work scared every day."

There was a trace, just a trace, of softness in her eyes now.

"Scared that I won't be able to think of anything good. Scared that I won't be able to think of anything period. Scared that someone else will think of something better. Or worse, scared that I'll think of something great and because of politics something mediocre will be hailed as being better. Knowing you're there at the end of the day, your midday calls, your funny e-mails—you get me through more days than you know."

DING!

"7. And no one knows you better than I do. No one. Not your parents, not your sister, not Kat—no one."

She looked skeptical at best.

DING!

"OK—then. Number 8. When you get stressed, your left shoulder gets tighter and hurts more than your right. But most people are right handed and so unless they know this, when they rub your shoulders, they'll be putting the most pressure on the part that needs it least."

She cocked her head ever so slightly as she looked at me.

"It's true. And I know that."

DING!

"9. You hate your ears."

She looked startled.

"You think they're uneven and that the right one is slightly pointed—like an elf. Which it's not. But you think it is—and it makes you self-conscious. Which is why when you're in a situation with people you don't know, you always pull your hair back over your left ear instead."

DING!

"10. You worry about what your father thinks of your career."

She looked at me with widening eyes.

"You're very proud of what you do, working here at Hadley—and even though he says it's great, you worry that it hurt your father that you didn't come into his firm. Hurt him more than he lets on."

DING!

"11. You're worried that eventually you're going to get a case at Hadley that you don't believe in. Part of what makes you a good attorney is your passion—the fact that you throw yourself emotionally into the case, that you commit yourself so personally to the cause. You worry that if you didn't believe it was a cause, you'd fail. And the inability to be committed no matter what might cost you your shot at partner."

DING!

"12. You worry about having kids."

She looked at me carefully.

"You worry that having spent your whole adult life taking all kinds of measures to make sure you didn't have a child, when the time comes that you want to—you won't be able to. Divine retribution, bad karma, bad luck, whatever—it scares you to death."

DING!

"13. You think I'm the one. It's why you're so hurt and so angry and so depressed. It wasn't just that your boyfriend slept with someone else—it's that *I* did. The one you'd really decided on. And even more than being angry, you're scared—scared about your judgment."

I looked at her.

"Scared," I said softly "that if I go away, how can you trust yourself to choose again?"

DING!

"14." I sighed and shifted gears. "I make you laugh. Every woman's magazine on the planet Earth runs article after endless article saying that the most important thing is finding a guy who makes you laugh. And I make you laugh. They all say it's the most important thing of all. Not looks, not killer abs, not money, not anything. Which is good, because as you well know, I have none of those other things."

She smirked—ever so slightly, infinitesimal even, but a smirk nonetheless.

"See?" I said spreading my arms in triumph.

DING!

The doors slid open and Alex stepped off the elevator and walked about ten feet into the 15th floor lobby.

And stopped.

She turned around to face me where I stood half in and half out of the elevator.

"What's 15?" she said.

There were lots of other young legal beagles walking through the lobby, crossing between us, passing by on their way to meetings, copiers and legal libraries.

"Number 15 is..." I paused. "I love you, Alexandra Emily Clarke."

Two passers-by were pretending so hard that they weren't paying attention to all this that they walked right into each other, releasing a blizzard of legal paperwork into the air.

Alex looked at me.

And blushed.

And smiled a little.

And shook her head in what I assumed to be disbelief at my idiocy.

She took off her glasses and rubbed the bridge of her nose.

"The bridge of your nose tingles when you blush," I said. "#16."

The buzzer in the elevator sounded, indicating that the door had been open too long.

"Get out of here," she smiled.

I stepped back inside the elevator, pressed 'L' and slumped onto the floor in the corner.

I was spent.

But, for once, I felt clean.

CHAPTER 69

Two weeks later, we got a call that a bunch of us should come to NY for The One Show.

Including me.

As I walked into Alice Tully Hall, I looked around and smiled.

Not a blood-soaked poster in sight.

I actually won another Pencil—Silver, for Magazine Campaign for the airline.

It felt good, I was proud of the work, particularly because of everything that had been swirling around at the time. I walked off the stage and back to my seat with Larry and everybody. I accepted the backslapping and handshakes.

Behind me, Mike Reston, a young art director who was a particularly rabid awards fan, shook my shoulders.

"Way to go, man! Way to go! Kick ass!"

"Thanks, Mike," I said smiling.

"Nice goin', dude," Keith said, nodding at me.

"Thanks," I said, returning the nod.

When the show was over, we all trooped out of Alice Tully Hall onto the plaza at Lincoln Center. It was a beautiful spring night in New York, breeze ruffling the flowering trees that dotted the plaza. The distance to Broadway muted the traffic sounds so that the vast plaza seemed quiet and far away from everything.

"Where we goin', man?" asked Reston of no one in particular.

"Per Se!" said Keith.

"Keith—do you really think we can just walk into Per Se?" Larry said smiling at him.

"Sure, man" he said. "I know this guy who–"

"Keith, it's like an eight-month wait for reservations," Larry laughed.

"No, really, man, he's a DP who–"

Larry started to laugh and clapped Keith on the back.

"Keith—I don't care if you know Martin Scorsese personally— it's not getting us into Per Se."

"I'm starved—how about Eatery?" asked Gail.

"Great idea" said Larry. "And then the bar back at the Hudson. I'm buying."

"Yeah."

"Absolutely."

"I'm in."

"Cool," said Keith, recovering from his momentary deflating. He was nothing if not resilient.

"Coming, Terry?" Larry asked.

"Yeah, I'll meet you there. I just wanna stop by the hotel for a second."

Larry smiled then reached out and squeezed my upper arm.

"OK" he said softly. "We'll see you down there. Or at the hotel."

The group headed off toward Broadway where I knew Larry had town cars waiting to take everyone downtown. I turned and started down Broadway on foot. We were all staying at the Hudson and it was only a few blocks away.

Because the night was so nice and particularly because I wasn't in any hurry, I turned down 64th St. and headed toward the Park. After just a few doorways, the bustle of Broadway began to recede behind me and the air, against all odds, had the subtle smell of lilacs.

About halfway up the block on the stairs leading up to one of the old brownstones was a homeless guy. His stuff was spread out around him and he was smoking a stub of a cigar. As I approached, he began quietly shaking a ragged Kangol cap at me.

A small handful of coins jingled in it.

"Evenin', sir," he said.

"Evening, my friend," I smiled and stopped.

"Enjoy the show?" he asked. For all he knew, I had just come from seeing 'South Pacific'.

"Yea," I said. I turned and looked back at the bright lights of Lincoln Center, glittering silently at the end of the street.

I smiled.

"Yea, actually, I did."

"Good for you, good for you," he enthused, nodding his head. "Do you think you could you help me out a little this evening?"

"Sure. I'd be honored." I reached into my pocket and took out a handful of folded bills. I looked at the bunch of ones on top and started to peel off a couple. I stopped and then peeled a twenty off the expense money on the back of the wad.

"Here you go, my friend," I said, holding the bill out to him instead of dropping it into his cap.

"God bless you," he said. "God bless you, sir. You take care of yourself."

"You take care of *yourself*," I smiled.

"Well, this will help" he cackled. "This will surely help."

"Take it easy," I said and started down the sidewalk. I took a few steps and was suddenly aware of the weight of the big, silver pencil in my jacket pocket. I stopped and fished it out, hefting it in my palm for a second as I looked at it.

I turned and walked back to the guy on the stairs.

"Everything all right, Sir?" he said eyeing me a little suspiciously this time.

"Yeah, everything's cool," I said. "I'll tell you what—why don't you take this, too."

He held out his hand and touched the glittering pencil.

"What is it?" he asked.

"Well, it's a prize. Not really worth much, though. I mean it's not worth money or anything."

"Well, then, why would I want it?" he said hefting the thing. The streetlight above us caught the beveled edges of the pencil as he turned it and it flashed in the darkness.

I shrugged. "Maybe it'll be lucky for you,"

"Do people think these things are lucky?"

"Yeah...they do."

"Why?"

I thought for a long minute.

"They think that it will protect them," I said.

He eyed me carefully but curiously.

"From what?" he asked softly.

I looked up into the night sky and smelled the soft spring smells.

"From everything," I said quietly. "From everything."

THE END

Two weeks later, I was sitting in my office cleaning out my e-mail and listening to one of the agency's many shared-play lists on iTunes—*bozomuzic* had some nice options today.

I was actually killing time until I had to go to a meeting Keith had asked me to sit in on. We were, apparently, pitching IBC Insurance, "...the 3rd biggest property/casualty insurer in the US, with a long history of integrity and innovation", according to the briefing documents.

"We can sell them something cool," Keith had promised us all in a meeting. "They're looking for something cool and edgy—'cause of all their innovations over the years."

At any rate, the IBC guys were here today, a little grip-and-grin session, get to meet everyone, hear the agency's capabilities, talk about the assignment, try to gauge the chemistry—the usual first meeting. Two dogs circling each other and sniffing cautiously at each other's butts.

"Hey, Ter?" Meghan said, leaning in the door. "That meeting's gonna be starting in a couple minutes..."

"Thanks, Meg," I said, looking up and smiling. "I'm on my way."

Grabbing a pad, a couple business cards, my Treo, and my coffee, I headed up the stairs and down the long green swath toward Empire.

The clients hadn't arrived yet and everyone was milling around, their collective anxiety making them all talk a little too loud and laugh a little too hard at things that weren't really funny in the first place.

"Hey, Ter," Haggerty said as I approached. "Have you met Adrian Townsend?"

"No, I haven't," I said, extending my hand. "Terry Wilson, nice to meet you."

"Terry's one of our Creative Directors," Mike said. "He writes all those great Brand Vision videos you've seen…"

"Among other things," I said, my annoyance starting to rise.

"Those are great," Adrian said, a soft British accent revealing itself. "Really compelling."

"Thanks," I said, settling myself down, going with it. "Nice to be famous for something."

"Adrian's our new Head of Brand Planning," Mike said, beaming as if he'd actually given birth to Adrian himself.

A British Head of Planning.

How incredibly fucking original.

"That's great," I said as convincingly as possible. "Welcome."

"Ah, here they are," Mike said, looking over my shoulder.

The IBC guys arrived in a wave of pinstripes, crisp haircuts, perfect teeth, and ties ranging wildly from indigo to cerulean. They looked perfectly nice and exuded loads of integrity. They did not, however, look even remotely like a group that was looking to further their reputation for innovation by buying something "cool and edgy".

Firm handshakes all around and then everyone arranged themselves around the table and dove in.

Paula was on her feet at the head of the table, Air mouse in hand; ready to commence the inevitable PowerPoint presentation.

"Well, good morning, everyone," she smiled brilliantly, eyes ticking over all the participants. "Thanks so much for coming. We're really excited to have you here today, to get to tell you a little about Cracknell, Burroughs and to hear a little more about IBC. I thought before we dive in, I'd just give you all a little of the agenda we've planned for the next few hours—just so you can see where we're headed."

She punched the air mouse and replaced the 'Welcome IBC' slide with the agenda slide.

"As you can see, we thought we'd spend a few minutes doing introductions and then get into a little agency history, a brief overview of our capabilities as a modern, full-service agency and one or two case studies that we think show Cracknell at our best and how we get to great. Then we thought we'd take a 10-15 minute bio break before we start to cover the assignment…"

I sat looking at Paula doing her thing up there.

I couldn't pinpoint when it had happened.

I must have been there, but I couldn't remember the exact moment.

Somehow, she had inexplicably gone from being the best Account person I'd ever known to being a game show host. And worse, everyone in management considered that transformation to actually be progress—improvement even.

Tragically, even Paula herself.

The realization gradually sank in and suddenly seemed so heavy I nearly groaned from the weight of it.

I began calculating about how long it would take until we got to the inevitable 'bio break'. If Paula could keep clicking robotically along doing her Pat Sajak impersonation and they could keep Mike from going completely off the reservation and giving the entire history of advertising as we know it, I figured that it would be about an hour—maybe an hour and 15.

I figured I could hang on that long.

Because as I sat there, listening, all of a sudden…I knew.

Clear as day, clearer and more certainly than I'd known anything in a long time, I knew.

I suddenly knew that when the bio break ended and the group reconvened and began to sit back down at the table with their refreshed coffees and replenished waters and their tiny plates of melon and kiwi and their pleasantly earnest, interested expressions...

I would be gone.

Long gone.

Already down the elevator, through the concourse and out onto the street—sputtering and gasping and gulping in great swallows of reality as I broke through the surface and back into the world.

EPILOGUE

Two months after going AWOL, I was sitting having coffee with Meghan at Dunkin' Donuts. I'd never really been a Starbucks guy and now I didn't have to be.

The burden of cool had been lifted.

After my rather unique departure from The Crack, I had caught a tremendous break from Meredith Mancuso, our head of HR—always a friend and never more so than now. Meredith had gone to Justin and made the case that I had clearly suffered a breakdown of some kind—brought on by the stresses of the business and all that had gone on in my personal life. She, apparently, had laid it on pretty thick that Justin's elevation of Keith had played no small role in my coming apart. Justin wasn't wired to feel guilt—but he did succumb to an Englishman's natural aversion to emotional mess. He agreed to allow me to leave the company on short-term disability, at the end of which I would be laid-off and receive a few months' severance.

And it'd be over.

"So you're working for Gail now?" I asked.

"Yeah," she said. "You know, they promoted her after you left—and I asked if I could be her assistant."

"I heard, that's awesome," I said. "You guys'll be great together."

"Yeah, I'm psyched," she said happily. "And it's really good for Gail—she deserved to be promoted."

"No one deserved it more," I nodded. "She'll do an awesome job."

"She says you taught her everything she knows."

"Oh, Gail had a pretty full body of knowledge and a pretty full set of opinions before I ever met her," I laughed. "I can't take credit for that."

"Well, she gives you full credit anyway," she said. "So how's the life of leisure?"

"It's very leisurely," I laughed.

"You look good."

"Thanks. Been trying to work out a lot."

"Look at you—gettin' all buffed up!"

"Well, it's as much for my head as anything," I laughed. "Maybe more."

"How is your famously messed-up head? People talk about you in hushed tones now, you know."

"They do?" I laughed.

"Oh yeah," Meghan guffawed. "Ever since the rumor got out that you'd had a breakdown, people see me in the elevator or come by the desk. They scrunch up their faces, all concerned and lower their voices...'How's Terry?' It's hysterical."

"And do you put them at ease?"

"Oh sure, I play right along with it. I slump my shoulders and look sad—'He's OK...getting stronger every day.'"

"Oh my God, you're awful."

"Are you kidding? It's the high point of my day!" she said.

She leaned over the table toward me.

"I did it to Keith last week..."

"You did not."

"Absolutely," she said with indignation. "That fuckin' weasel?"

"Interesting that The Weasel, as you refer to him, was even asking about my well-being."

"Oh, I don't think he gives a shit—he just knows that lots of people really were concerned about you so it seems like caring about you is the cool thing of the moment. He doesn't want to be left out."

I laughed.

"Hope he dies in a fiery crash," she said with contempt.

"Easy, there Meg."

"He's evil."

"Uh, yeah—I know."

"There's rumors he's after Larry's job now."

"Those aren't rumors, babe," I laughed. "He's got the knife out for whoever's got the job just above him on the food chain. He's a shark—literally. He has to keep moving forward and killing whatever's in his path or else he dies."

"Enough bad things can't happen to that guy."

"Ah, well," I shrugged. "As Alex likes to say: 'the punishment for being him, is being him.'"

"Damn straight," she nodded. "She's one smart lady."

Meghan stirred her coffee for a long minute.

"How is Alex?" she said, still concentrating on her stirring.

"She's good," I said.

"Yeah?" Meghan said looking up at last.

"Yeah, she is. Working on a new case, pretty excited about it."

"And, ah…you two are…?"

I smiled.

"Pretty good, actually."

"On the mend?"

"Yeah. Actually, that's a pretty good way of describing it," I smiled. "On the mend. The patient is stable and the prognosis is for a long, slow recovery."

"I'm glad."

"Yeah…me too."

She went back to stirring her coffee thoughtfully for a few seconds.

"Almost blew it there, buster," she said without looking up.

"Not almost."

She nodded softly and made a twisted little smile and held it for a second or two.

"I miss Sean," she said quietly.

"Yeah," I sighed. "I do too."

"When I think of what happened, it makes me so sad," she said. "But whenever I think about him, I can't help but smile."

"Yeah," I smiled. "I know exactly what you mean."

I sighed.

"I'd give anything to be able to have him here. To be able to change it all. But since I can't—you know, what you just said about him? That just thinking about him makes you smile? There are worse legacies to leave behind, I guess."

She nodded.

We were both quiet for a minute.

"So what are you going to do now?" she asked.

"I don't know, really," I mused. "Trying to keep an open mind. Been having a bunch of different conversations with a bunch of different people."

"Rumor mill says you're going to Halladay & Company."

"Nope. Haven't even spoken to them."

"Who have you talked to?"

"Bunch of different people. Couple headhunters, a couple corporate recruiters…"

"Corporate? Like client side?"

"Hey, I'd consider it."

"Wow, you do have an open mind!"

I laughed.

"Sounds like you're taking your time," she said. "Which is good."

"Yeah, I don't want to jump at just anything. I've got the luxury of a little time."

"So, in the meantime, what are you gonna do—just work out a lot?"

"I don't know," I said.

Now it was my turn to stir my coffee thoughtfully.

"I was thinking maybe I'd write a book."

"Really?" she said smiling.

"Yeah, maybe."

"About what?"

"Um," I hesitated. "About an agency, about life in an agency."

"Yeah?"

"Yeah, you know, what it's like to work there, the people, the clients, the whole thing."

"Huh."

"What do you think?"

"Fiction or non-fiction?"

"Fiction, you know, a novel."

"It would have to be," she laughed.

"Yeah, you're right," I laughed. "No one would possibly believe the shit we see every day is real!"

AND NOW, A WORD FROM OUR SPONSOR...

This book has been a long time in the making, mostly because it was written against a long series of self-imposed deadlines—and to an advertising creative, there's nothing in the world more pliant than self-imposed deadlines.

As a result of this passage of time, there are many, many thanks due to many, many people.

First, I suppose, would be everyone who ever had the sense of humor to employ me in this crazy business—Steve, Gene, Jim, Seamus, Tony, Dick, Jack, Jay, Rick, Tom, Peter, Brendan, Tom, Bruce, Bob, Gary, Peter, Ed and, of course, Ron. Over the years you have given me the rare opportunity to earn a living doing something I (mostly) loved. I owe you all. And learned so much from every one of you.

A special, heartfelt shout out goes to my early and supportive readers—Georgia, Margie, Deze, Bill, Kay, Ben, Sarah, Chris, Amelie, Brian, Patty and Phil. Your enthusiasm and encouragement in those early days meant more than you will ever know.

Of course, I owe an enormous debt of gratitude to Michelle, Masha, Matthew, Lisa, and all the good folks at Inkwater Press for helping to make this dream a reality. Thank you doesn't even begin to express my gratitude.

To The Book Club—Mary, Bill, Trish, Rush, Jane and Brian.

Thanks for all the books and all the laughs and all the support over the years. Sorry there are no elephants.

Thanks to my wife Margaret—for all the encouragement and the freedom to disappear for days at a time in order to write this.

A special thanks to my kids—Maddie, Nick, Tom and Peter—for their support. And especially for the look of absolute incredulity on learning that Dad had written a book. As they say in the commercials—priceless.

And finally, a very special thanks to my mother, Madeline—who gave me the tremendous gift of reading and a deep appreciation for a well-turned phrase. In so doing, she shaped my entire life.

ABOUT THE AUTHOR

JAY WILLIAMS is a writer, creative director, and veteran advertising executive.

Considered a writer's writer by his peers, he has won virtually every advertising award there is to win, including an Emmy. Three of his commercials are in the permanent advertising collection of The Museum of Modern Art.

He lives outside Boston with his wife and four children.

This is his first novel.